NEVER ENOUGH
Cowboy

JENNIE MARTS

sourcebooks
casablanca

Published by Sourcebooks Casablanca, an imprint of Sourcebooks
P.O. Box 4410, Naperville, Illinois 60567-4410
(630) 961-3900
sourcebooks.com

Printed and bound in Canada.
MBP 10 9 8 7 6 5 4 3 2 1

This book is dedicated to
One of my writer besties
Annie MacFarlane
You are my plotting partner, writing retreat cohort,
and all-around shenanigan starter.
You're my superhero.
I can't imagine doing this writing thing without you.

CHAPTER 1

SHE FELT HIS EYES ON HER THE SECOND SHE WALKED into the old barn.

Jillian Bennett dropped the fifty-pound bag of sweet feed she'd just lugged across the alley and into the storeroom and then stopped to roll her neck. Turning to go back for the other bag, she paused to look around the barn—the eerie feeling of knowing he was in there had a chill racing up her spine.

The barn itself wasn't creepy. She loved the smell of hay and leather and the soft sounds of the horses snuffling and moving around in their stalls. The pig was probably around here somewhere and there were numerous barn cats, but they wouldn't be any help if he decided to come after her. Jillian cocked an ear—the dogs hadn't come out to greet her when she'd pulled into the driveway and parked in front of the barn, and she didn't hear them now. Her friend Bryn—the owner of the horse rescue where Jillian and her son, Milo, volunteered—and Bryn's fiancé, Zane, must have taken them with them.

It was Saturday, and her morning had gotten off to a rough start. She'd overslept and only had time to pull her mass of curly hair into a messy knot on top of her head and swipe on a quick brush of mascara. She'd thrown on a T-shirt and one of the wrap skirts she used to wear all the time to the beach when she lived in California, and shoved her feet into her favorite pink pair of Chucks.

She'd found Milo, who was ten going on forty—the curse of an overly intelligent only child with a single mom—in the kitchen making pancakes, and he'd handed her a plate with a short stack covered in melted butter and warm syrup. The half she'd eaten before Milo's puppy, Gus, jumped on her and spilled the rest of the plate into her lap had been delicious. Her son was supposed to already be at his friend Mandy's house, and most of it had fallen on her leg anyway, so she'd just wiped it off as best she could with a wet cloth before grabbing her purse and racing out the door.

She was regretting that decision now as *he* finally stepped out of the shadows and faced her. The greedy gaze of his large beady eyes traveled over her body, and she shuddered.

"Stay where you are," she told him, using her most formidable librarian voice and holding up her hand. Her brain scrambled to process her escape routes. He was standing between her and the wide barn door, and she doubted she could get around him without him grabbing her.

Which left the corral to her right. But the gate was closed, so she'd either have to climb over or waste precious time trying to open the latch. Plus two of the rescue horses, Beauty and Prince, had plodded over, snuffling for apple slices, and they stood in front of the gate, adding two more obstacles to get through.

To her left was the ladder leading up into the loft, which held its own challenges, mainly that she was afraid of heights and, secondly, she wasn't sure she could beat him to it or that he wouldn't be able to follow her up there.

He took a menacing step toward her.

She knew she should have changed her clothes. He could probably smell the syrup she'd spilled on her skirt earlier. "I mean it, Otis, you ornery old goat, don't you take one more step toward me."

He kept his gaze trained on her as he sized her up again, then let out a loud bleat. Because Otis was in fact an ornery old goat. Stories abounded of people getting cornered by him, and Zane had once come home with the entire sleeve ripped off his shirt, which the goat had been rumored to have eaten.

"Stay back," she shouted, then let out a shriek as he lowered his head and charged.

She was always annoyed at the people in horror movies who went up instead of out when they were being chased, but she knew she'd never beat him out the front door as she feinted right, then ran left. The loft it was, then.

But he was faster than she'd imagined. She barely had her foot on the first rung of the old wooden ladder when his teeth clamped onto the edge of her maple-flavored skirt. She screamed again as she kicked out her leg, trying to free herself and gain another step.

She had one hand clinging to the ladder and the other gripping a handful of her skirt as she tried to both climb up to the next rung and wrench the fabric from the goat's mouth.

The Velcro fastener at her waist was great for wrapping

the skirt around her swimsuit at the beach, but it was no match for a tug-of-war with a determined goat hot on the scent of fresh flapjacks. The ladder shook as Otis rammed it with his head, and she let go of the fabric to clutch the ladder so she didn't pitch off. If he got her on the ground, who knew what he could do with those snapping teeth, big horns, and sharp hooves. She shuddered at the thought.

"Get away," she yelled again, trying to kick at him.

A ripping sound rang out in the empty barn as the Velcro released, and her skirt tore away from her body.

"You've got to be kidding me," she shouted to no one in particular. But at least she was free, she thought, as she scrambled higher up the ladder. "Go on now. You got what you wanted," she hollered.

But the goat continued to stare up at her, her skirt hanging from his mouth, as if he were contemplating going after her shirt next.

"Oh no you don't," she said, climbing the last few rungs and hauling herself over the top and into the loft. She peered over the edge, then let out a tiny squeal as the goat raised up on his back legs and planted his front hooves on one of the rungs. As a librarian, her mind was constantly cataloguing random facts about hundreds of odd topics, and her brain chose that moment to remind her that goats were notorious climbers. The ladder knocked against the frame of the loft as it shook with the goat's weight.

"Get off," she yelled, using her librarian voice again.

The goat was not impressed by her commanding tone and pawed at the ladder again. It shook with each strike of the goat's hooves, shifting to the side as the beast tried to ascend the rungs. The combined weight of the animal and the momentum of its already sliding motion caused the ladder to go skidding off the edge. It fell to the floor with a loud bang, scaring both Otis and the horses in the barn. Beauty, who had still been standing at the corral gate with Prince, let out a loud neigh and took off, the large gray following. Not that they were going to be of any help anyway.

Otis narrowed his eyes as he stared up at her, then took off out the barn door, dragging her skirt behind him. She let out a final cry of aggravation as she watched her cell phone drop from the pocket and bounce onto the barn floor.

She leaned back against one of the scratchy bales of hay behind her. Well, wasn't this just a fine kettle of fish? What the heck was she supposed to do now?

She couldn't call for help. And now she couldn't even read a book on her Kindle app while she waited for Bryn or Zane to eventually come home.

She heard a shuffling of feet and leaned over the edge of the loft as she hollered down into the barn, "Help! I'm stuck up here. Hello?"

She was answered with a snuffling oink as Tiny, the two-hundred-pound pig, lumbered into the barn. The pig, who had been raised by a teenage girl, thought of herself as more of a dog than a hog, and took offense at any porcine references. She had a hot-pink fabric peony tied with a ribbon around her stout neck, and she appeared to be smiling as she peered up at Jillian.

Another thumping of hooves sounded on the barn floor as

another one of Bryn's rescues, a mini-horse named Shamus, wandered in after his friend and frequent cohort-in-crime.

"Hello, Tiny. Hello, Shamus," she said with a sigh. "Think either of you could manage to put the ladder back or maybe toss that phone up to me?"

The pig let out another oink, then shuffled over to sniff the phone. Shamus just scoffed as he peered up at her. Tiny raised her head at the sound of a truck engine, and the two animals trotted out of the barn as if they were the official greeters of the horse rescue.

Thank goodness. Someone's here. She hurried over and pushed open one of the big loft windows in the side of the barn, thankful it kept her bottom half covered. Holding her hand up to block the sun from her eyes, she was relieved to see Zane's silver king-cab truck kicking up dust as it pulled a horse trailer down the driveway and parked in front of the barn.

"Zane! Help! I'm stuck up in the loft!" She waved her arms, yelling down as the truck door opened.

A tall man wearing a tan shirt and a brown cowboy hat stepped out of the truck. He lifted his head to look up at the barn.

Oh no.

She dropped down below the window, heat flaming her cheeks. *Seriously?*

It wasn't Zane. It was Deputy Ethan Rayburn, the guy she'd been semi-crushing on for the last few weeks. Which for her—someone who had vowed not to date or get involved with any man until her son was in college, or maybe never—was saying a lot. He'd been flirting with her and hinting at asking her out, but so far she'd been able to avoid his efforts.

"Jillian? Is that you?"

She cringed as she heard his deep voice call from below. He'd already seen her. It wasn't like she could pretend she wasn't up here—no matter how hard she wanted to. She peeked her head over the edge of the loft and tried for casual nonchalance, as if she'd just run into him at the supermarket, instead of half-naked and trapped in the barn loft. "Oh, hi, Ethan."

His brow furrowed. "What are you doing up there?"

I'm having a party. What does it look like?

"I'm stuck."

"Maybe I should repeat my question."

She let out a heavy sigh. "No. I heard you. And I really am stuck. Bryn's stupid goat chased me up here, then knocked the ladder down."

A grin tugged at the corners of his lips as he pointed to the fallen ladder lying on the barn floor. "That ladder?"

"Yes. *That* ladder."

"I can fix that, but you're making my first damsel-in-distress call this morning pretty easy." He picked up the ladder and leaned it back against the edge of the loft.

That's what you think.

"First off, I'm no damsel. I'm curvy and five-foot-nine. And I haul around stacks of books for a living, so I can take care of myself."

He grinned up at her. "Wait, you had me at curvy."

A warm flush heated her cheeks. "Stop it. Curvy is just a

nicer way of saying that I have an hourglass figure with way more sand in the bottom half."

"That just happens to be where I'm the most partial to sand."

"Oh my word." She rolled her eyes, but her insides were flipping around like she had jumping beans in her belly.

He lifted his hands off the ladder. "But if you don't need me, I can take off."

"No! Wait. I said I'm not a damsel, but I'll admit to being in the slightest bit of distress."

"At your service, ma'am," he said, deepening his voice and winking up at her.

Why did everything out of his mouth sound dirty? And why did she like it? Also, he wasn't usually this cool. He usually seemed more nervous and a little tongue-tied around her. Maybe he felt more comfortable in his official capacity as deputy.

"I'm sort of afraid of heights. And by sort of, I mean terrified. So I may need your help getting down."

He chuckled. "Okay. Not a problem. I can come up and get you." He lifted his cowboy boot onto the first rung of the ladder.

"No! Don't. I mean, that's nice of you, but there's another problem."

"What is it?"

She chewed her bottom lip as she tried to figure out how best to phrase it. "So when the goat chased me up here, we were having sort of a tug-of-war. With my skirt. And he won."

"Say again?"

"Please don't make me repeat it. I'm humiliated enough as it is."

"So, you're telling me there's a goat running around here somewhere with your skirt and you're up there in just your...uh...?"

There was the tongue-tied guy she was used to.

She nodded. "My underpants. Yes."

He raised an eyebrow. "Did you say *underpants*?"

"Yes. I have a ten-year-old son. That's what we call them in our house. Are you more comfortable if I call them *panties*?"

He cringed, and a pink blush crawled up his neck. "Nope. I'm good with underpants. Actually I'm good with not talking about them at all."

"Well, we don't have to talk about them, but from where you're standing, you're certainly going to get to see them."

"Let's just pretend I'm here on official duty. I'll try to think of you as a kitten stuck in a tree." Pink colored his cheeks again. "Okay, maybe not a kitten."

Jillian pressed her lips together to keep from laughing. It was kind of adorable the way he blushed. Especially since the man was a six-foot-plus, broad-shouldered hunk of a cowboy.

He scrubbed a hand across the back of his neck. "I just meant that I can stay professional. And don't worry, I've seen a lot crazier things in my line of work. Once I had to help save a three-hundred-pound naked guy who got his hand stuck in the toilet trying to save his phone from being flushed."

"Seriously, dude? Do you think telling me about a three-hundred-pound naked guy stuck in a toilet is helping me to feel better about this situation?"

"Well, uh, no, I mean, I didn't mean..."

"Let's just go back to you thinking of me as a kitten." Her heart pounded as she tried not to think about how high up she was. *I can do this.* Summoning her courage, she started to stand but then couldn't bring herself to swing her bare leg over the side of the ladder with him down there looking up at her. "I can't do this."

"Don't be afraid. I'm right here. I won't let you fall. And I'm still willing to come up there."

"No. I can do it. I just can't quite get over your vantage point."

"Oh. Do you want me to wait outside?"

"Heck no. I want you to hold the ladder steady."

"I've got it," he said, switching to the other side of the ladder and disappearing from her view. His voice came up from under the loft. "I'll just hold onto the ladder from this side while you get...situated."

"Okay. That works." She took a deep breath, thankful he was being such a good sport about this whole awkward situation. "I'm going to get on the ladder now. You sure you've got a good hold of it?"

"Yes, I've got it. And that first step is the hardest. Once you're on the ladder, it's smooth sailing from there. Just don't look down."

Her pulse raced as she turned around. She wiped her sweaty palms on her shirt, then took hold of the top rung and swung her leg over. She let out a squeal as her shoe slipped.

"You okay?"

"Ye-s-s," she said, her voice a little shaky as she regained her footing.

"Talk to me. Tell me about something you're thinking about."

"You mean besides my half-naked attempt to defy death as I descend a ladder that looks older than my grandma?"

"Yes."

She had to smile. "Okay, I'm thinking about how I've lived in California for the past ten years, and I've gone to the beach a million times. So I'm trying to pretend that I'm just wearing my swimsuit." She was fully on the ladder now, and she took another hesitant step down.

"Then do I get to be the lifeguard who is saving you? I'm certified in first aid, so I can administer mouth-to-mouth if the situation calls for it."

She could hear the humor in his voice as she took another step. "You're a pretty smooth talker when you're hidden under the loft." She descended another few steps, and Ethan's head came into view.

His eyes were wide, and his mouth was open as he stared at her mid-section. He made kind of a choking sound, then said, "Are you wearing Iron Man underwear?"

She'd been waiting for some kind of comment when her red and yellow bikini underwear came into view. Now it was her face heating up. "Yes. No. Sort of. It's my sister's fault. She has a weird sense of humor. She wanted me to be brave about making the move out here to Colorado, so she ordered me this value pack of superhero underpants. But when they came, we realized they were knockoffs, so I'm actually wearing *Ironed* Man underwear." She took another cautious step down the ladder, anxious to get her crotch out of his direct line of sight. "I'd like to tell you I'm only wearing them because I'm low on laundry, but if you must know, I often wear them when I need a little extra ounce of courage or superhero skills for the upcoming day."

"I've gotta know. What's happening in your life today that warrants *Ironed* Man's superhuman strength, genius level intellect, and acerbic wit?"

"I'd say if it was a tug-of war with a goat, Ironed Man failed me." She cocked an eyebrow, peering at him through the rungs of the ladder. "But I applaud your use of the word *acerbic*."

He smiled and lifted his shoulders in a shrug. "My mom was an English teacher. She raised her kids to have an expansive vocabulary."

Jillian offered him a coy smile. "You know, big words are a turn-on for librarians."

He swallowed. "*All* librarians or just you?"

She lifted one shoulder. "Why? Is there another librarian you're interested in turning on?"

He tilted his head. "Hazel Duncan works the desk at the library, and she's pretty cute."

Jillian barked out a laugh. "She's eighty-three."

"She's still pretty feisty."

"You make a valid point."

"I'm just asking to make sure I properly comprehend what kind of effects my usage of substantially large words might have on you."

She raised an eyebrow. "Don't think I don't know what you're doing."

"What?" he asked, obviously trying to sound innocent. He raised his hand on the side of the ladder. It was just the slightest movement, but it was enough for the top of his fingers to graze the underside of hers. "Because you shared that, I was just going to tell you that maybe women in superhero underwear are a turn-on for cowboys."

Jillian laughed, heat shooting up her spine at the soft touch of his hand against hers. "I think *all* women in their underwear are a turn-on for cowboys."

He shrugged. "You make a valid point."

She took the last step and heaved a sigh of relief as her foot touched the solid ground of the barn floor. Her knees shook as her other foot followed.

Ethan circled the ladder and slid his arm around her waist. "Hey, now. I got you." He peered down at her, offering her a coy grin as he picked a bit of hay from her bangs. "You made it out of the tree, Kitten."

Oh. Gosh. The word "kitten" coming out of his mouth in that deep slow drawl he had just about did her in. She wanted to swoon, and she was not a swooner.

But he *had* just been there for her in her hour of need. And had handled the ridiculously awkward situation with chivalry and tact.

She wasn't sure if it was because her knees were already weak or because with his arm around her they were already halfway there, but in a completely uncharacteristic impulse she turned to him and wrapped her arms around his waist. He smelled like leather and starch and the most delicious cologne, and she wanted to bury her face in his shirt and inhale him.

She gave herself just a moment to feel the strength of him, to relish the solid muscle of his chest against hers, to appreciate that amazing feeling of a man's arms wrapped around her, before her stone-cold willpower kicked back in.

She pulled away and smoothed the wrinkles in the front of his uniform shirt, all too conscious of the shiny gold star pinned to his chest. Another good reason to keep her distance from this man. "Sorry about that. Don't know what came over me."

"No need to apologize. I'll take a hug from a curvy librarian any day."

She smiled. "I'll let Hazel know."

He chuckled. "Seriously, don't be sorry to me. You just made my day, hell, my whole year has been made. I can't imagine anything that could top rescuing a damsel…er…I mean, a badass curvy librarian…in distress who was wearing Ironed Man undies."

"I can imagine," she said. "But I'd rather you *not* write this up in a report or share it with the guys down at the office."

"I won't say a word. We'll keep this one just between us."

"I appreciate it."

He shook his head, trying to hold back another laugh. "It's not like they'd believe me, anyway."

"As much as I'm enjoying our little chat here, I think I'm gonna go try to find some pants," Jillian told him, trying to pull the hem of her T-shirt down. "I think I've got my gym bag in my car."

She didn't need to tell him she'd had the bag in her car for weeks. It wasn't that she hated exercise, she just preferred to do it hiking trails and running around outside with her son and his newly acquired puppy.

"Good idea," Ethan said. "I'll try to track down the goat."

The back seat of her car was a mess of jackets, dog toys, and books. She spotted her gym bag on the floor and rifled through it, praying to find some pants. *Yes*. She pulled out a pair of leggings. Using the back of the car for support, she toed off her tennies and was wiggling into the leggings as Bryn and Zane pulled up next to her in *his* silver truck.

Bryn waved as she got out of the cab but had a quizzical expression on her face. "Hey, Jillian. What's up?"

"Hey, isn't that Rayburn's truck?" Zane asked, coming around the front of his pickup. "What's Ethan doing here?"

Bryn's eyes widened, and a knowing grin spread across her face. She was one of Jillian's closest friends in Creedence, and she knew all about the semi-crush and the flirting that had been happening between Ethan and Jillian. "Did we interrupt something? If so, we can leave and come back again later. What do you need? Thirty minutes? An hour?"

Oh brother. Could this day get any worse? "No. It's not like that."

At the same moment, Ethan sauntered out of the barn door holding up a wad of floral fabric in his hand. "I found your skirt."

Bryn peered from Ethan back to Jillian. "You were saying?"

CHAPTER 2

JILLIAN FELT THE HEAT RUSH TO HER CHEEKS AND IMAG-
ined they were the same shade of pink as the deputy sheriff's
currently were.

She just had to ask if things could get worse.

"No, it's not like that," Ethan said, as if trying to defend
her honor. "She just lost her skirt."

"That's what they all say," Zane murmured.

"No, really, it wasn't me. It was the goat."

Jillian smashed the palm of her hand against her forehead.

"Okay, that's a new one," Zane said with a smirk as he held
up his hands. "But hey, whatever floats your boat. I don't judge."

Jillian shook her head. "Stop. I dropped a pancake on my
skirt this morning, and your stupid goat wrestled it off of me
as he tried to eat it."

"Likely story," Zane said out the corner of his mouth.

At the same time Bryn said, "That sounds like Otis. I'm
so sorry."

"So what are you doing out here?" Zane asked, leaning
back against the hood of his truck. "Besides wrestling a goat
for ladies' undergarments. Or did you come to arrest Otis?"

"If only," Jillian said, stuffing her feet back into her
Converse sneakers.

Ethan shook his head, and his expression turned serious. "No, I actually came out here to get you all." He nodded to Bryn and Zane. "We need your help. We're doing a raid in about an hour of an illegal horse track operation in the next county over. There's evidence that beyond the gambling, there's also been some neglect and possible abuse of the horses. So we're calling on all the horse rescues in the area to show up and take as many as they can. It sounds like they have upwards of twenty-five horses." He jerked a thumb toward his truck. "I'm not a rescue, but I brought my rig just in case we need it. And I could probably house a couple of them temporarily."

Bryn and Zane immediately went into business mode. "I'll run in the house and collect our gear, then I'll find some of those extra halters we got last month," Bryn said.

"I'll hook up the trailer while you get ready," Zane said. He pointed toward the barn. "Jillian, why don't you grab some of those blankets in the tack room, and it wouldn't hurt to bring that half a bag of sweet feed and some little buckets to help get 'em in the trailers. Ethan, you can help me load up a few bales of hay. Wheels up in ten."

By the time they pulled out of the driveway, Bryn's cousin, Cade Callahan, and his fiancé, Nora Fisher, had shown up with another horse trailer in tow. They joined the parade of trucks heading out to the highway.

Ethan still wasn't sure how it happened, but Jillian was

somehow riding shotgun in the front of his truck, and they now had forty minutes to kill on the drive. At least she was wearing pants.

"So, thanks again for coming along," he told her. "I'm sure this wasn't how you were planning to spend your Saturday afternoon."

She shrugged. "I can't imagine many people plan to spend their Saturdays involved in a tri-county operation to raid an illegal racetrack betting ring."

He chuckled. "True."

"Seriously, I'm glad to be able to help. Milo talked me into volunteering at Bryn's horse rescue before we were even out of the driveway the first time we drove out there. I had no idea he'd be so interested in horses, but we've both had a lot of fun. It probably helps that his best friend, Mandy Tate, lives on a ranch, is the daughter of a veterinarian, and also volunteers there."

"I can see that. How about you? Have you always been interested in horses?" He couldn't believe how lame that sounded. Why couldn't he think of something interesting to ask her? Maybe it was distraction her legs presented with her feet propped on his dashboard. Or the heady scent of her perfume, or maybe it was her shampoo, that filled the cab of his truck. Whatever it was, it smelled amazing—somehow both sultry and light—like rich vanilla mixed with dahlias, or whatever those flowers were that his grandma had planted on the side of his house.

Geez, listen to him. He sounded like he was at one of those wine tastings he'd suffered through once on a blind date.

He snuck another glance at her. It was like the fifteenth time he'd done that in ten minutes. But he still couldn't believe she was here, in his truck with him. He'd liked her from the first time they met, which had also been at Bryn's horse rescue ranch. He couldn't put his finger on it, but there was just something about Jillian.

It was more than her looks, although those long tan legs of hers drove him crazy. And his hands itched to fill themselves with that mess of curly chestnut-colored hair that was always escaping whatever kind of knot or braid she tried to corral it into. It was mostly her sharp wit—although not as acerbic as Ironed Man's, she still made him laugh. The first time he'd met her, she was wearing a T-shirt that read LIBRARIAN BECAUSE BOOK WIZARD ISN'T AN OFFICIAL TITLE, and the one she had on today had a picture of a woman reading a book with the words BOOKMARKS ARE FOR QUITTERS on it.

She'd told him she liked to hike, so he knew she liked being outdoors. And she liked kids. Everything about her appealed to him. She was pretty, but when she smiled, it lit up her whole face. And if one of those smiles was aimed at him, it sent heat surging through his veins and a flurry of butterflies through his gut that rivaled anything he'd felt with any other woman he'd ever been around. Although that crack about her curves in the barn made him think she didn't see herself for the gorgeous woman she was. But he loved her curves. Even more now that he'd seen them wrapped in superhero underwear.

"What's so funny?" she asked, breaking into his reverie.

"Uh. What do you mean?"

"You just had this funny little smile on your face. I was wondering what you were thinking about."

"Actually, I was thinking about you." He held up his hand. "Not that I think you're funny. Well, I do think you're funny. But not in a I-think-you're-kind-of-weird way, but in a you-always-make-me-laugh way."

She nodded. "I think you're funny too. But in that first I-think-you're-kind-of-weird way."

He laughed. "Thanks. I probably deserved that one. Anyway, I was thinking about the first time we met. It was out at Bryn's when I came to get her help in rescuing a horse."

"And the second time we saw each other was at Bryn's too. When she had that benefit dance to help the horse rescue."

"And now here we are, going off to rescue a horse together again." He shook his head. "I'm worried I'm gonna keep having to find horses to save if I'm ever gonna get a chance to ask you out on a date."

"Oh gosh." She stared down at her lap, as if the seam on her leggings suddenly held all her interest.

Dang. He'd pushed too hard, too fast. He'd already figured out he needed to take it slow with her. She'd made that clear the first time he'd tried to ask her out at the benefit dance. But after the way she'd flirted with him in the barn earlier, he'd thought he might have a chance.

She took a deep breath, then her words all came out in a rush. "Ethan, I'm not much into dating. Nothing against you. I mean, I think you're ridiculously hot and so nice, and of course I'm attracted to you. And I'm not saying we wouldn't have fun together. It's just that I'm a single mom, and I just got this new job at the library. And I've just got a lot on my plate right now. Does that make sense?"

He shrugged. "I don't know. I didn't hear anything after that part where you said you thought I was ridiculously hot."

"Nice." She swatted playfully at his arm.

"Oh, and I also heard the part where you said you were attracted to me." He gave her a side-eye look. "No take-backs."

"Oh my gosh. You *are* crazy."

"And you smell really nice."

"What?" She furrowed her brow. "Way to make it even more awkward."

He shrugged again. "Well, you do."

She shrugged back. "Well, so do you."

His grin widened. Maybe he was wearing her down.

———

Jillian gasped as Ethan pulled his truck in behind the sheriff's Blazer. The ranch, if it could even be called that, was in a terrible state of disrepair. What was left of the paint was peeling off the old farmhouse, and the barn was leaning so far to one side a good gust of wind could knock it right down.

The yard had gone almost completely to weed and what grass remained was dry and overgrown. A dusty dirt track covered the pasture behind the barn, and at least a dozen horses stood in the paddock next to it, their coats dull and their bodies thin.

The raid had gone down thirty minutes earlier, so the

authorities had the culprits in custody, and they'd given the okay to let the animal rescue teams in. But the scope of the operation was much bigger than she'd anticipated. Cars from both the sheriff and police departments of three counties lined the road, as well as vehicles from the Humane Society, the Division of Wildlife, and a slew of other county agencies, including Brody Tate's veterinary truck.

It normally wouldn't surprise her that Brody would be here except for the fact that her son was supposed to be hanging out at some lake with him and his family this morning learning to fish. And from the looks of the two ten-year-olds perched on top of the vet box affixed to the back of the truck, the kids were most definitely not at the lake.

"I'm gonna kill Brody," she muttered, pointing out the kids to Ethan. Then she was out of the truck before he'd barely brought it to a stop and hurrying toward the vet truck. "What are you two doing here?" she called up to her son and Brody's daughter, Mandy.

"Hi, Mom," Milo answered with an excited wave. "Isn't this cool?"

"No, it's not cool. It's dangerous."

"Then why are you here?"

"Because I'm an adult."

Her son raised an eyebrow. "So, it's only dangerous to kids? That doesn't make sense. Especially since you're down there in the line of traffic, and we're safe up here."

"Quit dodging the question. What are you doing here?"

"It's my fault," Brody said, coming up behind her.

She turned on him. "You brought my son to a raid?"

"Not on purpose. We were fishing at a lake nearby when the call came in about the raid. They needed vets, and I didn't have time to take the kids back. Elle is on her way here to pick them up." He frowned at his daughter. "And they were supposed to stay in the truck."

"We are *technically* still in the truck," Mandy pointed out. "But we could see better from up here."

"Just make sure you stay up there," he said, opening one of the compartments of the work box and taking out a box of gloves. The tall cowboy had on coveralls and thick rubber Wellingtons over his boots and both were covered in mud and gunk.

Bryn, Zane, and Ethan walked up to the truck as Jillian took a step back, grimacing as she waved her hand in front of her face. "Wow. You smell awful."

Brody shook his head, his expression solemn. "It's a mess out there," he said, indicating the barn behind him. "They've got horses on top of horses in there, and haven't cleaned out their stalls in what looks like weeks. There's not enough hay, and what's in there is barely edible. Looks like half of them are malnourished and the other half aren't far behind. Doesn't look like they even give them enough water."

"Oh no," Bryn said, covering her mouth with her hand. "Poor babies."

"Yeah, it's bad. There's some evidence of abuse too."

"Thanks for coming out on short notice, Doc," Ethan said, shaking Brody's hand. "We appreciate it."

"Looks like it's gonna be a long afternoon."

Ethan gestured toward a couple of deputies standing outside the barn. "I'm gonna go see what's going on, and what we can do to help."

As the group waited by the truck, they were joined by Cade and Nora, who said hello to the kids, then cringed in unison as Bryn filled them in on the state of the horses.

"We brought our trailer so we can take a couple," Cade said. "I wish we could take more, but I just bought another fifty head of cattle, and I'm pretty snowed under with renovations at the new house."

"We just appreciate you taking any," Bryn said. "I know you all have a lot on your plates. This is good of you."

Cade nodded. "Happy to help. And Allie will be thrilled." He and Bryn looked like they could have been siblings instead of cousins. They shared the same dark-blond hair and both had the Callahan good looks. He was close to the same height as Ethan, but his expression was usually a lot more reserved whereas Ethan's was usually more open and friendly.

Although those weren't the expressions the deputy was using as he returned a few minutes later. His brow was creased with concern for the horses and anger at the perpetrators. "They've arrested the head guys," he told the group. "They're holding some of the others for questioning, but they want to get the horses out of here as soon as they can. The Humane Society has already been documenting them and their conditions, and are ready for us to come in and get them."

"We can get the ones we're taking trailered and give 'em

some fresh water and hay. At least they'll be dry and out of that shithole," Zane said. "Then we can come back and help with the rest. We'll do whatever's needed to help get them out of here."

Bryn nodded. She pointed at her cousin as she told Ethan, "Cade and Nora can take two, and we've got room for three, and you said you could take two. So we'll tell them we can take seven for now, but we can come back for more if we need to."

"Babe," Zane said quietly, sliding his arm around her waist, "we can't take them all."

She brushed off his arm. "We'll take however many we can."

"They've got other horse rescues here," Ethan said. "And they're all prepared to take several. The Humane Society is working out the particulars, so why don't we head over there and I'll introduce you and see what they want us to do."

"I'm still not super confident around all the horses," Nora said, climbing into the back of the truck. "So I'll just stay here and keep an eye on the kids."

"Thanks," Jillian said. "That would be great. I'd like to go over and see if there's anything I can do to help. If they don't need me, I'll come back to wait with you." She followed Ethan and the others toward the barn but veered off as she neared the paddock. "I'll catch up to you in a minute."

They didn't need her to work out the details with the Humane Society. But these horses did. Her heart broke as she surveyed the conditions of the corral. The water tank was rusted and sunlight shone through several holes in the side. One of the deputies had tried to fill the holes near the bottom with what looked like old rags. It was enough to slow the leaks as he filled the tank with fresh water from a hose. Several horses were already trying to drink from what little water he'd managed to get in the tank.

Two horses, one a buckskin color and the other brown, stood in the corner of the paddock. They both had black manes that were matted and tangled and long black tails that hadn't seen a brush in a long time. Their coats were dull and caked with patches of dried mud. The brown one was thinner than the other; his ribs were visible, but they both looked undernourished. The two of them had their heads bent together as if they were sharing a conversation, and they eyed her warily as she took a step closer to them.

"Hey there. It's okay," she said quietly as she moved closer still. "Nobody's gonna hurt you. Not anymore."

They didn't move away. They just stared at her, and she swore she saw sadness and defeat in their beautiful brown eyes. Her chest hurt looking at them. She ached for what they had gone through and was thankful for organizations like the Humane Society, and Bryn's horse rescue, and Ethan's department, who were all trying to help them.

Bryn had grabbed a bunch of carrots and apples from her house before they'd left, and she'd put a bag of them in Ethan's truck. One of the carrots had a notch like a gun, and Jillian had been joking around with it and another one on the drive here, sticking them in the side pockets of her leggings and challenging Ethan to a vegetable duel at high noon. She hadn't realized then that the carrots would be both terrible props for a joke and also come in so handy.

She pulled one of the carrots out now and leaned over the half-rotted fence, stretching her arm toward them. "Here ya go. You can have this."

The brown horse took a step back, but the other gave a huff and took a cautious step forward. Then another.

Jillian wiggled the carrot and kept up her soothing tone as she coaxed the buckskin toward her. The other horse, though cautious at first, seemed to stay in step with the first one as they plodded closer.

She broke the carrot in two and held a piece out in each hand. As if in tandem, the two horses each sniffed the carrots, then gently snuffled them off her palms. "Good horses." She pulled out the other carrot and let them have it too. Holding out her hand, she softly stroked her fingers over the buckskin's neck.

To her surprise, the horse took a step closer and nudged her nose affectionately into Jillian's shoulder. "Oh my gosh, aren't you just the sweetest?" she said, falling hopelessly in love as she gave the horse's neck another scratch.

"Looks like you made a friend," Ethan said, coming up behind her. He kept his voice low so as not to spook the horses. He carried two sets of halters and lead ropes and dropped them gently at their feet, then reached out to pat the buckskin's side.

"I did," Jillian said, blinking back the tears welling in her eyes. "And I'm not leaving without her. It's going to be a little cramped in the apartment we share with my sister, but we'll manage because I'm bringing this horse home with me."

He let out a soft laugh. "How about I bring her home with me? Then you can visit her whenever you want. And your sister doesn't have to share her bathroom with a horse."

"Oh, Ethan," she said, turning to him and wrapping her arms tightly around his waist. "Thank you."

She felt him hesitate for just a second, and she wasn't sure if he was just surprised by her display of emotion or if he thought she was crazy, but then he gathered her close and hugged her to him.

Pulling away, she brushed at the tear that had accidentally leaked out of her eye. "Geez. I don't know what is going on with me. I'm not usually a crier…or a spontaneous hugger. Well, I am a hugger, but not usually with men."

Ethan nudged her arm. "Just the ridiculously hot ones, huh?"

She shook her head. "I'm never gonna live that down, am I?"

"Not a chance."

She smiled, then gestured toward the horses. "There's some kind of connection with these two. That sounds silly, but they've been together the whole time I've been watching them, and they don't seem to leave each other's side. I feel like they just have to stay together. Can you take them both?"

He nodded. "Consider it done."

She swallowed, fighting another wave of emotion. "Oh gosh. I think I'm going to have to hug you again."

He grinned and opened his arms.

CHAPTER 3

JILLIAN STEPPED BACK INTO ETHAN'S ARMS AND LET HIM wrap her up. What was going on with her? Where was her willpower? She'd already told him she wasn't interested in dating, so how did she keep ending up in his arms and pressed tight against his hard muscular chest?

Because he feels so damn good.

He leaned down and pressed his lips to her hair. His voice was quiet as he spoke. "Don't beat yourself up about being emotional. It's tough seeing these animals like this. It makes me want to cry, too."

Yeah, that was it. She was just overwhelmed with the situation. Except that didn't explain why she'd hugged him earlier. Urgh. Stop thinking and just enjoy the hug.

He tightened his grip on her as he moved his mouth closer to her ear. His voice was still low, but this time his tone was flirty. "I feel like I may have played my hand too early. I love the hug, but if I would have held out longer on taking that other horse, could I have scored a date?"

A laugh bubbled out of her as she pushed him away. "You are terrible."

"Maybe not a full-on dinner, but coffee, at least."

"Let's just focus on the horses."

"That wasn't a no," he murmured with a laugh as he picked up the halters and handed one to her. Turning his attention to the horses, he spoke soothingly to the brown one as he carefully eased the other halter around his neck. He nodded to the one she held. "You want to try to get that one on your new best friend there?"

The buckskin had her head over the fence and leaned into Jillian again as she stepped closer and slid the halter around her head. She stroked the horse's neck, then finished buckling it.

Ethan slowly climbed over the fence, probably to both avoid scaring the horses and so the rickety thing didn't fall apart under him. He held out his hand to help her over. "I think it's best if we come in here, then lead them out the gate together."

"I agree." She let him help her over, sucking in the tiniest breath at the feel of his hands on her waist. It was a warm summer day, but it suddenly felt as if someone had turned the heat up. What had gotten into her? She was not usually affected by a man like this.

But she wasn't usually around a man like Ethan.

Focus on the horses.

He clicked the lead ropes onto the horses' halters and gently eased them forward. "I've got them if you just want to walk alongside and keep talking to them."

The same deputy who'd been filling the water tank crossed to open the gate for them. They stopped to let the horses get a drink, then led them out and across the yard, stopping again several yards from the command post.

"Why don't you go tell them which two we're taking while I stay here with them," Ethan told her.

She hurried over to a woman holding a clipboard and pointed out the horses. The woman made a few notes and then let her go. "We're good," she told Ethan as she caught back up to him, and they walked the horses across the property to where Ethan's truck and trailer were parked.

"I'm going to tie them to the sides for now instead of making them get in the trailer just yet," Ethan said. "I think we should give them some fresh hay and some of that sweet feed, earn their trust a little first."

"Good idea." She poured some grain into a couple of small buckets as he tied the horses to the back of the trailer.

The horses greedily devoured the grain and chomped on the hay Ethan offered them. He'd brought a rubber tub, and he filled it with some jugs of water, then set it on the ground between them. They lapped at the fresh water but didn't drink it as quickly as they had the water in the tank earlier.

"I think we need to take it easy so they don't end up bloated and colicky," Ethan said.

"I'm happy to just stand here with them," Jillian said. "I can watch them if you need to be doing other things."

He nodded. "I should probably check back in and see if there's something else I can do to help." He took a step forward as if he were going to hug her again, then stopped himself.

"If you walk back by Brody's truck, will you tell Milo he can come over here to wait with me and meet the horses?"

"Will do," he said, tipping his hat and sauntering away.

She tried to tell herself not to, but she totally checked

out his butt as he walked off. The buckskin nudged her side again, and Jillian wasn't sure if the horse was reading her mind or just prodding her for more food or affection.

Jillian gave her both. After petting both the horses' necks again, she took an apple from the cab of the pickup and had just finished cutting it into slices when Milo came racing up to her.

"Hey, Mom," he said, giving her a tight hug.

She hugged him back, then studied his face as he pulled away. For a kid who was almost always in a good mood, his brow was creased with anguish. "You okay, honey?"

He shrugged. "Yeah, it's just tough to see the way they treated all those horses. It makes my stomach hurt a little. I feel so bad for them."

She brought her son back in for another hug—he was the one guy she wanted to hug all the time. He was growing up so fast, and sometimes she was afraid he would get too old to want her cuddles. "I love you. You've got a good heart, son. And I know what you mean. This all makes my stomach hurt a little too." She gestured to the two horses tied to the trailer. "These are the two Ethan is taking back to his ranch. They're both really sweet. You want to meet them?"

"Yeah, totally."

She handed him a couple of apple slices. "These two seem to have some kind of bond. They wouldn't leave each other's sides when they were in the corral. But this one came right up to me." She patted the buckskin's side. "She's really affectionate. I think we should call her Nudge."

"Nudge? That's a weird name," Milo said, holding out an apple slice for each horse. They nibbled the slices from his flattened palms, then the buckskin nudged her nose into his armpit and nuzzled his arm. He laughed as he rubbed her neck. "Okay, I get it now. And actually, Nudge seems like the perfect name." He pointed to the other horse. "And what are you going to call her buddy?"

"Hmm. I think you just said it. Why don't we call him Buddy?"

"I like it." He rubbed the brown horse's side. "What do you think, Buddy? You okay with that name?" The horse stamped his foot and lifted his head as if he agreed. Milo laughed. "I think he likes it too. But isn't Ethan taking these horses? Maybe he'll want to name them."

"You're right. But I think he'll be okay with it. He's a pretty easy-going guy. And he's got a lot of other things he's thinking about today besides coming up with names for these two."

"Hey! What do you think you're doing with those horses?"

Jillian turned to see a large beefy man heading their way, an angry scowl on his face. His head was clean-shaven, and tattoos circled his neck and covered his thick arms. She took a step in front of Milo. "We're taking them somewhere safe and far away from here."

"You're not takin' them anywhere," he said, reaching for Buddy's halter. "They belong to the ranch, and we're keeping them here."

"Get away from them," Milo said, stepping between the man and the horses.

"What'd you say, you little punk?"

"I said get away from them. You don't deserve to have *any* horses, the way you've treated them."

"You should watch your mouth, kid." He reached down and grabbed a handful of the front of Milo's shirt, pulling him up by the fabric. "Now you'd better get out of my way."

Adrenaline shot through Jillian, like a protective surge of "mother bear" flowing through her veins, as she stepped toward the man. "*You'd better* get your hands off my kid. Right. Now."

A sinister smile crept across the man's face. "Who's gonna make me?"

A creepy skull with a snake slithering out of its mouth was tattooed across his neck, and he had the letters F, E, A, and R across the back of his fingers, but she'd run across his type before. They liked people, especially women, to cower in their presence.

She planted her feet and stood taller, the training of years of self-defense classes running through her head as she noted his most vulnerable spots. He was wearing a ratty T-shirt, jeans, and thick work boots crusted in mud, so better to go for the throat or the nose rather than his feet if things went dicey. She drew her fingers into tight fists and jutted out her chin as she stared him hard in the eyes. She prayed he would only hear the steel in her voice, and not a tremor of fear. "Take. Your. Hands. Off. My. Son. Now."

———

Ethan tried to tell himself he just wanted to check on the horses, but he knew it had more to do with the woman tending them. He couldn't seem to keep his mind off her. Or his hands.

He came around the side of the barn trying to think of a way to score another hug, but his heart lurched at the sight of her and Milo in what looked like an altercation with a large rough-looking man. He took off, not quite running, but moving quickly through the parked vehicles.

He couldn't hear everything, but caught snatches of their conversation and knew it wasn't good.

"Hey, Rayburn, can you take a look at this?" another deputy called to him as he waved a clipboard.

"Yeah, give me a few minutes, and I'll check back with you," he called back, not slowing his pace. The guy had hold of Milo's shirt, and Ethan couldn't get to them fast enough.

Apparently, it didn't matter though because Jillian seemed to have the matter in hand as she stepped between the man and her child.

Her jaw was set, and her body was positioned in a stance he recognized from self-defense training. Her fingers curled into fists, and even though the guy had fifty pounds on her and looked like he'd just gotten out of prison, she got right in his face and wasn't backing down.

He was one car length behind them now, but neither of them had seen him. He paused for a second, not wanting to escalate the situation further but ready to step in if she needed him.

But she seemed to be holding her own.

She was a sight to behold. *Fierce* was the word that came to mind. Even in her comical T-shirt and Converse tennis shoes, she had a strength and a fearlessness about her. He had to swallow back the emotion at watching this mother protect her son like a grizzly would a cub.

And forget about his heart.

He was pretty sure he fell in love with her, right in that moment.

The man held her stare for an extra beat, then dropped his hold on Milo's shirt. "Whatever. Take your stupid kid."

"Who you calling stupid?" Milo asked. "I'm not the one who can't figure out how to feed and water some horses."

Geez. That kid was as gutsy as his mom.

The guy opened his mouth to say something, then caught sight of Ethan and closed it again. He made a sort of a growling noise in the back of his throat, then turned and stomped off in the other direction before Ethan had a chance to give him a piece of his mind. He wasn't worried though; he'd find time to deal with him later.

Jillian stood her ground as she watched the guy huff away. When he'd rounded the corner of the trailer and was out of sight, she dropped her shoulders and pulled Milo to her in an intense hug. "Damn, kid. That scared the hell out of me. Are you okay?"

"I'm fine, Mom," the kid said, but Ethan could see he was hugging her back just as hard. "That guy was a jerk."

"Yeah, he was." She looked up, and her eyes went round as she noticed him standing there. "Hey, Ethan." She started to smile, then furrowed her brow as she took a few steps toward him. "Ethan? You okay?"

He opened his mouth to answer, or to say something about how brave she was, but instead the words that came out were "Will you marry me?"

CHAPTER 4

JILLIAN FROZE IN HER TRACKS. HER MOUTH WENT DRY. It felt like her heart stopped, then started again, pounding at a hundred miles an hour.

"Umm, what?" she finally managed to stutter.

Ethan held her gaze, his expression tender, as he repeated the words. "I said will you marry me?" He blew out a breath and pressed a hand to his chest. "That was amazing. I was coming to help you, but you stood up to that jerk all on your own. You were fierce, woman. And I think you just stole my heart."

She blinked, utterly at a loss for words. And words were her jam. She very seldom didn't know what to say. But this tall cowboy had completely knocked her sideways, and she wasn't quite sure how to respond. Her head knew he didn't mean it. He couldn't. They'd only known each other for a few weeks. But her heart was responding to the sincere way he'd uttered the words that she'd never been asked before.

"Wasn't she awesome?" Milo said, holding his hand out to Ethan for a high five. "My mom is a total B.A."

Ethan's lips curved into a grin as he finally tore his gaze from hers and gave Milo's hand a smack. "She sure is. Although I don't normally condone antagonizing dangerous men."

Jillian bristled. "How do you know he was dangerous?"

"Because he literally had the word 'dangerous' tattooed across his arm."

"Okay, I'll give you that one." She stared down at her son. "But *I* don't normally condone my son using swear words."

Milo shrugged innocently. "What? I didn't swear. I said B.A. I thought you'd prefer that over me saying the actual words 'bad ass.'"

"I'm about to use the words 'smart ass.' And not in a good way."

Her son ducked his head. "Yes, ma'am." He looked up at Ethan. "Sorry."

Ethan clapped him on the shoulder. "I appreciate that." He leaned lower, affecting a stage whisper that Jillian could obviously hear. "Between you and me, kid, your mom *is* a bad ass."

Milo grinned and just as loudly whispered back, "I know."

"Hey guys," a woman's voice called.

Jillian looked up to see her friend and Brody's girlfriend, Elle Brooks, heading in their direction. She waved her toward them, Ethan's impromptu proposal pushed even farther away. It wasn't like it was a real proposal anyway. Ethan had to have been goofing around. He wasn't serious. Was he?

"I'm so sorry Brody had to bring the kids out here," Elle said, striding forward to give Jillian a hug. Elle was shorter than her and smelled like designer perfume. She wore jeans, cowboy boots, and a simple white button-up, but still looked like she'd stepped off the pages of a fashion magazine. With her blond hair and slim figure, it was hard not to want to hate her. Except she was one of the nicest women Jillian had ever met. Sweet, kind, and generous to a fault—she was always picking up the check or donating to charities in an effort to use the life insurance money her husband had left her. Elle had seen her share of heartache when she lost him and their unborn child in a tragic car accident two years ago. "This is pretty awful. Is everybody okay?"

Jillian nodded. "Yeah, we're all fine. It's been tough, though, seeing the terrible conditions these horses have been kept in."

Elle shivered. "I can imagine." She said hello to Ethan, then put an arm around Milo's shoulders. "You ready to get out of here, kid?"

"Yes," Jillian answered for her son. "He is more than ready."

"But Mom," Milo said, "I want to stay with you and the horses."

"I know. But this place gives me the creeps, and I'd feel better if you weren't here."

"I agree with your mom," Ethan said. "Besides, we're almost finished anyway. So you're not gonna miss anything exciting. And the horses will be out at my house, so you and your mom can come visit them whenever you want."

Milo eyed his mother. "Can we, Mom?"

"Yeah, sure. If it's really okay with Ethan."

He turned back to the deputy. "How about tomorrow?"

Ethan grinned. "Fine by me. I'd love to see you *and* your mom tomorrow. In fact, you all should come out for supper. I can grill burgers."

That grin was doing funny things to Jillian's insides. "Well, we'll have to see what we're doing tomorrow. We might have plans."

Milo turned and gawked up at his mom. "What plans? We don't have any plans. And when have you ever said no to grilling burgers?" He turned back to Ethan. "My mom thinks cheeseburgers are the perfect food because they have all five food groups in one neat stack."

Ethan's grin grew wider. "Good to know." He nudged Jillian's arm. "So, how about it. Supper at my place? I can guarantee I make a pretty mean cheeseburger. *And* you can see the horses."

She leaned closer to him. "You're not even playing fair," she said quietly.

He shrugged. "Hey, all's fair in—"

She held up a finger. "Don't even say it."

He laughed. "It's just a cheeseburger. What do you say?"

"Fine. We'll come out for cheeseburgers."

"Good." He jerked a thumb toward the barn. "I'm going to go check in and see if I'm cleared to take off. I'd like to get these horses out of here and back to my ranch." He held up his hand to Milo. "See you tomorrow, bud. Bring your appetite."

Milo smacked his hand. "Always do." He turned back to Jillian. "I'm gonna say goodbye to the horses."

Jillian nodded. And since her friend *and* her son were standing there, she refrained from watching the deputy's butt as he walked away this time. But she caught the knowing grin Elle gave her as she turned back around. "What?"

Elle shrugged, the grin widening. "I didn't say anything." "It's just a cheeseburger."

Her friend chuckled. Milo's attention was on the horses, but Elle still kept her voice low. "Hey, burgers with a handsome cowboy sounds like a great night to me."

But he wasn't *just* a handsome cowboy. He was also a deputy with the sheriff's department. Which was just one more reason she should shut this thing down.

Elle winked, then reached out toward Milo. "Let's go, kid. Mandy's going to be wondering what happened to us. And with all this talk about cheeseburgers, I'm getting hungry. I think we should stop by the diner for fries and milkshakes on the way home."

Jillian gave her friend a quick hug. "Thanks, Elle. I'll pick him up in a few hours."

"Whenever is fine." She gave Jillian another knowing smile. "It's no problem if you want to stay longer with Ethan. Helping with the horses, I mean. Not because you're having fun. Just text me later."

Ignoring her friend's not-so-subtle innuendo, she gave her son a quick hug too, then sent him off with Elle. "Be good. Mind your manners. And—"

Milo nodded. "I know. Make good choices. See ya, Mom."

She watched them go, only turning around when she felt a warm snout nudge her in the back. "Hey, girl. Were you feeling ignored?" Jillian asked the buckskin. "Or did you just want another apple slice?"

The horse raised her head up and down and let out a whinny as if to answer "Both."

Jillian fed them each some more apple slices while she waited for Ethan, alternately petting them and reassuring them in a gentle voice that everything would be okay now. From her spot by the road, she saw Bryn and Zane load three horses into their trailer, a yellow palomino, a black and brown pinto, and another brown quarter horse. All three looked in bad shape, gaunt and malnourished, and their legs caked in mud and gunk. Jillian guessed they were some of the ones who had been in the barn, and it broke her heart to see the evidence of mistreatment. But she knew Zane and Bryn would be the best thing to happen to those horses. Both were great with wounded animals, Bryn with her huge heart and caring spirit and Zane with his well-known horse-whispering skills.

Within twenty minutes Ethan was back, and together they loaded the horses into the trailer.

"Since I'm taking two of the horses, Sheriff told me to go ahead and take off," he told Jillian as he held the truck door open for her. "They've got plenty of other guys here to finish securing the scene."

"I'm glad. I just want to get these two away from here and to someplace where they feel safe and dry."

Ethan eased the truck out onto the road, the trailer bouncing behind them. Jillian turned in her seat to look out the back window.

"They'll be okay," he said, setting his hand on top of hers.

"Anything is better than where they were," she answered, trying to focus on something other than the warmth of his hand resting on hers. She didn't know what to do. Should she turn her hand over and hold his? Or nonchalantly slide her hand out from under his? Or act like she sees something out the window and lift her hand up to point at it? Why was she so nervous? It wasn't like someone hadn't tried to hold her hand before.

Because this wasn't just someone. It was Ethan. And as much as she didn't want to admit it to herself, she liked him. He was kind and considerate and funny and sweet and charming. Just the kind of man she'd want to date, *if* she wanted to date someone. But she didn't want to date anyone. She had one very young man in her life who took up all her energy and focus.

Plus she was just starting this new job. And she wanted to do well at it.

And the last man she gave her heart to betrayed her and broke it into a million pieces. Not that Ethan was anything like Radley Mullins. In fact, he was the opposite of Rad—in so many ways, but especially the ones that involved holding up the law.

What would Ethan think if he knew about what had happened with Milo's dad? He probably wouldn't be offering to grill her burgers and trying to hold her hand. And he definitely wouldn't be proposing.

She pulled her hand free to roll down the window a few inches. The scent of hay and the floral fragrance of the wildflowers growing alongside the dirt road wafted in with the warm breeze. She lifted her hair off her neck and leaned back against the seat.

"You okay?" Ethan asked.

"Yeah, it's just been a crazy day." She dropped her hair

and turned sideways to look at him. He'd pushed his hat back a little, and a shock of dark hair fell across his forehead. His chiseled jaw was clean-shaven, and the quirk at the edge of his smile caused a funny little squirm in her stomach. *Quit looking at his mouth.* "I can't believe you asked me to marry you."

Oops. She hadn't meant to say that out loud. She'd planned on never bringing it up again. Like, ever. So much for that plan.

Ethan shook his head. "I can't believe the way you stood up to that guy. It took my breath away. You were so…fierce."

She swallowed, his description of her touching something inside her. "Only because he was threatening my kid."

"It was more than that. You looked like you were ready to take the guy out. I noticed something else. I've taught self-defense, and I don't know what it was, maybe the way you were standing, like you were poised to attack or something. It just seemed like maybe you've taken a few classes."

"I've taken a lot of them."

He frowned. "A *lot*? Any specific reason why?"

"You know, single mom living in California. I wanted to be able to defend myself."

"Against anyone in particular?"

She sighed. She might as well tell him—get it over with. He'd probably find out eventually anyway. And once she told him, she wouldn't have to worry about him trying to ask her out again. He'd probably drop her off at her car on the way back to his ranch. So much for trying out his "mean" cheeseburgers tomorrow.

Too bad. She did love a good burger.

"I guess maybe a lot of someones in particular," she said, twisting her hands together in her lap. "I don't really talk much about it, but I ran into a little trouble during my time in California."

"What kind of trouble?"

"The kind I'm not sure I want to tell you about."

"Why not?"

"Because I don't want to change the way you think about me. And I'm pretty sure once I tell you, you're going to conveniently have other plans tomorrow. And now that you've talked up your cheeseburgers so much, I was starting to really look forward to one."

He chuckled. "Don't worry. I can't imagine anything you could say that would take tomorrow off the table." He took her hand again, this time lacing his fingers with hers. "You know I'm a deputy sheriff, so I don't scare that easily."

"I know. You being a deputy is part of the problem," she muttered.

He didn't say anything, just waited for her to speak. He seemed totally casual as he leaned back in the truck seat, one hand on the wheel.

Here goes nothing. And everything.

She took a deep breath and dove in. "I was a bit of a handful as a teenager. I couldn't wait to leave home when I graduated. I had big plans to go to California and learn how to surf and live the boho lifestyle. So I cleaned out my savings, drove to the coast, rented a little dive apartment, and got a job as a waitress in a bar on the beach. I couldn't afford a surfboard or lessons, but I met a guy at the bar who was apparently a big deal in the surfing world. We flirted a little, and he offered to teach me. I started hanging out with him and this whole group of surfers he ran around with. I was charmed by their laid-back lifestyle, surfing all day and partying all night. I thought they were just this great group of beach-loving surfer dudes. But it turned out they were something more."

"Is that how you met Milo's dad?"

"Yes. He was a little older and an amazing surfer. All the young guys looked up to him. And he ate it up. But he deserved the praise. He was flawless, perfection on a board. He made it look so easy. And he was fearless. He'd try any trick, go after any wave. He loved surfing during a storm."

"You seem pretty fearless too. Did you surf like that?"

"Me?" She laughed. "Not even close. I was a terrible surfer. A total grommet. Sorry, that's slang for an inexperienced surfer. But for some reason, I caught Milo's dad's eye, and he took me under his wing. He offered me private lessons. And then it turned into something more, and before I knew it, I ended up moving in with the guy."

"So, it sounds like you found what you were looking for."

"No, that was part of the problem. I was young and dumb and wasn't really *looking* at anything." She pulled her hand away and crossed her arms over her chest. She didn't feel right holding his hand when she told him this part. "I was hanging out with all these guys and their girlfriends, and they surfed all the time and had top-of-the-line boards and equipment, yet none of them had jobs or ever worked. I don't know whether I thought they had sponsors, or if I just didn't let myself think about it too much, but it turned out they were into some bad stuff. Which is why Milo's dad is now serving time in a federal penitentiary."

CHAPTER 5

THERE WAS MORE TO THE STORY, MUCH MORE.

But Jillian wasn't ready to share all of it. Not with Ethan. Not now. Not when he acted as if he liked her so much.

"Oh." Ethan's calm composure didn't waver. Which was not the reaction she was anticipating.

"Oh? That's all you've got? I just tell you my son's father is in *prison* and all you have to say is oh?"

"What would you like me to say?"

She narrowed her eyes. "Wait a minute. You don't seem very surprised. Did you already know Rad was in prison?"

"*Rad*? Your ex-boyfriend's name is *Rad*?"

"It's Radley. Radley Mullins, but he goes by Rad—which, you have to admit, is a pretty cool surfer name. But you're changing the subject."

He held up his hand. "Okay, okay. I'll admit it. Yeah, I knew your ex was in prison."

"How? Why?"

"Because I like you. And I'm a police officer. So of course I'm gonna look into you." He glanced sideways at her. "Does that freak you out?"

She shrugged. "I don't know. I guess I'd do the same thing. I'm a librarian, so I'm always looking people up, or as we like to call it in the library world, *researching*. So I guess

I wouldn't expect anything less from you, especially with all the resources you have at hand."

He offered her a sheepish grin. "You wouldn't expect me to propose without running my new fiancée through the system, would you?"

Her heart leapt to her throat. "You ran *me* through the system too?"

"No. I'm just kidding. I wouldn't do that. But I heard your ex was in prison, so I looked *him* up. And to be honest, I guess I was also curious. Although he doesn't seem your type."

"Oh yeah? What does *my* type seem like?"

He lifted one shoulder in a cool shrug. "I picture you more with a tall, rugged, good-looking sort who might wear a cowboy hat and boots. Like a guy who's charming and funny and who works in law enforcement and rescues horses on the side."

She raised an eyebrow but couldn't hold back her grin. "I walked right into that one, didn't I?"

"Like a stroll in the park."

"How about we change the subject? Can we talk about something besides Milo's dad? He's not my favorite topic—in fact, he's one of my *least* favorite."

"Sure. What should we talk about instead?"

"The weather, the price of beef, how bad the Broncos have been doing since Peyton Manning retired."

He laughed. "I could talk about that all day. But I'd rather talk about you."

"Ugh. Haven't I spilled enough dirty laundry?"

"You don't have to spill any more secrets. I just want to

know about you. Tell me about your job, or what brought you to Creedence. Do you have any pets? What book are you reading now? What shows are you watching? What do you like to have for dinner? And would you like to have it with me later this week?"

She smiled. "Yeah, I caught how you snuck that last one in there. But to answer your first question, I love my job. It's amazing. After Milo was born, I lucked into a job at a big library and fell in love with it. I've spent the last seven years working my way up to librarian and taking classes on the side to earn my undergraduate degree. They had a great tuition reimbursement program, and I finished my master's degree in library science last year. You know my sister, Carley, and how stubborn she is. She's been trying to get me to move out here for years, and once she heard about the head librarian position in town, she begged me to apply."

"And are you glad you made the move?"

"Oh, so glad. I love it here, and it's been great for Milo. It helped that he found Mandy so soon after we moved here. Those two are thick as thieves. And I think he's going to flourish in the smaller school system."

"He seems like a bright kid."

She couldn't help the proud smile that stole across her face. "Oh, he's off-the-charts smart. He loves to read and devours books way above his grade level. He wasn't much into the beach scene in California, and he hated surfing. He's so much happier here. And he finally gets to have a dog."

"That's cool. What kind?"

"The kind that's half goofball, half adorable," she told him. "He's a golden mix and such a sweetheart."

"Oh yeah?" he asked, then raised one shoulder in an offhand shrug. "I guess you could say that's what I have too. A golden mix."

"Gus was one of two abandoned puppies someone dropped off at the vet clinic earlier this summer. Mandy ended up getting one, and Milo got the other."

"I wouldn't have picked my dog out of a lineup," Ethan muttered. "She was a hand-me-down who used to belong to my grandmother. And the only reason I have her is because I promised my grandma I would take care of the dog after she died."

"And she died? Oh no. I'm sorry." Jillian knew the pain of losing a grandparent, and her heart ached for him.

"Thanks. It happened earlier this year."

"Were you close?"

"Yeah, we were. She was the best. Like your boy, my brother and I were also raised by a single mom. My dad was a sheriff too, here in Creedence, but he was killed in the line of duty when I was eight."

"Oh gosh, I didn't know. I'm sorry." She'd lost her dad too, but he'd hadn't died. He'd just walked out on them and never come back. So he might as well be dead to her. But that was his choice. *Poor Ethan. And* his mom. "That must have been so hard for you all."

"It was. But we moved in with my grandparents after that, and they pretty much raised us too. My mom ended up getting remarried after we graduated high school and she moved to Arizona with her new husband. My brother went to school out east and got a job there. And I enrolled in the police academy, then came back here with a goal of eventually becoming the sheriff and carrying on my dad's legacy. I got hired as a deputy, then bought the ranch right down the road from my grandparents' farm so I could help take care of them."

Jillian couldn't help but admire his determination and commitment to his family. "Wow. That was good of you."

He shrugged. "It wasn't that big a deal. They were really good to us, and it might sound kind of weird, but my grandpa was always kind of like my best friend."

"That doesn't sound weird. I was close to my grandparents too."

While they'd been talking, he'd turned off the highway and onto a smaller dirt road. After a few miles of pasture land, he pulled the truck into a long driveway. White fences lined the drive leading up to a ranch-style log home.

A large red barn sat to the right of the house, a corral off one side. Pasture land covered the area behind the barn, and what looked like close to a hundred cattle grazed the grassy area. Two horses stood next to the gate of the corral and both looked up to watch them as Ethan pulled the trailer to a stop in front of the barn.

Jillian got out of the truck and stretched her legs as she checked out his ranch. A small chicken coop sat between the house and the barn, and she could hear the soft clucks of the chickens as they wandered around the pen. The house had a wide front porch with a porch swing on one end and two cedar rockers with a little table between them on the other. Neat flower beds lined either side of the porch steps, overflowing with colorful perennials like snapdragons and cosmos. Everything was well-kept and tidy, which she would have expected from a guy who valued order and wore ironed shirts with starched collars.

"I just need to let the dog out, then I'll get the barn ready for the horses," Ethan said as he hurried up the porch steps. He opened the front door, and a curly-haired tawny-colored dog came racing out of the house, circled her legs in a frenzy, then plopped down in a sit in front of Ethan, its butt wiggling with barely controlled excitement.

Jillian squatted down to pet the dog's curly head. "Oh my gosh, you have a *poodle*. I thought you said she was a golden."

His face twisted with a grimace. "I said she was a golden *mix*."

"You didn't say she was mixed with a poodle. You have a *doodle*." She pressed her lips together to keep from laughing. *And* because the dog was licking her face and she didn't really want its tongue in her mouth.

"I prefer not to use the word 'doodle.' It sounds so dorky."

"You mean a*dork*able. She's darling." The dog planted her curly paws on Jillian's chest in an attempt to lick more of her face. "What's her name?"

"Frankie."

Jillian's eyes widened. "*Frankie*?"

"Well, her name is really Francesca Princess Puffball but I can't bring myself to call her that, so I just call her Frankie."

"Yes, that's much manlier. Which is what I assume you're trying for."

"I told you she was my grandma's dog."

"She looks like a teddy bear." Jillian ruffled the dog's neck.

"Yes, I know. Which is just the kind of dog a deputy wants riding around in his truck with him—an adorable doodle that looks like a teddy bear." He talked tough, but he reached down to give the dog a sweet scratch on her neck as she plopped down on his boots. "You're a good dog, aren't you?" He pointed toward the trailer. "You want to go meet the new horses?"

The dog hopped up and trotted after them as they walked back toward the truck.

A green tractor was parked next to the side of the barn and tractor implements were lined in a perfect row in the grass near it.

"You have a tractor?" she asked as they approached the barn.

He grinned down at her. "Yeah. Why? Do you think it's sexy? I can take you for a ride on it later, if you want."

"I'll get back to you on that."

"Offer's always open." He pulled open the wide door of the barn. "I'm just gonna line a couple of stalls with some straw to get them ready before we bring the horses in."

"Good idea. I'll help," she said, following him into the barn. A wide alley went down the center of the barn with stalls on one side and what looked like a tack room and workbench on the other. Wooden pegs lined one wall holding bridles and lead ropes with saddle stands lined up underneath. It smelled like straw and dirt and leather and the faint scent of horses, even though the stalls were currently empty.

"You don't have to," he said.

"I know, but I want to."

"Okay." He passed her a pitchfork, then grabbed a hay bale and dragged it over to an empty stall. He dug a multi-tool from his pocket, pulled opened a knife blade and cut the baling twine holding the hay bale together. He stuffed the twine into his pocket, then pointed to the adjoining stall. "I thought we'd put them in these two. That way they'll be right next to each other."

"I think that's perfect."

They worked together to get both stalls ready, spreading out layers of straw and filling the troughs with fresh water and sweet feed. Both horses seemed glad to be out of the trailer and followed them easily into the stalls. It helped that Ethan led them in by shaking buckets of oats in front of them and then poured the extra into the sweet feed.

"It's killing me not to brush them and get them cleaned up, but I think I'll let them get settled for a bit before I try," he told her as they leaned on the stall gate and watched them devour the feed.

"I think that's a good idea." The buckskin finished her food and came over to Jillian, nosing her arm up with her muzzle. She'd told Ethan her ideas for their names, and he'd agreed they sounded perfect.

"You want to give them each a sugar cube?" he asked, grabbing several from a box on the workbench.

"Sure," she said, taking two from his hand and holding them out for the horses to nibble.

"You want one?" he said, popping one in his mouth and holding the other out to her.

She eyed the small white cube. "Really?"

"Haven't you ever had a sugar cube?"

She shook her head. "I don't think so. I've put them in coffee, but I've never eaten one out of the box."

"The secret is to let it dissolve on your tongue a little before you swallow it." He took a step closer to her as he held out the cube. "Open your mouth."

She swallowed, then did as he asked, the request setting off a spike of heat along her spine.

Slowly, he lowered the sugar cube to her mouth, running it along the edge of her bottom lip before setting it on her tongue. He kept his gaze on her mouth as he quietly instructed, "Now, hold it for just a second. Let it melt a little on your tongue first, then swallow it."

She felt the granules dissolving on her tongue as she peered up at him, her gaze enraptured with the intense way he was staring at her lips. She saw raw desire and hunger there, as if he were a starving man and she was his favorite meal.

When had he gotten so close to her? She could smell the woodsy scent of his cologne and see specks of navy in his crystal-blue eyes. Swallowing the sugar, she shivered at the rush of sweetness.

He leaned in, his gaze still intent on her mouth.

Oh. Gosh. He was going to kiss her.

Her pulse raced as she debated what to do. Once again, her mind told her to pull back, but no other part of her body was listening as she lifted her chin and drew closer.

CHAPTER 6

ETHAN LIFTED HIS HAND AND LAID IT ACROSS HER cheek, cupping her jaw as he skimmed his thumb along her bottom lip.

Jillian drew in a tiny gasp of breath as he tilted his head and grazed his lips across hers. Softly at first, then he slanted his lips over hers and took her mouth in a hot rush of desire. The sweetness of the sugar mixed with the heat of his mouth combined to send her senses reeling. And she could not get enough.

His free hand slid around her waist and pulled her to him as her arms went around his neck. The hand cupping her cheek skimmed up her face, and his fingers tangled in her hair.

The kiss was so intense, she wasn't sure if she was breathing her air or his. She was drowning in him, all logic and reason slipping away as she melted into his arms, dissolving into him like the sugar had done on her tongue.

Must stop.

She couldn't do this, couldn't let herself fall into him. Dragging her hand down, she pressed it against his chest, but instead of pushing him away, she melted even more at the hard slab of muscle evident under his uniform shirt.

Her head finally won out, and she pulled away, trying to catch her breath.

He didn't say anything, just stared. He looked slightly dazed, as if he couldn't quite comprehend the intensity of the kiss either. "Wow," he finally managed to whisper. "That was—"

"I should go," she said, taking a step away.

"But—"

"I'll see you later." She took another step back, then turned and hurried from the barn, calling over her shoulder, "I'll call you about those cheeseburgers tomorrow."

"Jillian, wait."

But she was already to the barn door, practically running as she burst into the sunshine. Frankie came running over to her, racing around her legs. She bent down to pet the dog as she tried to regain her composure.

She couldn't remember ever having a kiss affect her so hard. She couldn't think straight. She stood and peered around the ranch.

Well, crud. She obviously wasn't thinking at all. Her dang car was at Bryn's.

She slunk back into the barn to find Ethan casually leaning against Buddy's stall. "So, I'm actually gonna need a ride. I don't have my car."

He seemed to have recovered from his earlier stupor as he offered her a knowing grin. "Yeah. I know. That's what I was trying to tell you."

A grin tugged at the corners of her lips. "That kind of ruined my grand exit."

He laughed and pushed off from the stall. "I was still impressed." He gestured toward the door. "Come on, I'll give you a ride back to Bryn's."

The next day, Jillian couldn't seem to concentrate as she went about her normal duties. It was her day to take the bookmobile over to the nursing home, a task she normally relished. She loved visiting with the residents and helping them to pick books and discover new authors. But today, she couldn't seem to keep her focus. Unless her focus was supposed to be on the amazing kiss she'd shared with Ethan the night before.

This was the very reason she was reluctant to get involved with him. Well, one of the reasons.

But her job was important to her. And she was still learning the ropes. She needed to give it her full attention. And the only thing holding her attention today was the memory of the hot cowboy's lips pressed to hers.

Maybe she should cancel their plans to go out to his ranch for supper. She could get a great cheeseburger at the diner—without the complications of considering dating it.

But Milo was so excited to go. He'd talked about it all through breakfast that morning, how excited he was to see the horses again.

"Are you gonna come in and bring me a book or just stand at the door daydreaming all afternoon?"

She blinked and turned to look at the old man sitting in the recliner in the room she'd stopped outside of. He'd only been at the nursing home a few weeks now, but he'd already become one of her favorites. Not due to his charming personality—he was one ornery old cuss—but he also had a softer side, especially when she got him talking about his late wife. Today he had his red plaid pajama pants tucked into his cowboy boots and a straw cowboy hat perched on his thinning gray hair.

"I'm so sorry, Amos. I was lost in thought." She wheeled the book cart into his room.

"It must have been some pretty good thoughts because you were smilin' like you'd just had a bite of a great piece of pie."

Warmth flooded her cheeks, and she busied herself searching the cart for the books she'd set aside especially for him. "I found you a couple more Louis L'Amour," she told him. "And I've got some new books I think you might like. They're not necessarily westerns, but they're mysteries and the heroine is a park ranger."

"I'll give 'em a try. Anything's better than sitting around here waiting for a nurse to bring me a bowl of lumpy tapioca."

She raised an eyebrow. "Isn't tapioca supposed to be lumpy? Like, by its very nature, it's a bowl full of individual lumps?"

He narrowed his eyes. "Are you gettin' sassy with me, Miss Bennett?"

She chuckled. "I wouldn't dream of it, Amos." She passed him a new stack of books and took the pile he'd finished the week before. She perched on the edge of his bed. "How are you feeling this week? Any better?"

He'd been brought to the assisted living section of the nursing home to recover from hip surgery. It wasn't bad enough for him to stay in the hospital, but it wasn't good enough for him to be able to go home yet, and he was able to attend daily physical therapy sessions to improve his recovery.

He shrugged. "Fair to middlin'. I'd like to say I can't complain, but I find that I can almost always come up with a few complaints. This room's too noisy. I can hear the traffic through my window. And the mattress is too hard, and the sheets are too stiff." He'd had the same grievances, plus a few more, the week before.

"Last time I saw you, you showed me a picture of your wife and promised to tell me about her."

His brow, which had been creased in a tight furrow, unwrinkled as his expression softened. "Damn, I miss that woman."

"Oh no. I'm sorry, Amos. I didn't mean to upset you." She pushed off the bed and reached to put a hand on his shoulder.

He waved her back down. "Sit down. You didn't upset me. There isn't a day goes by that I don't miss my Trudy. You asking about her isn't gonna change that one way or another. And I like talking about her. She was a special lady. And my best friend."

Jillian's heart ached a little at the sentiment. She wondered what it would be like to be so certain of your partner and to have the kind of relationship that feels like you're totally in love but still spending your life with your best friend.

———

Ethan checked his watch…for the third time. It was only a few minutes past the last time he'd checked. He'd already cleaned the grill, made the hamburger patties, cut thick slices of cheddar and Monterey jack cheese, and set out the plates, napkins, and silverware. He'd bought potato salad and chips at the store and stopped at the bakery to grab a chocolate cake.

Everything was ready. He just needed Jillian and Milo to get here. What if she'd changed her mind and decided not to come?

That kiss the night before *had* been pretty intense. It'd knocked him senseless for a good several minutes. Even though it had baffled him why she'd practically run from the barn, Jillian's oddly-timed retreat did give him time to collect himself and come back to his senses.

But that hadn't stopped him from thinking about it all day and most of the night before. He couldn't remember a time when a single kiss had shaken him to his core. He knew Jillian was special. Which was why, as much as he'd enjoyed it, he'd blasted himself most of the day for pushing her too fast.

He knew he liked her. And felt as if she liked him. But she reminded him of a skittish colt—he'd have to take things slow if he had any chance of winning her over.

Relief washed over him as he heard a car coming down the driveway. He wiped his sweaty palms on his jeans and pushed through the screen door. Raising a hand to wave, he tried to control the thumping of his heart as she got out of the car.

Her hair was down in a riot of chestnut-colored curls cascading around her shoulders. She had on an outfit similar to the day before, or at least similar to the outfit she'd been wearing *before* she'd wrangled with the goat. She wore a short black skirt, sports sandals, and a snug pale-pink T-shirt that, as she got closer, he saw read I'M A MOM AND A LIBRARIAN— NOTHING SCARES ME.

"Hey, you made it." Frankie raced around him and made a beeline for Milo, practically jumping into the boy's arms as he knelt to pet her.

"Wow, I love your dog," Milo said, turning his head to fend off the lick-fest Frankie was having on his chin. "She looks like a teddy bear. Is she a goldendoodle?"

"Yep." He grimaced as he snuck a glance at Jillian, who was grinning widely. Dang, but she did have the greatest smile. It was weird how just seeing her smile lit up something inside of him. "Hope you're hungry," he called to the boy.

"I'm starving. But I really want to see the horses. Is it okay if we go visit them first?"

Jillian bumped his elbow as they followed Milo toward the barn. "It makes me pretty proud that my kid's heart is bigger than his appetite."

"I think you'll be excited to see the horses too. You would have *lost* your appetite if you would have been around this morning when I gave them each a flea bath and cleaned all the dirt and gunk from their coats. I also trimmed and cleaned their hooves, which was another nasty job. But they look a lot better already."

"Yeah, they do," Jillian agreed as she approached the horses' stalls.

"It's amazing what a shower and a few good meals will do for you," he said, patting his hand along Buddy's side.

Nudge had come over to the stall gate when they walked into the barn and prodded her nose into Jillian's side when she got closer. "Maybe we should have named her Cuddle Bear," she said, laughing as the horse nuzzled into her, eating up all the affection.

"Yeah, that's just what I need. I've already got a dog named Francesca Princess Puffball, why not have a horse named Cuddle Bear too?"

Jillian raised an eyebrow. "Worried about your man card, Deputy Rayburn?"

He chuckled. "I wear a badge and carry a gun. I think my man card's pretty secure."

"What's a man card?" Milo asked. "And when do I get mine?"

Jillian and Ethan laughed, but Milo looked confused.

"What's so funny? Does it come in the mail? Should I have already applied for it?" He ran a hand along his chin. "I think I found a whisker the other day, so we should probably get on it."

Jillian ruffled her son's hair. "You did not find a whisker. It was probably a dog hair. And I'll explain about man cards on the way home."

"I could explain them," Ethan said, offering her an amused grin. "Just as soon as I feed some sugar cubes to Cuddle Bear, here." He passed Milo a cube. "You can give this one to Buddy. We'll bring some carrots out for them after supper."

"Cool," the boy said, taking the sugar cube and holding it out on his palm.

"Now, who's ready for a burger? I say we go fire up the grill."

━━━━━━━━━━

An hour later, Jillian leaned back in one of the rockers and pressed a hand to her stomach. "Okay, you were right. You do make an amazing cheeseburger. I'm stuffed."

He raised his eyebrows. "That's just *one* of my amazing skills."

"Ha. I had enough cheese on my burger, thank you," she said, tossing a chip at him.

Ethan had found another chair for Milo, and they'd eaten outside on the front porch. She'd been impressed at the spread of food he'd set out, and he did have mad-talent with the barbeque grill.

Milo had already finished eating and was playing fetch in the yard with Frankie as she helped Ethan clear their dishes and put away the extra food.

"I hope you saved a little room for dessert," he said, coming up behind her at the sink and leaning down to speak closer to her ear. The deep timbre of his voice sent a surge of heat racing through her, and her mind went to all sorts of dirty places with thoughts of what he had in mind for *dessert.* "I have chocolate cake."

Okay. So chocolate cake was good too. And would get her into a lot less trouble than the other kinds of desserts she was imagining.

She heard Milo calling her as an SUV turned into the driveway. "Is that Brody and Elle?"

"Yeah, he called earlier and said he wanted to stop by and check on the horses. I think he's bringing out some dewormer and some vitamins for them too."

They went outside to find Mandy already with her arms full of a squirming Frankie, who couldn't seem to cuddle close enough to the girl. "She's so cute," Mandy squealed as the dog licked her chin.

Ethan led Brody and the kids into the barn while Elle stayed behind to chat with Jillian.

"How was the barbeque?" her friend asked, as she settled into the rocker opposite Jillian on the front porch. "What'd you think of Ethan's meat?"

Jillian almost choked on the sip of iced tea she'd been taking. "Oh my gosh. You are terrible." She waved a hand at Elle. "You look so nice and classy, but girl, you have a dirty mind."

Elle let out a little cackle. "I know. I think Aunt Sassy has been rubbing off on me," she said, referring to Sassy James, the octogenarian who had taken them all under her wing and become an honorary aunt to the whole group of girlfriends. "So, tell me, how did last night go? And supper tonight? You picked Milo up in such a rush last night, we didn't have time to chat."

She stared at her lap and plucked at a piece of lint on her skirt. "There was nothing to chat about."

Elle gasped. "Oh my gosh. Something happened last night."

"I didn't say that."

"You didn't have to. It's written all over your face." She pointed to Jillian's glass. "I know it's only iced tea and not margaritas, but swill it and spill it, girl," she told her, calling out the signature phrase their group of friends used during their weekly Taco Tuesday and margarita get-togethers.

"There's nothing to spill. Not really. We just kissed."

Elle gasped again, then leaned closer. "Tell me everything. Was it like a quick peck on the lips kind of goodnight kiss? Or was it more like a toe-curling, can't-think-straight, hands-up-your-shirt kind of kiss?"

A grin tugged at Jillian's lips. "More like the second one."

"Ohh." Elle offered her a coy smile.

"Except his hands definitely did *not* go up my shirt."

Her friend's smile fell, and she frowned. "Oh. Too bad. But I'm sure you'll get another chance."

She swatted playfully at her friend's leg. "No. I'm not looking for another chance. This thing with Ethan is a terrible idea."

"What? Why? You're both single. It's obvious you like each other. It seems perfect to me."

"It's not perfect. I just got this new job at the library and between it and trying to get Milo adjusted to the new town and ready for a new school, I don't have the time or the inclination for a serious relationship."

"Who said anything about a relationship? I'm not saying you have to marry the guy."

Jillian grimaced, but didn't share the deputy's recent proposal.

"But you can still have a little fun," Elle continued. "And enjoy the attention of a good-looking man." She waggled her eyebrows. "And by attention, I mean…"

She held up her hand. "I know what you mean. But I'm a single mom with a ten-year-old kid who has a terrible situation with an absent father. My goal in life right now is to be the best mom possible for that kid and to raise him in a way that he feels loved and makes him believe for as long as I possibly can that he has a decent dad. Not to get involved with another man who I barely know and who could end up leaving too. Which would only make things worse in the end for my son."

Elle lifted one shoulder in a shrug. "I hear what you're saying. But Ethan's a good guy. He can actually provide a good role model for Milo. And he might be the one who stays."

"I don't think I can take that chance."

Elle put a hand on Jillian's knee. "I admire you, and I know you're an amazing mom. But don't overthink this to death. You're allowed to have a little fun too. And between the way Ethan looks at you and the amount of muscles he has under those uniform shirts he wears, I think he could offer quite a bit of fun. Like, *hours* of fun. And by fun, I mean..."

Jillian laughed. "Yes, I know what you mean."

The kids came running out of the barn then and raced across the yard and up the porch steps.

"Mandy's family is going out for ice cream, then watching a movie tonight. They invited me to come over. Can I go, Mom?"

Jillian raised an eyebrow at Elle—had this been part of her friend's plot to add more "fun" to Jillian's life? "I think Ethan was planning on having us for dessert. He said he bought a cake."

"He won't care if I miss it," Milo said. "Or I could always take a piece to go."

"It's fine with us," Elle said. "In fact, since the kids have swim lessons in the morning anyway, why doesn't Milo just sleep over? We can stop by your place on the way home and pick up Milo's swim gear and grab Gus too. Then the puppies will get to be together too."

"Please, Mom," Milo said, pressing his palms together.

"Okay, fine."

"Yes." Milo gave Mandy a high five.

"Let's go get my dad and tell him we're ready to go," Mandy said.

"Thanks, Mom," Milo called over his shoulder as the two kids ran back toward the barn.

Elle patted Jillian's leg. "See? This is working out perfectly. We'll keep Milo overnight, and then you all can hang out as long as you want. And you did say Ethan was planning to have you for dessert."

"I didn't mean *that*," she said, trying for another swat, but her friend had already jumped up and scooted out of the way.

"Hold on. I've got something for you," Elle said, racing to her car. She rummaged in the back, then came back carrying a small lime and two bottles, one of margarita mixer and the other of tequila. "I got this for girls' night, but I'm leaving it here instead. If you all want to have a margarita, great. If not, no pressure, just bring the rest with you to Bryn's on Tuesday night. I'll just pop this inside." She disappeared into the house before Jillian had a chance to argue.

Then the kids were back and piling into the car, and Elle was hugging her, and Brody was waving as he climbed into the driver's seat. Then they were gone, and she was left standing in the driveway with Ethan.

"Ready for some dessert?" Ethan asked, heading for the house.

She swallowed, unable to stop herself this time from watching Ethan's butt as he sauntered away and imagining all kinds of dessert.

"Hey, what's this?" Ethan said, gesturing to the drink

mixer and tequila sitting on his kitchen counter. "Did the margarita fairy stop by while we were in the barn?"

"Yes, and her name was Elle. She just gave it to me to bring to girls' night on Tuesday in case she couldn't make it," she explained, trying to think of a plausible reason for Elle to have dropped off the booze. "But she said we should have some too. If we want."

"I could go for a margarita," Ethan said, already reaching into the cupboard for some short glasses that looked like small jelly jars. "You want one?"

"Sure. But just a small one."

He sliced the lime and ran it around the rims of the glasses. "I don't have margarita salt. You good with sugar?"

"Sure."

He dumped some brown sugar in a bowl and dipped the tops of the glasses into it before dropping in several ice cubes, then filling each one about three-fourths full with margarita mixer. Opening the tequila, he poured some into his drink, then passed the bottle to her. "You can be in charge of making yours as weak or as strong as you want."

She poured in a little. Then added another small splash.

He squeezed in some extra lime, then stirred their drinks and lifted his into the air. "Cheers."

"Cheers." She clinked her glass to his and took a sip. "Mmm. That's a good mix. And I love the sugar." She took another sip. "So good. I've never had brown sugar with a margarita. It's delicious."

His gaze dropped to her mouth as she licked the loose

granules of sugar from her lips. The alcohol and the look of desire combined to form a swirl of heat in her chest, and she felt warmth rush to her cheeks.

"You want to sit?" He tore his gaze away and gestured to the living room.

"Sure," she said, crossing the room as she debated where to take a seat.

Ethan's house was an open concept with only an island separating the kitchen from the living room area. A stone fireplace covered the center of the far wall, and a big-screen television sat on the mantle. The room was decorated in browns and blues, with an overstuffed sofa facing the television and a recliner to its side. A stack of books lay on the floor next to the recliner, and Jillian was dying to know what Ethan was reading.

A pile of logs was already laid in the fireplace, and he spent a few minutes getting a fire started as she perched on the edge of the sofa. He took a sip of his drink as he peered around the room. Jillian tried to act casual and stop holding her breath as she waited for him to decide where to sit. His denim-clad leg brushed her bare one as he dropped onto the sofa next to her, and her shoulders shook as a shiver ran through her. Her mouth had gone dry, and she took another big gulp of her drink.

"Are you cold?" he asked, wrapping his arm around her shoulders.

Tonight, instead of his uniform, he wore a soft navy T-shirt with faded jeans and his cowboy boots. He smelled like fabric softener and the same cologne she'd started to think of as *his* scent, and part of her wanted to sink into him and cuddle up against his side.

She took another sip of her drink, feeling awkward and unsure of herself. "I don't know why I'm nervous," she admitted. "I can't think of a time when I haven't been able to think of something to say or some question to ask."

"We don't have to talk." He dropped his arm from her shoulders and scooted an inch away. "Listen, Jillian, I like you. A lot. But I don't want to make you feel uncomfortable. And I sure don't want you to be nervous around me." He ducked his head. "Although would it make you feel better to know that I get a little nervous around you too?"

She smiled. "Yes, that would make me feel a little better. You're supposed to be the big strong lawman. I wouldn't think much scares you."

"You'd be surprised." He nodded to her front. "But you're the one wearing a shirt claiming that nothing scares you."

"I put up a brave front."

"Is that what you're doing now?"

"Maybe." Her voice was breathy as he leaned closer to her. She took another sip of her margarita, surprised to see she'd finished it. Holding up the empty glass, she shook the ice cubes. "I might have one more." At least having a drink gave her something to do with her hands, and her mouth, so she wasn't tempted to launch herself at the cute cowboy.

Ethan pushed up from the sofa. "Here, I've got it." He carried their glasses into the kitchen and refilled them with margarita mix.

"Just a tiny bit of tequila for me," Jillian said, watching

him pour in just a small splash. She was having the second one more for something to drink, but she could already feel the effects of the small amount of alcohol she'd put in the first one.

He squeezed in more lime, stirred the drinks, then brought them over and sat back on the sofa next to her.

"Thanks," she said, taking another healthy swig. "So, how are the horses doing?"

"Good. Brody said he could already see an improvement in them just from yesterday."

"It was really good of you to take them."

"It's never been my intention to get into the horse rescue business, but this was a special situation. I'd seen the conditions of the horses out there and knew I had to do something to help. I figured I could keep them here for a while, at least until Bryn can find someone to adopt them. I'll give them a week or so, then Zane and I can see if they're saddle-ready. It would help them get adopted if they're good at taking a rider."

She caught herself staring at his mouth, remembering the way his lips had felt against hers. She put down her drink as she tried to think of something else to say. "How about that cake?" she asked, pushing to her feet.

The room spun a little, and she reached out to support herself, but the only thing to grab onto was Ethan's shoulder. She felt tipsy already, but how could she be? She hadn't put that much tequila in her first drink, and she'd watched Ethan only put a small splash of it in her second.

She tried to take a step forward, but her feet got tangled in each other, and she pitched backward. Right into Ethan's lap.

CHAPTER 7

"Whoa there," Ethan said, sliding his arms around her. "You all right?"

She reached out and touched the pads of her fingers to his mouth. "Damn. You've got great lips."

His eyes widened, then his lips slowly curved into a flirtatious grin. "Thank y—"

He didn't get the rest of the word out before she leaned in and pressed her mouth to his. His response was immediate as he pulled her close and tilted his head to deepen the kiss.

His tongue slid between her lips, and he tasted both sweet and tart like sugar and lime and tequila. She drove her fingers through his hair—dang, the man had great hair too. Everything about him was amazing. She just wanted to touch him. And *be* touched by him.

The feel of his big hands as they slid across her back felt incredible. She gasped as his fingers slid under the tail of her T-shirt and gripped the bare skin of her waist.

She wasn't sure if he flipped her over or if she pulled him down on top of her, but suddenly she was lying back on the sofa with his body covering hers. She tried to catch her breath as he kissed her cheek, then her jaw, then her neck as his hands moved up her waist. A small cry escaped her as his long fingers grazed the sides of her breasts. Her nipples tightened, aching to also be touched.

She jerked up the bottom of his T-shirt and slid her hands under the fabric and over his back, marveling at the hard muscles she discovered there.

Their legs were entwined, and she could feel how much he wanted her. She ground into him, trying to sate the need that radiated from her core.

"Jillian." He breathed her name into her neck, and she almost came undone. She wanted this man. Logic and reason were replaced with pure carnal need as she gripped his broad shoulders.

His lips found hers again, and she moaned at the delicious press of his mouth against hers. His fingers were splayed out over her ribcage, and she moaned again as his thumb grazed over the rounded cup of her bra.

Then he drew his hand out of her shirt and pulled away. "Hold on." His breath came hard as he managed to sit up next to her. Her shirt was twisted, and a line of bare skin lay exposed above the band of her skirt. He kept his hands possessively around her waist as he peered down at her. "I need a second to catch my breath." His gaze was intense as he raked his eyes over her body. "And I'm dangerously close to picking you up and carrying you to my bed."

His words sent a thrill through her. As a tall woman, she didn't often get offers to pick her up and carry her anywhere. Her hand lay across his thick bicep, and she was pretty sure Ethan would be able to pull it off.

His expression changed from seductive to caring. "I was

getting carried away, and I don't want to take advantage of you. Are you okay with all this?"

A minute ago, she'd been a ball of lust and desire, but now he was touching her heart as well, and she just wanted to melt into him. "I think I kissed you, so I should be asking *you* if you're okay with all this."

His flirty grin returned. "Oh, darlin', I'm more than okay with all this. I've been fantasizing about this for weeks." He cringed. "I don't know why I just said that. This sounds crazy, but I feel like I'm a little drunk."

She blew out a breath. "I do too. I know I was working on a second drink, but they were in small glasses, and I swear I didn't put that much tequila in them."

"I didn't put that much in mine either." He scrubbed a hand through his hair. "Maybe we should take a break and have some of that cake." He stood and reached for her hand to pull her up next to him.

The dizziness hit her again, and she gripped his arm to steady herself. "Yeah, cake sounds like a good idea."

"You good?" he asked, still holding one of her hands while his other had a firm grip on her waist.

"Yes, I'm tipsy, but I'm fine." She followed him into the kitchen and picked up the tequila bottle. "Is this tequila extra strong or something?"

"Holy crud. I think I solved the mystery," he said, holding up the margarita bottle. "This margarita mixer *already* has tequila *in* it."

"Oh no. So when we were adding tequila, we were just doubling the alcohol?"

"Yep. No wonder we feel tipsy."

She boosted herself up to sit on the island. "I think I'll take that cake now."

He cut them both a piece, then handed her a plate and fork and leaned back against the counter next to her.

She sank her fork into the layers of cake and frosting, then took a bite. The chocolate dessert tasted like heaven and melted in her mouth. Groaning, she closed her eyes and savored the deliciousness. She opened them to find Ethan staring at her, his fork partway to his mouth.

He shook his head. "Sorry, but that was the same sound you made when I was kissing your neck, and I just got a little lost in it for a sec."

"You say some of the sexiest things," she told him.

"Is that you talking or the tequila?"

"Probably me. If it were the tequila, I'd also be telling you how crazy hot I think you are. And might even mention how badly I want to rip your shirt off and smear some of this chocolate frosting on your chest, then lick it off."

His eyes went wide again. "Dang. I don't know whether to cut you off or add more to your drink and pass you the frosting."

A giggle bubbled out of her. Oh geez, she *was* tipsy. But she also felt kind of fun. And why couldn't she have fun? She'd told Elle earlier that she wasn't getting involved with Ethan because of her son, but she was a mom, not a nun. Wasn't she allowed to have a little fun sometimes too?

Now that really *was* the tequila talking. And it wasn't just talking. It was whispering sweet nothings in her ear that were telling her to grab the hot cowboy and get back to that toe-curling, can't-think-straight, hands-up-her-shirt kind of kissing.

She put down her plate and offered him a seductive smile. "I think I've had enough of the tequila, but I'm pretty sure I haven't had enough of you."

His fork went sliding off his plate as he practically dropped them into the sink, then turned and stepped into the space between her legs. He planted his hands on the counter on either side of her hips and leaned in to press a soft kiss to her neck. "I'm pretty sure I haven't even begun to have enough of you either."

She slid her arms around his neck and gave him a slow, sensual kiss. He made a noise that sounded like something between a growl and a moan. She loved it. Grabbing the hem of his T-shirt, she pulled it over his head and leaned back to admire his broad muscled chest. She dragged a finger along his pec and reveled in his small shiver.

This is crazy.

She knew it was, but at that moment, she didn't care. All she cared about was pressing her bare skin to his. *Here goes nothing. And everything.* She pulled her T-shirt over her head and dropped it next to his.

His gaze traveled over her, hunger and desire evident in his eyes, then he grabbed her hips and pulled her against him as he dipped his head and kissed her again.

She wrapped her legs around his waist and pressed against him, arching her back as he laid a trail of kisses down her cheek and along her neck. Hooking his fingers under the strap of her bra, he drew it over her shoulder, then pressed a kiss to the spot where the strap had been.

His other hand had slid up her thigh, then stopped as he got to the edge of her skirt. He drew back, taking her hand in his and holding it to his chest. "I'm gonna ask you again. Are you *sure* this is what you want?"

She stared into his crystal-blue eyes. "I'm not sure about much, but I do know that I want you."

"And it's not just the tequila talking?"

"Oh, the tequila *is* definitely talking, and it's telling me to rip your clothes off."

"Well, that's a hell of a coincidence, because it's telling me to do the same thing to you."

"Right here in the kitchen?"

"Might be easier in my bed." Her legs were still wrapped around him, and he lifted her off the counter and carried her toward his bedroom.

"Wait," she said as they passed by her purse sitting on the table in the hallway.

He stopped and grinned down at her. "You want to go back for that frosting?"

"Not now, but I'm not ruling it out." She laughed as she reached down and unzipped her purse, then grabbed a smaller bag from inside it. "Okay, go."

He gave her a quizzical look. "Why do you need your wallet? Are you going to offer to pay me? Because that might be a little too much pressure."

She laughed again. "This isn't my credit card. It's a...you know, protection. In a little foil packet."

"Gotcha." He carried her the rest of the way into his bedroom and laid her back on his bed. He stood back to pull off his boots and shimmy out of his jeans. He reached for the hem of her skirt but she pulled a tab at her waist and the tearing sound of Velcro ripped through the air as her skirt fell away.

The sun had gone down but it was still dusk outside, and there was just enough light coming in his bedroom window for him to see what she had on under her skirt.

A sexy grin spread across his face. "Damn, woman. And here I thought I couldn't get any more turned on. Then you go and land in my bed wearing Wonder Woman undies." He glanced at the bag she'd tossed down beside her. "I hope you've got more than one foil packet in that little wallet of yours."

She hoped there was too. "They're actually 'Wonderful Woman' undies," she said, laughing as she pulled him down on top of her.

"Of course they are."

His lips found hers—he was a great kisser and she wanted to melt into the mattress. He felt so good. It had been so long since she'd felt the weight of a man on top of her. She hadn't realized how much she missed it—how much she missed the feel of a man's hands roaming over her body, touching, caressing, exploring her curves.

Not to mention how much she was enjoying exploring his incredible body. The guy had muscles on top of his muscles. All he had on was a pair of black boxer briefs, and she ran her fingers under the band circling his lean waist.

Oh gosh. She was in Ethan's bed and they were down to their underwear. They were really doing this. She'd spent so much time wondering what being with him would be like, and so far, even just kissing him had far exceeded her expectations. Her body was wound so tight with anticipation, it would only take one stroke and she'd shatter into a million glorious pieces.

But once they took this step, there was no going back. It could change everything. And she liked the way they were.

Stop overthinking. Just enjoy this man.

Her body overruled her head as Ethan dipped his chin and pressed a kiss to the lacy edge of her bra. Her nipples were tightened into hard nubs, and he closed his lips over one. Even through the fabric, she could feel the heat and pressure of his mouth on the sensitive tip.

She caught his small smile when he discovered the front clasp of her bra and with one quick flip of motion, he had it undone and was slowly peeling back the lacy cups to reveal her full breasts. He filled his hands with the weight of them, then bent to taste, to nibble, to suck the pebbled tips between his lips. His mouth was warm as he circled the nub with his tongue, and she curled the sheets into her fingers as she inhaled a sharp gasp of breath.

She wanted him. But hated how much she wanted him. And once they crossed this line and were together one time, it would be so easy to do it again. And again. And then she'd start looking forward to seeing him and feel let down if he didn't call. And she couldn't afford to let herself get wrapped up in all that relationship stuff right now.

She swallowed hard as the fear and emotions rippled through her.

Ethan looked up. "You okay?"

She shook her head, overcome by the concern she saw etched on his face. Ethan was a good man. A man she could really fall for.

Who was she kidding? She'd already fallen. Margarita mix-up or not, she wouldn't be half-naked in his bed and using her emergency condom if she weren't halfway in love with the guy.

"No," she whispered, reaching out to touch his cheek. "I'm not okay. I don't care what that stupid shirt I was wearing says, I *am* scared."

He frowned. "Of me?"

"No. Not *of* you. Of my feelings for you. I've worked so hard to keep my focus on raising my son. I hardly ever date, and I haven't had…" She looked down at their bodies wrapped up in each other. "You know…*sexy times* in over a year."

His lips curved into a grin. "Sexy times?" He tilted his head. "Wait, did you say a *year*?"

She covered her face. Why did she just tell him that? Stupid boozy margarita mix. "There was a guy I worked with, back in California, kind of a friends-with-benefits thing that only happened once a year or so, usually after the annual Christmas party."

His brow furrowed as he leaned on one elbow. "Is that what you're looking for? Another friends-with-benefits kind of thing?"

"I don't know. I wasn't looking for anything. But then you came along, and you're so cute and charming, and I love the way you flirt with me and the way you look at me as if I'm some kind of treasure you've discovered. Plus you're a realllly great kisser." What was wrong with her? It was like she couldn't get her mouth to stop talking.

Ethan grinned. "I think you're a really great kisser too. And you *are* like a treasure." He looked down at her and ran the backs of his fingers over her chest. "I've never met anyone like you, and you stir something in me."

Oh.

It felt like all the air in the room had just disappeared. Or at least she couldn't seem to find any to breathe. He stirred something in her too. And that's what scared the heck out of her.

His eyes narrowed as his mouth drew down in the slightest frown. "That's why I'm not so sure about this friends-with-benefits idea. I mean, don't get me wrong, I'm all in for the benefits. In fact, I think about the benefits. A lot. But I also really like you. And I'm hoping someday we can be more than friends."

"Okay, I hear you, but for right now, can we just focus on the benefits?" She stared down at his muscular chest. "Although it is a little intimidating being naked around you since you're in a thousand times better shape than I am. And I obviously eat way more ice cream than you do."

"But your job doesn't require you to be as physically fit, and you don't have to be ready to run down a perp or chase after someone with overdue library book fees."

She cocked an eyebrow. "Do you run down a lot of perps here in Creedence?"

He shrugged. "Not a lot. But I don't want to be huffing and puffing if I do have to. So I jog and do a little lifting." He tilted his head. "And I did have to rescue a sexy librarian in her underwear from a hay loft the other day."

"Speaking of underwear," she said, giving him what she hoped was a seductive smile as she pushed herself up on her elbows. "How do you feel about taking mine off?"

His eyes widened, then he grinned. "I feel pretty good about that."

"I think I'd feel pretty good about it too."

He hooked his fingers under her waistband and slid her underwear down her legs and dropped them on the floor. A second later, his fell on top of hers and then he was between her legs, skimming his fingers along her skin, touching, stroking, exploring. He kissed her mouth and her neck and her breasts and her stomach, his lips and tongue grazing over her body, pausing to give and take pleasure.

Fumbling with the zipper of the bag she'd taken from her purse, she finally retrieved the one lone condom inside and tossed it toward Ethan. He tore the packet with his teeth and sheathed himself, then he was inside her and she cried out, unable to hold in how amazingly good it felt.

Everything else fell away. She was utterly at his mercy, lost in the heat of desire and the passion that coursed through her, as she surrendered to the intensity of the sensations that crested and seized her muscles.

Their bodies seemed to be made for each other, already

knowing what the other needed, as they moved together, finding that perfect rhythm that had her teetering on the edge, then pulling back, then finally reeling as she went over, clutching the sheets and calling out his name as the tremors quaked through her and she gave in to the intimate connection.

—————

Jillian froze as she woke the next morning. This wasn't her bed, these weren't her sheets, and she didn't normally wake up naked and spooned against a hard-muscled chest or to a large hand holding her bare breast like it was palming a basketball. Okay, more like a softball, but that wasn't the point.

The events of the night before came swimming back to her, and she clutched the sheets to her chest. Holy hot cowboy—what had she done? And why was her body coming alive and aching to do it again?

She turned her head, and her heart melted at the sight of Ethan snuggled against her. He was so damn good-looking, it almost hurt to look at him. Plus the dog was curled at his feet, and she had her fluffy head resting on his ankle.

Placing her hand over his, she paused for just a second, relishing the feel of his strong hand holding such an intimate part of her. She remembered how those same hands had felt the night before as they roamed over her body, caressing and touching as they explored all of her intimate parts.

Letting out a sigh, she lifted his arm and carefully eased out from underneath him. She found her bra and undies on the floor and quickly pulled them on. A half-empty bottle of water sat on the bedside table, and she grabbed it and glugged it down.

"Good morning," Ethan said, rising up on one elbow and grinning at her like he'd just won a prize at the fair. "Now there's a sight I could get used to waking up to." His hair was tousled and his eyes were still sleepy, and Jillian's heart tumbled in her chest.

Oh man. She was falling for this guy, and she had it bad. She needed to get out of there or else she might crawl back into bed and ravage him. Again.

"You want breakfast?" he asked while absently scratching the neck of the dog who had woken and inched up closer to his hand. "I can make eggs, or pancakes, or there's still more cake."

She grinned. "That cake already got me in enough trouble last night."

"The cake? I thought it was the tequila."

It was you. And all these crazy mixed-up feelings I have for you.

"I think it was a combination of the two." She spotted her skirt on the floor, tangled in his jeans, and snatched it up. She wrapped it around herself. Now where the heck was her shirt?

"How about some coffee, then?"

"Really, I should go. I've got to get to work, and I don't want Milo to come home and not find me there." She'd texted her sister the night before to tell her she'd be staying later, just so her sister didn't worry and call the police. Especially since she'd been *with* the police. Or at least one of them.

Ugh. She really needed to get her own place.

"I thought he was with Elle."

"He is. But with kids, something is always happening to throw your best-laid plans awry."

"Okay. When I can see you again?"

"Um…" She shifted from one foot to another, her head and her heart having a knock-down-drag-out debate. Part of her wanted to put the brakes on right now, and the other part of her wanted to move in with him.

"How about we just *go* for coffee sometime?" he suggested. "That's something a couple of friends would do."

"I guess coffee would be okay."

"Like, later this morning?"

She raised an eyebrow at him.

He gave her a sheepish grin. "Can't blame a guy for trying. Especially a guy who is using all his self-control not to drag the half-naked woman standing in his bedroom back into his bed."

"If it makes you feel any better, it's taking all my self-control too."

"Yeah?" He pulled back the covers and patted the bed next to him. "You could at least give a guy a kiss good-morning."

She knew what one kiss would lead to. Especially since he was naked and all of his glorious muscles were on display and rippling as he beckoned her to him. She told herself she needed to walk away, but instead her traitorous body took a step forward.

He reached out and fingered the hem of her skirt. "That was a pretty slick trick with this skirt last night. I'm gonna make a motion that more women wear Velcro clothing."

"Everyone wears these around the beach because they're so easy. You just wrap them around you and go."

He shooed the dog down as he sat up in bed. The sheets fell away as he scooted toward her. He slid an arm around her waist and pulled her closer, leaning his head forward and pressing a soft kiss to the spot next to her belly button. "And how does the Velcro part work again?" he murmured as he laid a line of warm kisses all along the waistband of her skirt. The shadow of whiskers along his jaw scraped across her delicate skin, but she didn't want him to stop.

She inhaled a quick breath as he placed his hand next to her knee, then slid it lightly up the side of her leg and along her thigh. He stopped just at the edge of her skirt and looked up at her.

This was a really bad idea. Her head knew it, but her body was in full-on denial. And it wasn't like she hadn't had bad ideas before.

She pointed to the tab securing the Velcro. "You just grab this part and pull." It was easy. And apparently so was she.

He leaned forward, took the tab in his teeth, and pulled. He dropped the skirt to the floor, then ran his eyes up her body. Stopping at her midsection, he grinned like a wolf who had just discovered a sheep sandwich. "After last night, I think I know what your superpower is."

A grin tugged at her lips. "Oh yeah?"

"Yeah. But I think I might need one more shot to know for sure."

He might think she had superpowers, but all she felt was power*less* as she surrendered to her heart and tumbled back into bed with him.

CHAPTER 8

Bryn, Elle, and Sassy were already at Bryn's that night for their weekly Taco Tuesday night when Jillian showed up carrying a box holding her seven-layer dip and the rest of the tequila and margarita mixer.

"Nora couldn't make it," Bryn told her, taking the box from her arms and giving her a one-armed hug. "She had a physical therapy client to meet, but she'll be here next week."

Jillian followed her into the kitchen and was greeted with more hugs from Elle and Aunt Sassy.

"You've got to try this salsa," Bryn told her, setting the box down and pushing the bowl of chips toward her. "Elle got it at a new place when she was in Denver yesterday."

Jillian picked up a chip and eyed the salsa. She wasn't sure she should trust it after the last stuff Elle had given her. The salsa might be spiked with tequila.

Elle held up a glass. "Ready for a margarita?"

She shook her head. "Not tonight. I had enough last night." She pointed to the mixer. "And just to let you know, that mixer already has alcohol in it, so I wouldn't pour more tequila in it or you'll end up loopy after one drink."

"What? No way. It's a new kind I thought I'd try," Elle said, picking up the bottle to read the label. "I didn't know."

"That kind of stuff happens to me all the time," Aunt Sassy said, peering over her shoulder at the label. "I have to make sure I keep the Preparation H in a separate drawer because once I almost mistook it for toothpaste."

"Eww," Jillian said.

"And one time I bought a frozen quiche instead of an ice cream pie at the store. Let me tell you, that made for an interesting dessert night at Bible study." Sassy laughed at the memory.

"That's only because you refuse to wear your glasses in public. If you wore your readers, you wouldn't make those crazy mistakes. I'm surprised you didn't get kicked out of Bible study."

Sassy waved a hand at Bryn. "I hate wearing those stupid reading glasses in public. They make me look old."

"You *are* old."

She planted a hand on her hip and glared at Bryn. In her trademark style, she had on lime-green-and-white-checked ankle pants and a hot-pink top. A trio of blingy bangle bracelets sparkled and jangled at her wrist. Her silvery white hair curled in a soft cloud around her head and it looked like she'd had the beauty parlor put in a few streaks of light-pink at her last appointment. "Well, I don't need to advertise it by standing in the grocery store squinting through a pair of readers."

Bryn shrugged good-naturedly. "Fine. Then be prepared to brush your teeth with hemorrhoid cream."

Jillian laughed as she shook her head. "Can we please quit talking about hemorrhoid cream?"

Elle had set down the margarita bottle and was studying her as she leaned back against the counter. She had on khaki shorts, a flowy floral tank top, and a pair of black designer sandals that probably cost more than Jillian made in a week. "So let's go back to that comment you made about getting loopy after one drink. Did you and a certain hot deputy go on a margarita bender last night?"

Jillian winced. "I wouldn't call it a bender. But we both ended up a little tipsy."

"And were any bad decisions made?" Elle waggled her eyebrows. "And by bad decisions, I really mean *good* decisions."

Warmth flooded her cheeks, and she avoided Elle's eyes as she reached for another chip.

"Oh my gosh," Elle squealed. "I was just teasing, but you are blushing like crazy. Something *did* happen." She grabbed a glass and passed it to Bryn. "Quick—get her a drink so she can swill it and spill it."

Aunt Sassy bumped her hip into Jillian's. "Did you do the horizontal hustle with the dashing deputy?"

"The horizontal hustle? Really?"

Sassy gave her a feisty grin. "Oh, sorry. Would you rather I say bumping uglies? Or that he gave you the hot beef injection? Or drove the beef bus into tuna town?"

Jillian covered her ears. "Gah. I'd rather you not talk about it at all."

"Yeah," Bryn said, sliding a margarita toward her. "We'd rather hear *you* talk about it. What happened?"

Jillian sighed and dropped onto one of the bar stools next to the counter. She took a small sip of the drink and the taste brought all the memories of the night before—and that morning—back to her. "Okay, so yeah, we had a couple of drinks and ended up..." She paused, then snuck a furtive glance at Sassy. "...doing the horizontal hustle."

"Yay," Elle said, clapping her hands.

"I don't know why you're so excited," Jillian said. "Or why you're clapping for me like you're giving me a round of applause."

"Was it applause-worthy?" Aunt Sassy asked, waggling her eyebrows.

"I'm just happy for you," Elle said, ignoring Sassy's comment. "Ethan seems like a great guy, and he obviously likes you. I just want you to stay open to the possibility of something happening with you two."

She'd left his place that morning thinking the same thing. What if she and Ethan really could have something? They seemed to connect in a way that she hadn't with another man in a very long time. And not just physically—although that was a pretty amazing connection—but their personalities too. He was kind and thoughtful, and they made each other laugh. Which counted for a lot in her world. But still.

"I don't know," she told the other women. "We did have a great time last night, and I mean a *really* great time, like, it was not only applause-*worthy* but also earned a standing ovation again this morning." She laughed as Elle and Bryn clapped again and Aunt Sassy let out a whoop. "But that doesn't mean I've changed my mind about getting involved with him. I still have my new job and my son to think about. And they both take up all my focus right now."

Aunt Sassy rested a hand on her arm. "You can do all that and still let yourself enjoy the company of a good man. And I don't just mean his 'company.' I mean it's nice sometimes to have someone to go to dinner with or to snuggle up with and watch a movie."

Jillian shrugged. "I don't need a man for that stuff. I've got you all to go to dinner with, and I snuggle on the sofa and watch movies with my sister and Milo like three times a week. Speaking of which, if anyone has a lead on an apartment or a house to rent for cheap, let me know. We're all on top of each other in my sister's small place, and the neighbors aren't thrilled with the dog barking every time someone knocks on the door."

"I wouldn't get too worked up over everything happening with Ethan," Bryn said. "Just take it slow, have fun hanging out with the guy, and see what happens. And besides, he's going to be pretty busy the next several months anyway with the election."

Jillian stopped as she was raising a chip to her mouth. "What election?"

"I saw it in the *Creedence Chronicle* this morning. The current sheriff is getting ready to retire and everyone thought Ethan was a shoo-in for the position since he was running unopposed, but the paper said Conway Peel just threw his hat in the ring and is making a play for the job."

Aunt Sassy huffed. "Well, Ethan should still win by a landslide. Who wants a sheriff named Con?"

Oh no. Jillian's heart sank. Ethan was running for sheriff? She slumped back in her chair, the chip forgotten. "Well, I guess that answers that. We can just end this discussion now because any chance of a future with Ethan just went swirling down the drain. If he's running for sheriff and going to be caught up in an election, then that means people will be digging into his past. *And* into the past of everyone associated with him."

Bryn frowned. "So?"

Jillian sighed. "So, it's not going to help his chances to be dating a single mom whose baby daddy is in prison." And who barely escaped ending up there herself. She hadn't shared that part with Ethan, or with her friends. They knew about as much as she'd told him in the truck a few days before.

"Oh, pshaw," Aunt Sassy said, waving her concerns away. "Nobody's going to care about that."

"Wanna bet?"

———————

The next few days went by in a blur. Jillian had a million things going on at the library, and she'd thrown herself into every task in hopes of keeping her mind off a certain cute cowboy. He'd texted her as she'd left Bryn's house Tuesday night and again yesterday. They'd exchanged a few messages, all of them light and funny, and her heart had leapt in anticipation of his words every time she heard the little chime notification of a new text.

He'd asked her for coffee again, but so far she'd put him off.

It was late afternoon when she heard the whoosh of the

library door. They'd received a big shipment of new books at the library, and she was trying to get them catalogued and ready to be shelved before her shift ended.

She looked up to see a dark-haired woman enter and make a beeline for the information desk where she was sitting. The woman was dressed professionally in a sleeveless silk blouse, pencil skirt, and sleek black pumps.

There were only a few patrons scattered around the library, so Jillian used her normal voice to address the woman. "Hi there. Is there something I can help you with?"

"I hope so. I'm Cynthia Dresden," she said, holding out her hand.

"Jillian Bennett," she said, smiling as she shook the woman's hand.

"Oh, I know who you are."

Of course she did. Creedence was a small town. Everyone knew who everyone was. Especially someone who was new to town and who had taken a prominent position in the community.

"So, what was it you needed help with?"

The woman studied her for a moment before answering, as if she were a bug under a microscope. "Oh yeah, I just wanted to use one of the computers. Do I need to sign up for one?"

Jillian glanced over at the reference section where the six computer stations sat empty. "I think you're good. Take your pick."

The library door opened again, and a swirl of butterflies performed loop-de-loops in Jillian's stomach as a familiar tall deputy sauntered in. The flirty grin on his face felt just for her, and she hoped her sports watch didn't go off with an alarm notification that her resting heart rate had just gone through the roof.

He tipped his hat. "Ladies."

"Well, hello, Ethan," Cynthia Dresden practically purred, the pitch of her voice triggering Jillian's internal notifications that there was something between these two.

Ethan nodded at the dark-haired woman. "Cynthia."

The woman narrowed her eyes to study the two of them, much like she'd done to Jillian when she'd first walked in the door. She pointed a long red-polished nail from her to Ethan. "I didn't realize you two knew each other."

Hmm. The way she'd said it made Jillian think she knew full well that they knew each other. She tried to think back to the benefit dance she'd hung out with Ethan at earlier that summer, and if she'd possibly seen Cynthia there. But nothing was coming to her.

"Yeah, we've been friends for a while now," Ethan said, his voice casual, and Jillian loved him for it.

Her job at the library was already a source of contention with some that it hadn't gone to a local person, and she didn't need any rumors flying around that she was now also trying to steal one of Creedence's most eligible handsome bachelors. She didn't want to give anyone more fuel to add to the new-woman-in-town fire.

Cynthia paused a beat, her eyes still squinted into narrow slits. Then she waved a hand in their direction. "Well, I'd better get to my research and let you two get back to whatever it is you're doing."

As if by unspoken agreement, they both waited for

Cynthia to make her way to the computers and sit down before resuming their conversation.

Ethan turned his back to the computer stations and lowered his voice. "So, I was thinking if I couldn't get you to come to coffee with me, I'd bring the coffee to you."

"What does that mean?" She hated to admit how intrigued she was.

"You'll see." He glanced up at the clock. "You get off in, what, fifteen minutes or so?"

She nodded.

"I'll just look around then, maybe check out a book or two, while I wait." He leaned forward, lowering his voice further. "Got any recommendations for books about romance? I'm kind of interested in this woman, and I feel like I need to up my game with her."

She pressed her lips together to keep a giggle from escaping. "Your game is plenty up," she told him, playfully nudging his arm. "I don't think you need any more inspiration."

"Good to know." He walked a few steps backwards. "Let me know when you're ready to go."

They left the library together twenty minutes later. Jillian could have been finished right on time, but she didn't want Ethan to think she was too eager.

"You good with leaving your car here for a bit and taking my truck?"

"Sure." Her car was secure in the library parking lot. And he seemed so pleased with himself, it made her curious to see what he had up his sleeve. "But can't we just walk to the coffee shop? It's only a few blocks away."

"Nope," he said, holding the truck door open for her. "That's not where we're headed for this coffee."

Hmm. She did love a good mystery.

She settled back against the seat as Ethan started the truck and pulled out onto the road. "So what's the story with you and Cynthia?"

"No story. She's asked me out to dinner a few times is all."

"Have you gone?"

"Once. And that was enough. We got along fine. But she's not really my type, and I wasn't interested in pursuing anything more."

"But she was?"

He shrugged. "I don't know. Maybe. I guess."

"Did she ask you out again?"

"Yeah."

"More than once?"

He shrugged again. "I guess."

"Then yeah, she's still interested."

"It doesn't matter. The only woman I'm interested in right now is a sexy librarian who wears superhero undies." He glanced down. "Who are you wearing today?"

She offered him a coy grin. "Wouldn't you like to know?"

He groaned. "Yes, I would. Sooo bad."

Over the last few days, she'd forgotten how fun it was to flirt with him. And how much she enjoyed his attention and witty banter. He was smart and clever, and she loved that in a man.

They'd driven a few miles out of town when Ethan pulled off the highway, went a ways down a dirt road, then turned into a field full of freshly harvested hay. He jumped out and opened a gate, then pulled through and got out again to close it.

"Where is this coffee shop?" Jillian asked, leaning forward to peer through the windshield.

"I never said we were going to a coffee shop. I just said we were going *out* for coffee."

"This is definitely *out*. As long as this isn't some kind of practical joke where you're planning to serve me cowboy coffee and a cow pie."

He chuckled. "That's a good one. But don't worry. I take coffee very seriously." He drove through the pasture, and they bumped along a small path that led into an outcropping of trees at the base of the mountain.

"Are we trespassing?"

"No. This is my grandparents' land." He pointed through the windshield. "It's just ahead."

They pulled out of the tree line and into a clearing where a small blue pond sparkled in the sun. A tall waterfall trickled over the rocks on the side of the mountain and into the pond.

Jillian covered her mouth with her hands. "Oh my gosh. It's gorgeous."

He pulled up to the shore and cut the engine, then got out and ran around to her side to open her door.

She stepped out onto the grass, thankful she'd worn sandals today. The air smelled of hay and pine trees and the faint scent of algae from the pond. The day was still hot, and she was tempted to run over and splash into the water. That would certainly show Deputy Rayburn that he wasn't the only one full of surprises.

Opening the back door of the king cab, he brought out a large Rubbermaid tub and carried it to the back of the truck. He dropped the tailgate and set the tub on the edge.

"What's that?" she asked, foregoing her thoughts of splashing in the water as her curiosity was even more piqued.

"It's our coffee." He opened the tub and lifted out a fancy coffee maker, a small cooler, a clear canister of ground coffee, a large bottle of water, a small porcelain pitcher, and two cups, one a dark green mug and the other a fancy floral tea cup with a matching saucer.

He plugged the coffee maker into an outlet in the bed of his pickup and filled the top with coffee and the basin with the contents of the water bottle.

The rich scent of coffee mingled with the pine-scented air as the coffee brewed and trickled into the carafe. With a flourish, he brought out a quart of her favorite creamer from the cooler.

Her eyes grew wide. "How did you know what my favorite creamer flavor is?"

"When it's important, I make it my business to know things."

"And my favorite creamer flavor is important?"

"It's important to you."

She narrowed her eyes. "Are you just trying to make me fall madly in love with you?"

He grinned. "Maybe. Is it working?"

Oh, it's working all right. But she wasn't about to tell him that.

"I'll have to try your coffee first."

"Coming right up." He poured the creamer into the small pitcher and frothed it with the steamer affixed to the side of the coffee maker. Then he filled the two cups with coffee and carefully poured the frothed milk on top. He gently stirred the creamer in, then handed Jillian the cup and saucer.

"This cup is gorgeous," she said, admiring the purple, pink, and yellow pansies painted around the sides of the cup and on the matching saucer. "So who told you that pansies are my favorite flower?"

He raised an eyebrow. "You just did."

"What?"

"Pansies were my grandma's favorite flower. And she loved drinking tea from fancy cups. I just picked that one from the collection of teacups she left at my house because I thought you'd like it."

"I do. Like it, I mean." She took a sip of the coffee, marveling at the delicate porcelain of the cup and feeling a little fancy herself for drinking it outside at the edge of a waterfall. "Mmm. You do make good coffee, Deputy Rayburn."

"Just another one of my many talents." He pulled a blanket out of the tub and spread it on the grass next to the pond and below the branches of a cottonwood tree.

She kicked off her sandals and settled on the blanket as he brought over his cup and sat down beside her. They were in the shade, but the air was warm, and after taking another sip of coffee, she set her cup down to lift her hair off her neck.

"You have great hair," Ethan said. "I don't know that I've ever told a woman that before, but yours is just so cool. I love all the curls."

She ducked her head, trying to hide her grin and not about to admit she'd worn it down and curly today with the secret hope she might see him. "Thanks," she said, peeling an elastic off her wrist and corralling the curly mass into a messy bun on top of her head. "It's a lot, though. And in the summer it gets hot."

"We could always cool off with a dip in the pond." He lifted one eyebrow as if issuing a challenge.

She eyed the sparkling water. It did look refreshing. "Is it safe to swim in?"

"Sure. We've been swimmin' in it since we were kids."

Her gaze bounced from him to the water, then back again. "Let's do it."

His eyes widened. "Yeah?"

"Yeah." She laughed and stood up on the blanket, then held out her hand to pull him up. She lifted her shirt over her head, revealing a lacy pale-pink bra, and dropped it to the blanket. Unzipping her cropped ankle pants, she shimmied out of them and waited for Ethan's comment about her underwear.

He'd left his hat in the truck and had yanked off his shirt and boots, but stopped to admire her bright-green undies. "Come on. I gotta know…"

She flexed a muscle. "The Incredible Bulk."

He let loose a laugh. "Seriously? The *Bulk*? I think I'm in love."

She ignored the tingle of heat that surged through her at his words. "I wore them specifically today because I'm trying to be super strong and not get all caught up in wanting to kiss you."

"How's that working out for you?"

"Not so great."

"Then it sounds like it's working out perfectly for me." He reached for her and got one arm around her waist before she ducked and feinted and ran toward the pond.

"You gotta catch me first," she called over her shoulder.

"I do love a challenge," he muttered as he jerked off his jeans and went running after her.

"It's freezing." She shrieked as she splashed into the water.

"Come on. You think the Incredible Bulk would be put off by a little cold water?" he said, wading in after her. He shivered as he made it in up to his waist. "Holy crap. This *is* freezing."

She splashed at him before dunking down to her neck in the water. He dove in and came up next to her, shaking the water from his hair, then pulling him to her.

"Now what were you saying about a kiss?"

CHAPTER 9

THE SUN FELT WARM ON ETHAN'S WET BODY AS HE AND Jillian sprawled out on the blanket after their swim. Making out in the water had already brought his blood to near-boiling, but having her lying so close to him wearing nothing but a couple of scraps of wet fabric that clung to her most intimate bits was sending him over the edge.

She gave a shiver, and he reached out his arm. "Come over here, I'll help warm you up."

"I'm only doing this because I'm cold," she told him as she scooted closer and pressed her body against his.

"Oh yeah. Me too. Otherwise, there's no way I'd want a sexy wet librarian in hot lime-green undies pressed up against me." He peered down at her and brushed a stray lock of damp hair from her forehead.

The top of her hair was still mostly dry, but locks of loose wet tendrils curled around her neck, clinging to her skin. A drop of water fell from one and made its way lazily down her neck and chest, then disappeared into her bra. His gaze followed its progress, then he bent to press his lips to the spot where it had vanished, as if he could catch it in his mouth.

Her skin was cool, and goosebumps rose on her flesh as another shiver ran through her. The wet fabric was practically translucent and clung to the tightened peaks of her nipples, making them even more enticing. He closed his lips around one and reveled in her soft gasp. Even through the fabric, he knew she could feel the warmth of his mouth and the gentle scrape of his teeth.

He cupped her other breast in his free hand, drawing from her another intake of breath as he grazed his thumb over the taut nub. Then he leisurely skimmed his fingers over her stomach, her waist, over the rounded contour of her thigh.

He looked down at her lush wet body, feasting on it with his gaze. Her eyes were closed and her back was slightly arched, as if beckoning his touch. She must have pulled the band from her hair because it was spread out in thick curls around her on the blanket, making her look like a goddess.

And he couldn't get enough.

Watching her body react, he slid his hand between her legs, then slowly slipped his fingers under the elastic of her panties. Dipping his head, he circled her nipple with his tongue as his fingers found her feminine core. She let out a soft kitten-like sigh as he caressed and stroked, but her fingers tensed as she tightly gripped his shoulder.

"Ethan?" She breathed his name, and he almost lost it. Her eyes were open now, and her smile was seductive, her voice husky and sexy as sin. "Any chance you brought a box of condoms in that tub with the coffee maker?"

"A *box*?" His lips curved into a grin. "No. But now I'm

planning to buy one on my way home. I do have *one* in my wallet though."

Her grin widened. "Not for long you don't."

━━━━━━━━

Ethan couldn't keep the smile off his face as he drove them back to the library where they'd left Jillian's car.

He was a few blocks away and had just braked at the four-way stop in front of the Creedence Country Market when Jillian gave a soft gasp, then opened her door.

"I'll be right back," she said before slamming the door and hurrying across the street toward a homeless woman sitting on the curb.

That woman has a heart of gold, he thought, assuming she was going to give the woman some money.

Instead, as Jillian got closer, she held out her hands, then pulled the woman up and drew her gently into a hug. And not just an awkward pat on the back kind of hug he'd give someone at a Christmas party. No, this was a full-on bear hug as Jillian wrapped the woman in her embrace. And the woman was hugging her back as if her life depended on it, clinging to Jillian's back and burying her face in the librarian's shoulder.

They stood like that for what seemed like a long time, Jillian just holding the other woman, as he slowly drove through the intersection then pulled into a parking spot. It wasn't until he got closer that he saw the woman's sign she'd had next to her.

He blinked back a sudden sting of tears as he read the words: JUST NEED A LITTLE KINDNESS.

He watched in awe as Jillian finally pulled away, then spent a few minutes speaking to the woman, then waved and hurried back to the truck. She climbed in and reached for her seat belt. "Thanks for waiting. I'm ready now," she said, clicking in the buckle as if nothing had happened.

But he knew something had. He'd just witnessed something extraordinary. And it made his throat thick as he reached down and took her hand. He wanted to tell her how amazing he thought she was, how kind and thoughtful, and what an incredible person she was. Instead, he opened his mouth and asked her again, "Will you marry me?"

Jillian came out from the back office of the library the next afternoon and was surprised, and a little excited, to see Ethan sitting in one of the reading chairs, his nose buried in one of the newest thrillers they'd just got in. Her skin heated as thoughts of their time spent together at the pond the day before flashed through her mind.

For someone who was determined not to start anything with this man, she sure did seem to find herself naked and in his arms a lot lately. And fending off another proposal. When he'd asked her the day before, she'd brushed it off like he was teasing, but his voice had held a sincerity that had her heart pounding harder even now as she remembered the moment.

It had to have been the emotion of the hug she'd given the

homeless woman. He'd told her how much it had moved him when he'd dropped her off and snuck a quick last kiss.

Almost as if he had radar that detected her, he looked up from the book and grinned in her direction. Dang, but that grin did funny things to her.

She waved as she crossed the room to him. "What are you doing in here?"

He held up the book. "Reading."

"I can see that. But why are you doing it here?"

He glanced around the room. "Because this is a library. It's a place where they have a lot of books. And they let you read them for free."

She planted a hand on her hip and stared at him.

"And there's a sexy librarian who works here who I've been trying to get to go out with me."

"How's that going?"

He shrugged. "Tough to tell, but I think I'm winning her over with my charm and charisma."

She finally smiled at him as she perched on the arm of his chair. "You are pretty charming."

"I'm glad you think so. I spent two hours canvasing downtown businesses and shaking hands this morning trying to remind people of that."

She nodded to the novel he was holding, anything to steer the conversation away from talking about the election. "How's the book?"

"Pretty good, actually," he said, glancing down at the cover, then back up at her. "I've read enough that I want to see how it ends, so I guess I'll be checking it out."

The library doors opened, and Milo walked in. He scanned the library, spotted Jillian and Ethan, and raced over to them. "Mom, guess what?"

"What?" she asked, pulling him into a quick hug. His hair was still damp, and he smelled like chlorine and sunscreen and ten-year-old boy.

"I swam a fifty off the blocks without coming up for air once. *And* a kid blew a snot bubble almost as big as my fist."

"Wow. Both of those sound quite impressive."

"I agree," Ethan said, tilting his head toward Milo. "Good job on the fifty."

"Thanks." He nodded to the book in the deputy's hand. "I read that one. It's good."

"Oh yeah? I like it so far. I was going to check it out."

"When you're done, we should talk about the ending. I have some definite thoughts."

Ethan chuckled. "Okay, we will." He nodded to Milo's backpack. "Are you done with swim practice for the day?"

"Yeah. I just walked over from the park. Mom doesn't get off for another few hours, so I usually just hang out and read while I wait for her."

"I just got off work and need to run out to the country to check on Miss Miriam. She was a friend of my grandma's, and I usually take some groceries out to her and see how she's doing once a week or so. She's got a pretty neat old farm, and her mini-horse, Applejack, is about the cutest thing you'll ever see," Ethan told him. "You want to come with me? Then we can come back and pick up your mom when she gets off and maybe go grab a pizza."

Milo bobbed his head. "Yeah, sure." He looked toward his mother. "Is that okay? Can I go with Ethan? Please."

"Umm, why don't you go put your stuff in my office and grab some water, then I'll let you know."

"That means she wants to talk to you without me here," he explained to Ethan. "You want some water too?"

"Sure."

She studied Ethan as Milo disappeared into the back-office area. "You don't have to offer to babysit my kid."

"I'm not offering to *babysit*. I'm just asking if he wants to hang out with me. He makes me laugh. And I could use the company."

"Okay. But you should be prepared to hear a lot of stories about his dog, books, and superheroes. Those are his favorite subjects."

He offered her a coy grin. "Superhero *attire* has become a favorite subject of mine as of late, as well."

She nudged him with her elbow, then pushed off from the arm of his chair. "See you at five. And Milo and I only eat pepperoni pizza."

"Perfect. That's my favorite too."

"Can I ride in the front seat?" Milo asked, racing out from the back room with two bottles of water and a couple of snack bags of Goldfish in his hands.

"Sure," Ethan said.

"Can I turn on the siren?"

"Yeah, sure. Once we're out in the country."

"Can I hold your gun?"

"No," both Jillian and Ethan answered at the same time.

"Don't even think about it, buster," she told Milo. She chewed on her bottom lip. "Maybe this isn't such a great idea."

"We'll be fine," Ethan told her. "I promise I won't let him hold my gun." He pointed to the snacks in Milo's hands. "Tell you what, though. I'll let you flash the lights if you give me one of those bags of Goldfish."

"Cool." Milo grinned as he passed him a bag and a bottle of water. "I got these for you anyway."

"Cool." Ethan nudged Jillian's arm. "Hear that? We're just a couple of cool guys hitting the open road with some Goldfish crackers." He winked, then headed toward the door with Milo in tow, calling over his shoulder, "We'll see you at five."

―――――――――――

"That was so awesome," Milo said, his eyes bright with excitement, after Ethan had let him run the siren and flash the lights. "How fast does this truck go? Have you ever gone over a hundred? Like, in a high-speed chase?"

Ethan grinned. "Yes, I have gone over a hundred, but not in a high-speed chase. Not a lot of opportunities for them here in Creedence."

"Not yet, at least."

He laughed. "True. I can keep my fingers crossed. But Creedence is a pretty quiet town. What do you think of it? Must be a little different from where you lived in California."

"Yeah, it is. But I like it. It's cool here. And my mom really likes it."

"Do you miss California?"

He shrugged. "Not much."

"What about your dad? Did you see him much?" *Wow. Really sly, Rayburn. Just slip in a little comment about his dad. Not fishing at all.*

Milo shook his head. "Nah. I don't really even know him. He writes me a letter once a month or so and sends me fifty dollars in a birthday card every year. But other than a box of letters, he's never had much else to do with me."

"Ever visit him?"

"No. It was pretty far from our town, and plus my mom didn't really want me to see the prison."

"That makes sense. Did you want to go see him, though?"

What was wrong with him? This was none of his business. Yet he couldn't keep his mouth shut. He was curious about Milo's dad, but he should be asking Jillian about him, not her son.

The boy turned his head to look out the window, his small shoulders tense. "Not really."

Ethan couldn't tell if he was done talking about it or wanted to say more. He let the silence hang in the air for a minute as he focused on turning down the dirt road that led to Miss Miriam's small farm. When Milo still hadn't said anything, he figured it was time to change the subject. "Hey, thanks for the tip on that book. I'm going to check it out. And I think it's cool that you like to read."

"Actually, I love to read." Milo ducked his head, but eased back against the seat, his shoulders relaxing again. "Some of the kids back in California used to make fun of me for it, but then I met Mandy, she's my best friend here, and she totally likes to read all the time too. Sometimes I go to her house and Elle makes us popcorn and we hang out all afternoon and don't even talk to each other because we're both reading good books. That probably makes me sound kinda nerdy, but I don't care."

"If it does, then I must be kinda nerdy as well because I love to read too. I've always got a book going, and I read pretty much every night before I go to bed."

"You do?"

"I do." He pointed toward the dash. "Click open that glove box."

Milo opened the glove box and pulled out a paperback of a popular thriller. "Hey, I've read this one. I think I've read the whole series."

"Wow."

The boy regarded him with a slight smile. "I can see you putting it together in your head. Yeah, I do read above my grade level."

Ethan laughed. "I'd pretty much figured that out. I am a deputy and have *some* detective skills, you know."

"My mom isn't thrilled when a book has a ton of swearing, and she says I have to wait until I'm twelve to start reading Stephen King, but otherwise she lets me read pretty much whatever I want. I read all the Jurassic Park books, and I really like Matthew Reilly's books. I haven't read the new one yet. I'm waiting for Mom to get it at the library."

"I read a couple of those too. I might even have the new one. If I do, I'll let you borrow it," Ethan said, making a mental note to order it online as soon as he got home.

"Cool." Milo tilted the top of the book toward him. "But if you're really interested in dating my mom, I wouldn't let her catch you dog-earing the pages of a book. That kinda makes her lose her mind."

Ethan chuckled, making another mental note to fix all the dog-eared books in his house. "Good to know." He gave Milo a quick side-eye. "So, how do you know I'm interested in dating your mom?"

Milo gave him a look that suggested he might be dumber than a box of rocks. "*Dude*. I might only be ten, but I've got ears. My mom and my Aunt Carley talk about you *all* the time."

Ethan leaned closer to him. "Oh yeah? Like what kind of stuff do they talk about?" He waved his hand. "On second thought, don't tell me. I don't want your mom to think I was interrogating you for info."

"I don't know that much anyway. Just that my mom thinks you're…" He raised his voice to mimic his mother. "…soo sweet and soo cute. She thinks you look like that guy who played Superman, Henry whatever. And my aunt keeps telling her she's crazy not to go out with you."

Ethan tucked the comparison to Superman comment away and asked, "What about you? How would you feel if your mom went out with me?"

Milo shrugged. "Doesn't bother me. Although I could be persuaded to put in a good word for you if you let me hit the siren again."

Ethan hesitated, then grinned as he shrugged back. "Deal." He liked the way this kid made him laugh. He pointed to the farm up ahead, then down to the manual button on his console. "But we're almost there, so you'd better use the manual button to just do a quick chirp, otherwise Miss Miriam will think we're coming to arrest her."

Milo bounced in his seat as he hit the button, and the siren reverberated through the air.

They pulled into the driveway, and Ethan grinned as he spotted one of his campaign signs stuck in the front of her yard. He pointed out the small barn and the chicken coop across from the house. Two cows stood inside the fence lazily munching on some hay as they watched them get out of the truck. The house was a two-story farmhouse with fading yellow paint and quaint blue shutters.

"Miss Miriam's lived here as long as I can remember," he told Milo as they carried the box of groceries he'd brought up the porch steps. "She used to run it with her husband, but he died close to ten years ago now."

The front door was open, and he rapped on the screen. "Hello. Miss Miriam? Anybody home?"

"I'm in the kitchen," a voice called out. "Applejack's coming to let you in."

Milo let out a laugh as a miniature horse came trotting to the door and peered at them through the screen. He nudged the door open with his nose to let them in.

"Neat trick," Milo said, grinning at the horse.

Ethan pointed to the leather strap affixed to the front of the door. "He can open it from the outside too by biting that strap nailed to the front of the door and pulling it toward him," Ethan said.

The horse followed them through the main living room and into a large sunny kitchen where Ethan set down the groceries. The cabinets and sink were on one side, and a large kitchen island filled the center of the room. A long row of windows facing the mountains filled the outer wall of the kitchen, and a dining room table was set up in front of them on one side and a small reading nook area was set up in the corner of the other.

An antique wingback chair with faded chintz fabric held a petite old woman, and she smiled and waved as they came in. Her hair was pure white and plaited into a braid, and she wore a faded pink housecoat. Her feet were clad in teal-blue slippers and propped up on an ottoman in front of her, and she had a knitted afghan tucked around her. An open book sat propped against a black tabby cat curled on her lap.

Her eyes sparkled and her voice was warm with affection and mischief as she reached to fold Ethan into a hug. "Hello, Ethan dear. I heard the siren and figured it was either you coming to visit or the police had finally figured out I was the one who stole that hideous dragon statue from in front of the courthouse and had come to arrest me."

Ethan's mouth dropped. "That was you who stole the dragon? That was a town scandal for years. You never told me that."

The woman shrugged but a satisfied grin creased her wrinkled face. "A woman has to have some secrets." She let out a soft cackle, then waved her hand. "And the town should thank me. The shyster who created it did a terrible job and then ran off with the money before he'd finished. And who decided a dragon should represent our town? Especially one that everyone thought looked like a giant tallywhacker on the front lawn of the courthouse. Good riddance." She let out a shiver, then squinted at Milo. "Who's your friend?"

Ethan closed his mouth—although he was still speechless from Miss Miriam's use of the word "tallywhacker." "This is Milo Bennett," he finally managed to say. "His mom is the new head librarian in Creedence."

"Nice to meet ya. I've met your mom a few times when she's brought me some books, and I really like her. She stayed and visited with me instead of running off like most of them do," she said, then gestured to the mini-horse who had clopped along behind them and was standing next to Milo, sniffing at his pockets. "That's Applejack. He's hoping you might have some apple slices or a carrot."

"He's so cool," Milo said, starting to reach his hand out, then hesitating and looking back at Miss Miriam. "Is it okay if I pet him?"

"Absolutely. He would love it. The crazy horse thinks he's a dog." Her tone was meant to come out gruff but there was no mistaking the affection in her voice for the little horse. "I'm sure Ethan brought some apples, and I'll bet you could get him to slice one up for you to feed to him."

"I'm already on it," Ethan said, lifting a bag of apples from the box. He quickly washed and sliced one, then handed a few slices to Miss Miriam and the rest to Milo.

He held one out, and the mini-horse nibbled it delicately from his flattened palm, then nudged his ribs for another.

"He likes you," Miss Miriam said, after taking a small bite

of an apple slice. "He doesn't usually warm up to strangers so quickly. You must be special." She gestured to the cat stretching on her lap as Ethan noted Milo standing a little taller. "This is Shadow, on account of the fact she follows me everywhere I go—has since she was a kitten. She likes everyone, especially if they rub her belly. I love her, but I still think she's a bit of a hussy."

"Have you eaten today?" Ethan asked, unloading the rest of the groceries and sticking them into the pantry.

"No, honey. Not until this apple." She set the rest of the slice on a saucer holding a half-empty cup of coffee. The cup and saucer were perched on a tall stack of books next to her chair, the books seeming to double as an end table. She frowned for the first time since they got there. "To tell you the truth, I've been feeling a little peaked lately."

"Peaked?"

"Best word I can think to describe it. Just not quite myself, I guess."

"Have you called your doctor? Do you want me to see about bringing him out here? I could give him a lift."

She waved his concern away. "No. I'm fine. Old Doc Hunter stopped by yesterday with Sassy James, and he looked me over. Visiting with the two of them was the best medicine he could offer—that Sassy does make me laugh—but he had the nerve to mention I was getting old." She turned to Milo, who was scratching Applejack's neck. "Young man, do you know how old I am?"

"No, ma'am. And my mom raised me to never ask a woman her age. In fact, she says to tell anyone who asks that they look as young as a spring daisy. So that's how old you look to me."

Miss Miriam let out a laugh that turned into a cough. Ethan took a step toward her, but she quieted it with a sip of coffee he imagined had grown cold. He started a fresh pot as he listened to her chatting with the boy. "I like you, Milo. Your mom did a good job raising you. As much as I appreciate being compared to a spring daisy, I'm actually ninety-one years old. You ever met anyone that old before?"

"No, ma'am. I don't think so."

"Well, now you have."

"Cool. I've also never met anyone who let a horse in their house before."

"Applejack is more than a horse. He's my best friend. I've had him since he was a colt, and he's close to fifteen now. My husband gave him to me for my birthday one year. To keep me company, he said, since I'm allergic to dogs. He had no idea how much I'd come to rely on that little horse."

"Does he always stay in the house?"

"No, but he spends most of the day here. And has since he was born. You saw him. He knows how to open the door and let himself in and out. He's got a little corral outside where he sleeps at night."

"I've never heard of a horse being housetrained before."

"My Applejack isn't like any horse you've ever met. He's a smart one. He knows what I need before I even know myself." She pointed to the afghan on her lap. "I swear to you I shivered earlier, and he picked up this blanket from the sofa in the living room and brought it to me."

"Wow," Milo said, sounding duly impressed.

Ethan had moved into the kitchen and was rummaging

through a drawer for a can opener. "I got some of that soup you like—the chicken noodle. I'm going to heat you up some before we go. I'll put it in a mug for you."

"Suit yourself. Although if you're going to the trouble, maybe I'd take a few crackers too."

Ethan listened to Milo chatting with Miss Miriam and Applejack as he heated the soup and checked the fridge to see what she was running low on. He poured the soup into a mug and then set it on a plate with a spoon, a napkin, and a sleeve of saltines.

"Now don't let this be all you eat today," Ethan told her, bending to press a kiss to the side of her weathered cheek.

She clasped the hand he'd just placed on her shoulder. "You're a good boy, Ethan. Thanks for bringing Milo out to see me. He's a good boy too."

"Anything else we can do for you?"

"I can't think of a thing," she said.

"We're gonna head back to town then, but you've got my number if you need anything. And I'll be back to check on you in a few days."

"You're too good to me, honey."

"Yeah, I am, especially now that I know you're the one responsible for the theft of that dumb dragon."

She laughed again. "Bring an arrest warrant next time. I think it would be fun to spend the night in jail again before I die."

"Again?"

She looked out the window, a small smile on her face, but her gaze was fixed on another time, another place. She patted his hand again. "Remind me the next time you're here. I'll tell you all about it. It's a pip of a story."

"You're a pip of a lady," he told her with a wink. "And you know I mean that in the best possible way." He gently squeezed her shoulder. "See you in a few days."

"Bye, Miss Miriam," Milo said, waving as he followed Ethan to the door.

"Bye, Milo. Come back anytime. See you soon, Ethan. And don't forget your promise."

"I won't," he called before giving Applejack one last pat and closing the screen door.

"What did she mean? About not forgetting your promise?" Milo asked when they were back in the truck.

"I promised her that if anything ever happened to her, I'd make sure Applejack and Shadow were taken care of."

"That's nice of you."

"She was a good friend to my grandma and was always kind to me as a kid. And I don't take promises lightly," he said as he pulled the truck back onto the dirt road.

"Me either." Milo watched out the window as they passed a long field of corn, then he turned back to Ethan. "Can I ask you something else?"

"Sure."

"What's a hussy?"

CHAPTER 10

"WHAT'S EATING YOU?" AMOS ASKED JILLIAN THE NEXT morning at the care facility as she folded a blanket and smoothed it across the end of his bed.

"Who said anything was eating me?"

"You're not being your normal annoyingly chipper self," he said. "So what is it? You got man troubles?"

She stopped and planted a hand on her hip. "What in the world makes you think I'm having man troubles?"

He gave a gruff chuckle. "Besides the fact that I was married for over fifty years?" He circled his finger at her. "Your face keeps changing from that moony look women get when they're being courted to that broody look that says they're also a little annoyed at who's doing the courting." He pointed to the blanket. "Plus you've folded that blanket three times now and haven't even asked me how I liked the books you left me last week, which you usually do first thing."

She perked up, trying to push back her conflicting thoughts about how much fun she and Milo had at the pizza place with Ethan the night before while trying to convince herself of all the reasons getting involved with him was such a bad idea. "Oh yeah, how did you like the one with the lady park ranger?"

He waved his hand. "I liked it fine. I'll take the next one in the series when you think of it. But let's get back to you and what's troubling you."

She sighed and slumped on the corner of his bed. He was propped up in the chair across from her, wearing blue flannel pajamas, and he leaned forward and tipped his cowboy hat up as if that could help him to listen better. "You really want to hear this?"

He lifted his palm. "Does it look like I have somewhere to be? The next most interesting thing on my schedule is a game of dominoes after supper tonight with Walt Anderson, and I swear that guy cheats."

"How do you cheat at dominoes?"

"How do you keep changing the subject?"

"Fine. If you must know, I *am* having man troubles."

"I already knew that. What's the trouble? He's not stepping out on you, is he? Because I might look old but I've still got a good right hook and I can have a 'talk' with him, if you get my meaning."

She shook her head. "No. No. It's nothing like that. This guy treats me well—he's kind and funny, and if I let myself, I could really fall for him. But I can't. There's too many obstacles in our way. But we do have fun together, and I like him. He's a good man. Which is also part of the problem. He's *too* good—especially for someone like me."

Amos screwed up his face. "What the devil's that supposed to mean?"

She shrugged. "I have some things in my past that I'm not too proud of."

He offered her a mischievous grin. "All the best women do."

She let out a laugh. "Oh yeah? Even your Trudy?"

He laughed with her. "*Especially* my Trudy." His voice took on a wistful tone. "That woman tied me in knots with her crazy stunts. You know, I fell in love with her the first day I met her. We were eighteen, and she'd come to spend the summer with her cousin. It was a hot day. I can still remember every detail of it. A bunch of us were out at the lake, and Ruth, that's her cousin, showed up with this leggy blond in a turquoise-colored bikini with white polka dots all over it. She'd never met any of us, but she strutted out onto that beach and plopped down on the blanket *right* next to me. I thought I was gonna have a heart attack. I'd never seen anyone that confident. She had a spray of freckles across her nose and just the slightest gap between her teeth, but she was the prettiest thing I'd ever seen, and I was just a ball of dad-blamed nerves."

Jillian's shoulders eased, happy to get off the subject of Ethan. "So did you talk to her?"

"I'd given her my best smile and was getting up the nerve to say something when Ruth tripped on the edge of the blanket and fell forward, and the lunch she'd packed went sprawling everywhere. I liked Ruth well enough, we'd been in school together forever, but she wore glasses and was kind of clumsy, and some of the kids gave her a hard time. You know how they do."

"I do." She thought of the way Milo had been treated back in California and was thankful again for the move to Colorado.

"Well, this one fella, Paul, he played football for our school and thought he was kind of a big shot, he started giving Ruth a hard time. But Trudy was having none of it. I can't recall exactly what she said, but she put that guy in his place faster than you can spit a watermelon seed. I think I fell in love with her that instant."

"Wow. She sounds pretty great."

"She was. When she saw that I'd helped Ruth up while she'd been telling Paul off, she grinned and informed me that we were going to be best friends for the rest of the summer."

"How long did that last?"

Amos blinked at the sudden well of tears in his eyes. "For over fifty years. That woman was the best friend I ever had."

Jillian choked back her own emotion. "Oh, Amos. I'm so sorry."

"Don't be. I like talking about her. And I haven't even gotten to the good stuff."

A woman wearing light-green scrubs in a playful kitten print poked her head in the door of the room. "Hey Amos, you'd better get yourself down to the dining room. Lunch started ten minutes ago."

Jillian hopped up off the bed and collected the books he'd left for her. "Oh jeez. I don't want you to miss lunch." She set the new stack she'd picked for him on his nightstand. "By the way, I knew you'd love those books, so I already brought you the next two in the series."

He winked. "Pretty *and* smart. Don't go talking yourself out of a good thing before you've even given it a chance. Just because *you* think you don't deserve it doesn't mean that you don't."

"Thanks, Amos."

"Remind me next week and I'll tell you the rest of the story of what happened that summer with Trudy and me."

"I can't wait."

———————

Girls' night was a welcome reprieve for Jillian the following Tuesday. It was great to listen to stories of the other women's lives and focus on someone's problems other than her own. It was a bonus that talking and laughing with her friends helped keep her mind off a certain handsome deputy who'd been taking up more than his share of her headspace.

She was still amazed at the friendships she'd found in these women. All because her son had befriended Mandy and they'd rescued some puppies. After what had happened with Rad, Jillian hadn't put much effort into making friends in California, female or otherwise. She'd had a couple of women at the library who she occasionally grabbed lunch with, and she'd formed an attachment to the grandmotherly woman in her apartment building who babysat Milo, but her life there had been centered solely around working, school, and raising her son.

Moving to Colorado, she'd been so glad to reconnect with her sister and give Milo that family connection, but she'd never imagined that she'd gained the friendship of Bryn, Elle, Nora, and Aunt Sassy—women who now also felt like sisters.

"Who needs another margarita?" Elle asked, as their conversation about the newest rescues wound down.

"I'm in for one more," Aunt Sassy said, passing Elle her glass.

"I'm good," Nora said, popping another chip into her mouth. "I've got patients in the morning."

"I'm good too," Jillian said, turning toward Nora. "It sounds like things are really going well with your physical therapy business. I'm so glad."

Nora smiled. "I'm glad too. I never could have imagined how much my life would change in such a short time. Just a few months ago, I was flat broke, lonely, jobless, nursing a broken heart, and back in my old room in my mom's basement. Now I'm living on a farm, have a thriving business, and in a relationship with an amazing man and his equally amazing daughter. Plus I have a horse." She slung an arm around Elle's shoulders. "All because my friend called me about a therapy job."

Elle shook her head at the attention. "I didn't do anything. But I'm so glad it all worked out so well for you. I love how happy you seem. And no offense to your mom, but your new roommate is way hotter."

"Speaking of roommates, I've been thinking about what you said last time you were here," Bryn said, turning to Jillian. "About how you were looking for your own place. And I think I've come up with a solution that will benefit both of us."

"Oh great. I'm all ears."

"Why don't you rent one side of the bunkhouse? It's been sitting empty since Cade and Nora moved out to their fairy-tale cottage in the woods. But he fixed both sides up really nice before they left. We just took in all these new horses so we could use the income, and it would give you and Milo a place of your own."

"What a great idea," Elle said, chiming in. "You've seen inside them, right? They're so cute. And they've got two bedrooms so one for each of you. It sounds perfect."

Jillian had to admit it did sound kind of perfect. "I like the idea, but I don't make a ton at the library. What were you thinking for rent?"

"Zane and I talked about it the other night. We're not trying to make a huge profit, but the rental income could go a long way to buying feed and supplies for the rescues." She quoted a figure. "If you think you could swing that, it would cover the feed and care of all five of the horses we just took in and give us room in the budget to take on a couple more."

"That's more than doable." She couldn't believe Bryn's generous offer. It sounded too good to be true. But that's how everything with Bryn was—her friend was generous to a fault. She'd give someone the shirt off her back—or the empty bunkhouse on her farm—if they needed it.

Bryn nudged her shoulder. "Plus you would get the added benefit of hanging out with us. *And* Milo's dog can have the run of the place. *And* I'll even sweeten the deal with a standing invitation to Sunday dinners here at the farmhouse." She grinned. "What do you say?"

"I say it's a really great offer. But I need to think about it and talk to my sister. She really helps me with Milo, and we'd talked about renting a house or something bigger when her lease runs out at the end of the summer."

"Easy. She can move out here too. Ask her if she wants to rent the other side of the bunkhouse. Then it's like you're still together, but you each have your own space." Bryn clapped her hands. "This is perfect."

"I haven't said yes yet," Jillian said. "But you're definitely swaying me. Can I let you know tomorrow?"

"Absolutely." She picked up another chip. "And don't think this is all out of the goodness of our hearts. Having a volunteer on site means I may put you and Milo to work more often helping out around the place."

"We'd actually love that." She let her shoulders drop. "And helping out would make me feel better about accepting such a great offer of rent." She hoped her sister would be excited about the idea. The rent was much less than what they were paying at the apartment. She frowned. "But Carley works full time at the salon and running her own business keeps her pretty busy. I'm not sure you could expect the same kind of help from her."

Bryn waved her concerns away. "Don't worry about that. Having double the rent would more than make up for it." Her brow furrowed. "And let me talk to Zane, because if you're both going to be renting, then maybe we should cut the rate back even more."

Jillian shook her head. "No. As much as I'd like to accept the cut, your offer is more than generous. I don't want to feel like I'm taking advantage of our friendship."

"Stop. There's no taking advantage in a real friendship. I know you would help me if I needed it."

"You can count on it."

Bryn put her hand on Jillian's arm. "I mean it. We would love to have you and Milo *and* Carley here. And you'd be helping us too. The place is empty so you could move in tomorrow if you want."

"Oh my word," Aunt Sassy said from the other end of the counter. She tapped a spot in the *Creedence Chronicle* she'd been perusing while she listened to the conversation. "Jillian, you are not going to like this."

"What's wrong?" Bryn asked, leaning toward her.

"You know that new section they've got in the paper? They're calling it 'About Town,' but in my day, we just called it the gossip section."

"The gossip section sounds much more scandalous," Nora said.

"And that's totally what it is," Elle told them. "Last week it reported that Aunt Sassy had made a delicious French silk pie to take out to her nephews at the Triple J Ranch and that Ida Mae Phillips had gotten a new hairstyle at the Cut & Curl."

Sassy grinned. "I may have leaked that part about the French silk pie to the editor of the paper when I saw her at the grocery. I've been getting tired of hearing Madge brag about the spot they did on her homemade preserves *every* single week at bridge club."

"Forget about Madge's preserves," Jillian said, her heart thumping as she squeezed in on Aunt Sassy's other side. "What's in there that I'm not going to like?"

"It's just a small mention, but we all know who they're talking about." Aunt Sassy read the lines out loud: "Rumors are floating around that our recent candidate for sheriff was seen taking our new head librarian out for coffee last week. Could there be a romance brewing?"

Jillian slapped her palm to her forehead. "Oh my gosh. It's starting already." The tacos in her stomach rumbled with a queasy turn. "Who writes this column? And how could they have known that Ethan asked me out for coffee?"

"I don't know," Sassy said, squinting at the byline. "It says Ruby Dare—but that's obviously a pen name. I've never heard of anyone named Dare around these parts. But I can ask around, try to find out."

"Maybe they don't even know for sure," Bryn suggested. "They might have seen you two getting into his truck and just supposed."

Jillian groaned. "This is just the kind of thing I was worried about. The election has barely even started, and they're already looking for dirt on him. *And* on the people around him."

She couldn't let that happen. Even if she was starting to really fall for the guy and they had the kind of chemistry she'd only read about in romance novels. It didn't matter that she thought about him all the time or that he was the first guy who she'd even *considered* dating in years. She had to stop this thing.

They both had too much to lose.

CHAPTER 11

"WHO'S YOUR FAVORITE SISTER?" JILLIAN CALLED OUT AS she let herself into the apartment later that night.

Carley was sprawled out on the sofa, wearing pajama pants, flip-flops, and an old hoodie Jillian was pretty sure she'd had since high school. She hit the mute button on the television. "That depends on what kind of favor that sister is about to ask."

Jillian laughed and held up the plastic container Bryn had insisted on sending home with her. "I'm the one doing you a favor. I brought you some tacos."

Her sister's face lit up, and she pushed up from the sofa. "Oh yum. You *are* my favorite. I was so wiped out from work that I never got a chance to eat. Then when I got home, I hit the sofa and didn't have the energy to get back up and make something." Despite her sloppy attire, her hair was pulled up into an elegant up-do.

"How did the practice run with the wedding party go this afternoon? Did you get a good one or a total Bridezilla?" She gestured to Carley's head. "Your hair looks gorgeous, by the way."

"Thanks." She touched the side of her head as she slid onto a bar stool at the kitchen island. "I saw this in a magazine and wanted to show it as an option for her bridesmaid. And to answer your question, a little of both. She started out acting kind of outrageous, but after a little time in my chair and with her friends, she calmed down and ended up having a lot of fun."

"I've been in your chair—I'm sure the amazing head massage you give helped."

"That, and the three glasses of sangria she had."

Jillian filled a plate with several tacos, covered them with a paper towel, and put them in the microwave. "I'm gonna check on Milo while this heats up, then we'll catch up. I've got something to tell you."

She slipped down the hallway and peeked into her son's bedroom. Milo was asleep, his blond hair—sun-bleached over the summer—tousled across the pillow. His body was curled around the sleeping puppy, and his book lay on the bed next to his hand, as if he'd fallen asleep reading.

Her son slept like a rock, but she still tip-toed into the room, moved the book to his nightstand, and pressed a quick kiss to his forehead. He let out a small sigh and burrowed deeper into his pillow.

Pulling his door shut, she headed back to the living room where Carley had returned to her corner of the sofa and was tucking into the warm tacos.

"These are amazing," her sister said between bites. "Bryn is an awesome cook."

"Funny you should say that. Because we might get a chance to eat more of her cooking. That's what I wanted to talk to you about." She dropped onto the sofa and filled Carley in on Bryn's offer.

"Wow," Carley said when she'd finished. "That seems like a really generous offer. I don't know how we can pass it up. If I could save that much in rent, it would really help free up more of my money for the shop. And I could do some stuff to help with the horses too. I think we should go for it."

"Yeah?"

"For sure." She stuffed the last corner of the taco into her mouth and chewed thoughtfully. "I've got a few logistical things to work out and my lease isn't up here until next month, so it might take me a little longer to move out there, but if you're ready, I don't see why you couldn't go now."

"Thanks a lot."

Carley laughed. "Oh come on. You know what I mean. I love having you here, but this apartment *is* kind of small for the three of us, and Gus seems to double in size every day, plus we've gotten some complaints about his occasional barking. I think Milo *and* Gus would love it. And honestly, I wouldn't totally mind having my bedroom back."

The two of them had been sharing Carley's room since they moved in. They often took turns sleeping on the sofa and sometimes Jillian bunked in with Milo, but Jillian had to admit it would be nice to have a bedroom of her own again.

"Okay, that settles it then. I'll tell Bryn tomorrow and then move out there this weekend."

Her phone buzzed where she'd laid it on the coffee table, and her sister grinned as she peeked at the display.

"Deputy Dashing is calling."

Jillian glanced at the kitchen clock, surprised to see it was after ten. "It's kind of late."

"Just take it. We'll talk more after. Unless he's calling for a hot cowboy boot-y call—then I say go for it."

"Stop it," she said, giving her sister a playful swat before she picked up the phone. "Hi, Ethan."

"Hey, Jillian. I didn't realize it was so late until after I'd dialed. Are you still awake?"

"I answered, didn't I? And you're supposed to be the detective."

Carley swatted her back and mouthed, "Be nice."

"I'm just teasing. Yes, I'm still awake. I'm sitting on the sofa talking to my sister. What's up?"

"Me. I can't sleep. I've been trying, but my mind keeps thinking about this sexy librarian I'm kind of sweet on."

"I thought I told you that Hazel Duncan is too old for you. Besides, she's married."

"Just my luck."

She heard him chuckle and the sound of it sent funny darts of heat along her spine. "So, I have some news," she said.

"Oh yeah?"

"I was telling Bryn that we were looking for our own place, and she and Zane offered to let me rent the bunkhouse."

"Hey, that's great. I've seen the inside of them, and Cade did an amazing job renovating them. I think he even exorcised the ghosts of past cowboys and their smelly cigars and damp boots."

"Bryn didn't tell me about any ghosts. Hopefully she won't charge more in rent for those. As it is, she's giving me a great deal. And I'm promising that Milo and I will do more to help out with the rescue horse operation."

"Sounds perfect. When are you making the move?"

"This weekend, I guess."

"Wouldn't you know, I just happen to have some free time this weekend. Do you need some help?"

She grinned as she shook her head. "You don't have to do that. I don't have a ton of stuff. I sold all my furniture before leaving California."

"Jillian, don't you know that you should never turn down moving help from a guy with a truck?"

She chuckled. "This is Colorado. Every guy I know has a truck. Even old Doc Hunter has a pickup."

"Yeah, but try getting Doc to help you haul in those heavy boxes."

"Okay, you can help."

"Great. Text me what time you're starting on Saturday, and I'll be there."

⸻

Jillian took the following Saturday off work so she could focus on moving into the bunkhouse. She hated to miss her book-mobile rounds at the assisted living center—most especially the next chapter of Amos and Trudy's love story—but Miss Hazel had filled in before and Jillian knew she would do a great job. *And* that she could handle the cantankerous old cowboy.

Ethan had shown up at eight o'clock on the dot that morning and had come bearing coffees for her and Carley, hot chocolate for Milo, and donuts for them all. Sometimes the man seemed too good to be true.

She hated to admit it, but she was tremendously grateful for his help. Carley was scheduled to work at the shop all day, and Milo had swim practice for most of the morning. He'd helped carry several of the boxes from his room down to the car, then Elle showed up to take him and Mandy to the pool, promising to stop by the bunkhouse later to help move things in. She and Bryn had already done so much. The two of them had cleaned the bunkhouse the day before, scrubbing, dusting, and vacuuming it from top to bottom.

Jillian had spent the last several days boxing up the things they had at Carley's, and between her and Ethan, they'd had her car and his truck loaded in under an hour. Then she followed him out to the Heaven Can Wait horse rescue ranch— her new home.

And the funny thing was that the bunkhouse had felt like home from the minute she'd carried the first box up the steps of the long front porch. It had the look of a log cabin, with thick posts and galvanized steel buckets overflowing with pink trumpet flowers on either side of the stairs, and a cat curled up in the cushions of the glider swing.

Walking in the front door, she inhaled the subtle scents of vanilla, cinnamon, and cedar. She loved the open concept of the space and the modern farmhouse décor. The floors were the original hardwood and added an extra country touch. The main area had a kitchen to the right, a living room to the left, and a large kitchen island separating the two. A small dining room table was pushed up against the window, and a bouquet of wildflowers in a jar sat atop a light-blue tablecloth. A television and a small bookcase occupied one corner. An older sofa was against the back wall, giving its occupants a panoramic view of snow-capped mountains perfectly framed in the large picture window on the other side of the door. Jillian couldn't wait to curl up on it and enjoy that view with her coffee in the morning.

They propped the front door open to let in the breeze, and working together, it didn't take them long to bring in the boxes, luggage, and the few furnishings she had. Ethan offered to finish hauling in the kitchen stuff while Jillian got started on setting up the bedrooms.

"That's the last of it," Ethan said, setting the final box on the desk in Milo's new room.

"Awesome. I can't wait to unpack and start settling in," she said as she shook out a fitted sheet over the twin bed. "Thanks again for helping me. You were right about needing the truck."

Ethan grabbed the other side of the sheet and pulled the gathered edge around the opposite corner of the mattress, then held his hand out for the flat one. "Although I do appreciate being told I was right, you can stop thanking me now. I wanted to help and really, it was a pretty easy job. You didn't have that much stuff."

"Yeah. We travel pretty light." Jillian passed him one edge, and they spread the sheet across the bed and tucked it under the mattress at the end.

"Is that by choice or necessity?"

"A little of both, I guess. I'm already a bit of a purger *and* cheap, so I didn't want to pay to move a bunch of stuff across the country." She tossed a pillow and case toward him. "I told you I sold all my furniture. We also did a big moving sale before we left, and I made almost enough to cover the cost of the U-Haul we rented to get the rest of it out here." She took out the comforter and smoothed it over the sheets.

"That was smart."

"I'm nothing if not resourceful."

"I've gathered that." He placed the pillow against the headboard. "What's next?"

"I think that's it for in here," she said, surveying the bedroom. Besides the twin bed, it had a nightstand, dresser, and a small desk. "I think I'll let Milo move the rest of his things in, then he can decide where to put them. Although he's definitely gonna need a bookcase."

They froze as the sound of the television came on in the front room.

"What the heck?" Jillian whispered, taking a step closer to Ethan. "Is someone out there?"

Ethan frowned as he tilted his head toward the door to listen. "Sounds like it. I'll check it out." His hand automatically went to his hip as if reaching for his service weapon, but he was off-duty and out of uniform, wearing jeans and a T-shirt today.

"I'm coming with you," Jillian said, pressing against his back.

They inched down the hall, Ethan holding one arm out in a defensive maneuver while the other kept Jillian protectively behind him. As they got closer, Ethan stretched his neck out to carefully peer around the wall of the living room.

His shoulders relaxed as he let out a chuckle. He offered her a grin as he said, "Welcome to the country."

Her nerves jumpy, she hesitated before inching closer. What if it was a skunk? Or even worse, a snake? *Oh God, please don't let it be a snake.*

She took another step closer and cautiously leaned around the corner. A laugh bubbled out of her as she took in the scene in her living room. Definitely not a snake. Or a skunk.

"What are you two doing in here?" She planted a hand on her hip as she questioned the large pig who was lounged out across her sofa and the black-and-white billy goat who was standing in the kitchen eyeing the box holding the last of the donuts that was sitting on the counter. Tiny, the pig, who was anything but petite, wore a jaunty bright-pink flower tied around her neck, and she let out a happy snort as if to say "This is my favorite show" or maybe "Welcome home" or maybe "I'd take a donut too." Jillian wasn't completely up to speed on her hog facial expressions.

She pointed a finger at Otis, thankful she was wearing shorts today and there wouldn't be a repeat of the wrap skirt wrangle. "Don't even think about grabbing those donuts."

Ignoring her, the goat let out a bleat as he lifted his chin and sniffed at the box.

"I mean it," she said, using her best librarian voice.

The goat took one more sniff, then turned and sauntered, yes, *sauntered* toward her and rubbed its neck against her hip. She stood still and held up her hands as she looked at Ethan. "What is he doing?"

He laughed again. "He likes you. I think he wants you to pet him."

"*Pet* him?"

"Yeah, goats are really social animals. In some ways, they're a lot like dogs. But instead of petting their heads, goats like to have their front chest and their underarms scratched."

She shook her head. "I'm not petting this goat's armpit."

Otis let out a bleat as if he'd been insulted.

"Fine," she said with a huff and reached down to scratch the front of the goat's chest. Otis leaned into her hand and closed his eyes in bliss. He let out what sounded like a contented sigh, then walked over to the sofa and sat down next to Tiny. An episode of *Friends* was on, and both of the animals appeared to be engrossed in the show. "Nora warned me the goat knew how to turn on the TV by pushing the power button with his nose, but I thought she was kidding."

"Goats are smart animals. Especially when it comes to getting something they want."

"Yeah, but who would have thought what they want is to see if Ross and Rachel ever get together."

"Maybe they like Phoebe's singing." Ethan laughed, then waved a hand at the animals. "You want me to shoo them out?"

Jillian shook her head. "Nah. They seem to really be into this show. We can let them finish this episode."

"Way to embrace life in the country."

"No one told me that living on a ranch meant sharing the remote with a pig and a goat. But I'm working on being adaptable." She offered him an amused grin. "Now where were we?"

"I was nonchalantly trying to get an invite into your bedroom." His lips curved into a flirty smile. "I mean, I was offering to help you make up your bed."

She laughed and shook her head again. "Come on then. We'll leave the 'kids' in here to watch TV," she said as she led him back down the hall. Her stomach did a little flutter at the idea of him helping her make her bed. It felt too much like what a couple would do, especially with that stupid comment she'd just made about the "kids."

"Man, I hope our *actual* kids are better lookin' than those two animals," he teased as he followed her into her bedroom. "Although you gotta admit, they are pretty well behaved."

She lobbed a throw pillow at his chest, but her heart was racing at his casual comment about *their* kids—as if them having a future together was already a given for him. But they would have beautiful babies.

Stop it.

"Let's focus on the bed," she told him, reaching for the laundry basket of clean bedding.

"Oh, believe me, I am," he muttered, not quite under his breath.

She'd ordered new bedding online and had washed it all the day before. She ignored his comment—and the slight flush heating her cheeks—as they repeated the same process with her sheets and comforter on the queen bed in her room.

"I'm not sure I would've pegged you for pink sheets," Ethan ribbed her as she tossed him a corner of the bedspread.

"I don't think I've ever had them before. My last bedding was blue and green and had a definite ocean feel to it. I just ordered this and wanted something that felt a little more country." She smoothed her hand over the pink-and-white floral quilt. "I like the idea of a fresh start in a new place that's completely different from the old. Makes me feel like good things could happen."

"I like that you're open to the thought of new possibilities. Like maybe dating a handsome cowboy instead of one of those cool California dudes."

She laughed and tossed another pillow at him. "I didn't date a lot of 'cool California dudes.' I barely dated at all. I've pretty much only had one guy in my life for the past ten years, and he takes up the majority of my time."

"Now that you're in Colorado and out in all this open air of the country, maybe you'll find some space for another guy." He shook a pillow into a ruffled pillow case and tossed it against the headboard. "I have to admit, this wasn't exactly the way I imagined getting into your bedroom."

She offered him a coy grin, thankful to be done with the heavier conversation about new beginnings. "Oh yeah? Have you spent a lot of time thinking about it?"

His lips curved into a roguish grin. "*So* much time." He reached for her, but she slipped out of his grasp.

"Hey now, no time for fun. We've still got a lot of unpacking to do."

He reached for her again, wrapping an arm around her waist and pulling her close. "There's always time for a little fun." He leaned down and took her mouth with his.

The kiss was deep, gentle but demanding, and she lost herself in it. He tasted like coffee and the rich chocolate frosting from the donuts. His palm cupped her cheek, holding her face captive as he slanted his mouth across hers. Hunger and desire swirled through her as she clung to him, helpless to do anything but kiss him back.

The staggering rush of adrenaline that surged through her threatened to buckle her knees. His hand slipped under her T-shirt, and she hitched her breath as his fingers grazed across her back.

We're going to have to remake this bed, she thought. But instead of tumbling into it with her, he let her go and took a step away, leaving her breathless and trembling.

"What do you want me to start working on next?" he asked innocently, as if he hadn't just rocked her world.

Me. Start working on getting me into this bed, she wanted to tell him. But she didn't. She was too stunned and bewildered by the intense reaction she'd had to his kiss to say anything.

After what had happened with Rad, she swore she'd never let a man have that much power over her again. And she hadn't. She'd taken back her control, created this steady manageable life, where she made her own money and her own decisions and wasn't swayed by the demands of a man. But this thing with Ethan—this feeling of being weak-kneed and completely out of control—was new and different and shaking her to her core.

Ethan was different. He wasn't demanding, didn't try to make choices for her, or belittle her independence. In fact, he'd always done the opposite. He was giving and kind and respected her independent streak.

She kept telling herself she didn't want a relationship

with him, that she needed to back away, yet right now the feelings that swelled in her and the yearning and absolute desire she had for him scared the heck out of her. Especially because all she wanted to do was toss him onto her bed, rip off his clothes, and spend the afternoon exploring his hard-muscled body. But sleeping with him—again—wasn't going to slow down whatever this thing they were doing was.

And that kiss only had her wanting him more.

Which by the sly grin he was giving her was exactly the reaction he was hoping for.

She took a deep breath and pointed to the boxes on the dresser. "You can open those. I think one of them has the towels and stuff for the bathroom." She busied herself emptying a small suitcase of shirts and pants into the dresser drawers.

She heard the rip of tape and cardboard, then a soft murmur of surprise. She turned to see Ethan gingerly pulling a small metal box from the folds of the bathroom towels. *Crud.* She'd meant to unpack that first.

He carefully held the box up. "Is this a firearm?"

She nodded. "Yeah. But don't worry. It's not loaded, and that box is locked. I do have a carton of ammo in there with it though."

His brow furrowed. "Did something happen to precipitate the need for a firearm?"

She shrugged. "You know. Single mom. California." She gave him the same pat answer she'd used before when he'd asked her about why she'd taken self-defense classes.

He studied her face as if not quite convinced of the answer.

She let out a sigh. "Okay, yeah. There was something that happened. My boyfriend went to jail. And there were some people in Rad's circle who weren't real happy that he and his cohorts were in prison. Especially with the talk about me helping to put them there."

"Was there any truth to that talk?"

"Some."

He waited, but she wasn't quite ready to fill him in on the rest.

He nodded to the box. "Can I take a look?"

"Sure." The lock had a three-digit combination. "I bought it with the plan to use it only in an emergency, so that's how I chose the combo." She made air quotes with her fingers around the word "emergency."

He looked pensive for a moment, then grinned and turned the dials to the numbers 9-1-1. The lock clicked open. "Smart."

"Carley and I are the only ones who know the combination. And now you, of course."

He lifted out the gun, checked to make sure it wasn't loaded, then tested the weight of it in his hand. "It's a nice piece. A Ruger is a solid firearm. It's powerful enough to deal with most threats and has a manageable recoil. Have you shot it?"

"Yes. There was a firing range not too far from our neighborhood. I took a few lessons," she answered, hoping that she sounded offhanded.

In truth, she'd attacked purchasing the gun like she did with all the new things in her life. She'd googled the best handguns for women, studied videos on how to use them, and took enough lessons and classes to feel comfortable shooting it and confident in the fact she could use it to defend herself and her son if it came down to it.

"If you ever want to go shooting or do some target practice, I can take you. I've got a place set up at the far end of my ranch."

"Thanks."

He started to put the gun back when a curious expression crossed his face.

She realized too late what else was in the box as a frown creased his mouth. "Ethan. It's not what it looks like. I can explain."

CHAPTER 12

"WHAT DO YOU THINK IT LOOKS LIKE?" HE ASKED, LIFTING out a small plastic rectangle.

"I don't know. But I know it's not whatever you're thinking."

He scratched the back of his head as he studied the thing in his hand. "To tell you the truth, I don't know what to think. But I'm curious as hell as to why you have a *California Correctional Facility* stamp? *And* why you have it locked up with your handgun."

"I know it seems weird. But I promise I have a logical explanation."

"I'm listening."

"I didn't steal it or anything. I ordered it. Online."

"Why?"

"Because my son is too smart for his age. And he watched some documentary about the life of an inmate and it talked about their correspondence." She held up her hands as she sank onto the edge of the bed. "So I knew he'd figure out the letters I've been sending him weren't really from the prison if they didn't have an official stamp."

Ethan's eyes widened. "Letters *you've* been sending him? I thought all those letters were from his dad."

"Yeah. That's what Milo thinks too."

He put the stamp back in the box, relocked it, spun the dials, and then placed it on the top shelf of the closet before crossing to the bed and sitting down next to her. "I'm listening." His expression wasn't judgmental or disapproving, more one of curiosity, and possibly amusement.

She took a deep breath, then let it out in a long exhale. "My dad left when Carley and I were little and he never looked back. I barely even remember him. My mom raised us on her own—and she did a great job—but we still missed that fatherly influence in our lives. You were raised by a single mom, so you know what I mean."

"I do. Although I had a good dad for a while. And I was fortunate to have my grandpa in my life so he filled some of that role of dad for me."

She lifted one shoulder. "So, I guess that's what I'm trying to do for Milo—fill some of that role for him. By writing him the letters, I'm giving him a father who cares about him, who takes an interest in his life, and who frequently tells him he's proud of him and loves him."

Ethan nodded. "Just the kind of things a boy needs to hear from his father."

"Right?" She twisted her hands together, and her heart hurt for her son. "His father is a real shit. I know I told you a little bit about Rad, but I barely scratched the surface of his winning personality. He's tried to contact me a few times, mainly to ask for money or to try to get me to pass some kind of message on to one of his flunkies." She glanced up at him. "Which, by the way, I refused to do both things. Just in case you were wondering. But the thing he hasn't done is ever asked about Milo or tried to arrange any kind of contact with him."

"Bastard," Ethan muttered, which made Jillian fall a little bit harder for him.

"You don't know the half of it," she said. "He's not just a criminal and a slime ball, he's a user too. I didn't see it at the time." She dropped her shoulders.

She'd put off talking about this, but it seemed like the universe was driving her to have this conversation. And if she really wanted to curtail this relationship, or whatever it was with Ethan, telling him the rest of this story would most definitely end it.

"I was young and caught up in the glamour and thrill of being his girl. I was totally gaga for the guy, or I guess I was gaga for the guy I thought he was. You have to understand, Rad was a star in the surfing world, really good-looking and a total charmer. He flirted with everyone and had this way of making women, and men too, fall for him. Everybody loved Radley and vied for his attention. So when he shined that bright-star light on me, it made me feel *really* special. Like I was chosen. And make no mistake, I *was* chosen by him. But not because he thought I was pretty or kind or smart—just the opposite. He thought I was stupid—young and dumb and someone he could control and get to do what he wanted. He didn't trust me with the illegal stuff—hell, I didn't even know he was running drugs or guns or any of that stuff until I saw the footage of the DEA and SWAT confiscating it all on the news. So maybe I was stupid, or naïve at the very least. Which I guess was why he didn't fill me in on the bank robbery, even though he gave me one of the most important roles to play."

Ethan raised an eyebrow. "You were involved in a bank robbery?"

"No. I wasn't. But I *almost* was. If I hadn't forgotten my phone, I might be in prison right now too." She paused to wait for his reaction, but his expression seemed interested and not judgmental. *So far*.

She took a deep breath, then dove in. "Rad had planned for me to drive the getaway car. He didn't tell me what we were doing, just said he needed me to drive him and a couple of his guys downtown to pick something up. I was sitting in the driver's seat, waiting for them to come out of the house, when I realized I'd left my phone on the bench inside by the front door. I went back in, and the three of them were standing in the kitchen arguing about all this stuff on the table. They didn't see me, but I saw several guns, a couple of duffel bags, and these weird rubber masks spread out in front of them, and I could hear enough of their conversation to know they were planning to rob something." She swallowed and pressed a hand to the pressure building in her chest. "Contrary to what Rad thought, I was *not* a total idiot. But I was scared shitless, and I knew I didn't want any part of whatever they were doing. So I grabbed my phone and snuck back out the door. I'd been working part-time at this snack shack on the beach by our place, so I texted Rad and said I got called in to work, then I hid in the neighbors' shed until they were gone."

"You didn't have any idea what he was planning?"

She shook her head. "Although I remember later thinking I should have known something was up. He was on hyper-alert, amped up like he got when he was in a surfing competition. His knee had been shaking that whole morning, and his eyes were extra bright, like maybe he was on something. I could feel this kind of crazy energy coming off him, but I never in a million years would have guessed that he was planning to rob a bank."

"Had he robbed other places before?"

"I honestly don't know. Probably. I can't imagine he would be dumb enough to just start with a bank." She blew out a breath. "You have to understand, he was a god in the surf-ing world, bigger than life, and he could do no wrong. So he might have been just cocky enough to think he could get away with it. I'm sure he believed he was above the law, and that he was so clever he could pull anything off and not get caught."

"I've known plenty of men who believed the same thing. And most of them are sitting in jail because of that belief."

"I could have been there too. Everything happened so fast. I knew he was pissed that I'd left. I heard him come flying out of the house after I sent him the text and start yell-ing for me. He sent me these angry messages telling me to blow off my job and to get back there. I said my boss really needed me, then told him my phone was dying. I'd scooted all the way back into the corner of the shed and was hold-ing my breath, trying not to cry, or scream, or vomit. I was so scared they were going to find me. I finally heard the car drive away, but I didn't move for what seemed like an hour. I just sat there, trying to figure out what the hell to do. And while I was thinking, it dawned on me that there were only three masks on the table. One for each of them. But nothing for me. Rad hadn't even told me to grab a baseball cap or sunglasses. He hadn't cared enough about me to disguise my looks. Which I realized, as I sat there shaking and crying, meant I was so insignificant to him that he didn't even care if I got caught." She turned to Ethan, tears threatening to fill her eyes. "And that's a feeling I would never wish on anyone. To know with perfect clarity that you mean so little to someone that they don't care what happens to you. I'd felt that with my dad, but couldn't stomach feeling it with the man who I foolishly thought I was in love with."

"I'm sorry."

"I'm not. It was that feeling that finally spurred me into action. I knew I had to get out of there. I didn't want to have any part of that kind of life. I didn't know how long I'd been hiding, but I figured I didn't have much time, so I ran back into the house and just started throwing everything I had into a bag. I had a little money saved, but not enough to get me very far..." She stared down at her hands and picked at a loose cuticle on her thumb. She'd already told him more than she'd intended—his opinion of her had to have already been ruined so she might as well tell him the rest. "So I took all the cash I could scrounge, a watch I had bought him, and some small electronics I thought I could pawn." She held up her hands. "I know it was wrong. How was my taking his things any different than him stealing from those people at the bank? But I was desperate."

She snuck a quick glance at his face, expecting to see...

what? She wasn't sure…judgment maybe, or condemnation, or him reaching for his cuffs to arrest her. But he wasn't doing any of those things. He was just sitting there. Listening.

"I also took some food, whatever I could fit in my bag. I wasn't really thinking. I was just trying to get out of there as fast as I could. I was terrified he and his buddies were going to come in the door any minute. I had no idea what he'd do to me for leaving, but Rad had a temper, a mean one, and I knew it wouldn't be good. So I just grabbed what I could and ran. I hitched a ride with a truck driver who took me a few hours down the coast, then I used that money to start over. I thought about going home, but couldn't face my mom and Carley knowing how bad I'd screwed my life up and failed at all my big dreams."

"What happened to Rad and his guys?"

"They got caught. Because of me. I saw the footage of the bank robbery on the news that night. It was a huge deal because they'd used assault weapons and had shot one of the guards. He lived, thank goodness. But I recognized the masks and the clothes they'd been wearing." She huffed out in disgust. "Who else would rob a bank in flip-flops? I called in to the anonymous tip line and told them I'd heard them plotting the robbery and the names and addresses of all three guys. They raided our place, and Rad and the other guys were taken into custody and eventually went to prison. I laid low—stayed away from the surf scene, found a super-cheap place to live, and got a job at a library. It wasn't until I'd been there a month or so that I realized I was pregnant." She raised her palms. "And I think you can figure out the rest."

"That's quite a story."

"I know." She swallowed back the emotion as she stood up. "I put off telling you because I like you and you seem to think I'm pretty great, which has felt amazing, but now you know the truth. It was a lot, I know." She took a deep breath, then plunged forward as she took a step toward the door. "Thanks again for all your help today, but I will totally understand any excuse you want to use to leave and lose my number. And I promise I won't hold it against you."

He stayed seated on the bed. "Lose your number? Why would I do that?"

"Um…because you're a deputy sheriff, soon to be the sheriff, and don't need to be hanging around with someone who has the kind of criminal past that I do." She stared down at a small stain on the rug she'd put at the end of her bed. "I didn't want to tell you because I didn't want you to think poorly of me, but I know this has to change how you think of me. I may not have driven the car that day, but I lived with a guy who was apparently into some pretty bad stuff. And even though it's true, most people won't believe that I was too young and dumb to know what was going on right under my nose."

He stood, and she braced herself for him to leave. But instead of leaving, he took her hand and pulled her closer. "Jillian, first of all, I'm not *most* people. And I *don't* think poorly of you. Believe me, I understand about getting involved in a bad situation with the wrong sort of people. I have a story of my own I'll share with you someday. But Rad's choices don't reflect on you. He's the one who chose to rob that bank and break the law."

"But I broke the law too when I took his stuff."

"Yeah, maybe. Although you lived together, so it could be argued that it was communal property. My point is sometimes we do things we're not proud of in situations where we don't have any other choice. And it sounds to me like you made the right choice by getting yourself the hell out of Dodge and putting as much distance between you and Rad's crew as possible. *And* you made the call to turn him in. That couldn't have been easy. But you made the decision to break away from him and start over. And not just in a new place, but with a whole new life. You got a job and went back to school and raised a baby whose father was in prison—none of those things had to have been easy." He squeezed her hand. "I actually admire you."

She'd been steeling her heart to let him go, but instead he'd just scaled one of her defensive walls and jumped down on the other side. "You do?"

"Yeah, I do." He lifted her chin to force her to look at him. "I think you're amazing. You're kind and smart and a great mom."

Her eyes went wide as she stared at him. Could he really mean those things? "You're just saying that because you want to test out those new pink sheets."

He let out a soft huff of laughter. "No, I'm not. Although I wouldn't turn down the invitation. But I'm being serious. You make me laugh, and I love how feisty you are. All that stuff happened a long time ago. You were still a kid. Maybe some of those experiences shaped you as a young adult, but the woman you are *now* is the one I'm falling in love with.

And there is *nothing* you could tell me that would change how I feel about you."

Falling in love with?

She took a shuddering breath, blinking back tears. "Oh, Ethan" was all she whispered before launching herself at him, throwing her arms around his neck and pressing her lips to his. What started as a soft kiss quickly turned into something more as his hands went around her waist, flattening against her back, as he pulled her tight against him. Then they were inside her shirt, sliding over her skin, gripping her waist, then cupping her breasts.

She kissed him with a hungry desire, a wild abandon she didn't know she was capable of. She'd just shared her darkest secret with him, and he hadn't run. He hadn't even turned away. Instead, he'd stepped forward, opening his arms and saying he admired her and that he was falling in love with her.

Her head was screaming that this was all a bad idea, that sleeping with him again was just going to make it harder to pull away, but the needs of her heart and her body drowned out the sound. Maybe just for this afternoon, for the next hour, she could pretend she and Ethan could have a future, that her past wouldn't come back to haunt them and cost him the future he was planning for himself.

Maybe just for now, they could forget about everything else and focus on how good they felt together.

Jillian reached behind her and pulled back a corner of the bedspread as she shamelessly flirted with him. "You willing to help me remake this bed?"

"Is that an invitation?"

"You bet it is."

He pulled off his boots, shimmied out of his jeans, and hauled his shirt over his head. She sucked in a quick gasp at the display of hard muscle and toned abs. Reaching out to touch him, she skimmed her fingers over his chest, reveling in his soft inhale of breath. She couldn't ever remember feeling like this—wanting someone so bad that it hurt.

The air around them sizzled with their chemistry, and she wanted to take her time, to savor every inch of him, while at the same time she couldn't wait to get naked and have his skin against hers. Grabbing the hem of her shirt, she pulled it over her head and tossed it to the floor. Her voice was breathless as she said, "I sure hope you brought another wallet condom, because I haven't unpacked that box yet."

"Are you kidding? I'm a lawman—it's part of my duty to be prepared." His lips tugged up in a sheepish grin. "I've actually got three."

"*Three*? What exactly were you preparing for?"

He pulled her closer and brushed the backs of his fingers down her cheek as he gazed into her eyes. "Whatever you're willing to give me. Along with being prepared, I'm also a patient man, and I'm not going anywhere. I'm in this thing, and I'm here for it all."

She swallowed, not able to respond, the intensity and earnestness of his words touching her heart. Instead of answering with her words, she answered with action, as she wiggled out of her shorts and pulled him into the bed with her.

Then, finally, his hands were on her, touching, caressing,

stroking. Her body was feverish, desperate for each sinful sensation as he kissed, licked, and grazed his tongue and teeth over it. He ravished her in the most delicious of ways, and she surrendered to his carnal demands, gripping fistfuls of pink sheets as she cried out in release.

Just when she thought she was spent, he teased and tantalized and took her back to the edge of ecstasy. The way he kissed and touched her, like she was a priceless treasure, was an addictive rush. But it was more than that. It was the soft catches of words he murmured in her ear—telling her she was beautiful, how soft her skin was, how much he wanted her—that had her melting into a molten pool of desire and need. He made her feel voluptuous and wanton, as she both reveled in his attentiveness and offered him the same delicious torture as she tormented him with her lips and tongue.

Finally spent, she sprawled on his chest as they lay naked and tangled in the sheets, their legs entwined. He lightly combed his fingers through the curls of her hair, then she heard him chuckle and felt the deep rumble of his laughter under her cheek.

"What's so funny?" she murmured.

"It looks like we have an audience."

An audience? She lifted her head and looked toward the door, instinctively knowing Ethan wouldn't be responding so casually if it were her son or Bryn. She let out a laugh as she spotted Tiny and Otis standing in the doorway of her bedroom. Otis had a smear of what looked suspiciously like chocolate frosting across his beard.

Tiny raised her head and snuffled a small snort.

Jillian dropped her head back onto Ethan's chest. "I'm not sure if she's letting us know the show is over or if she's asking if there are any more donuts."

"Depending on how long they've been standing there, they might have already gotten a show."

She groaned as she pressed her forehead into his chest. "Ugh. I liked it better when they were just watching the television."

"Maybe they came back here because Bryn doesn't pay for cable." He laughed even as Jillian whacked him with a pillow.

CHAPTER 13

"I LIKE IT HERE," MILO TOLD JILLIAN THE NEXT AFTER-
noon as he sank into a chair on the front porch next to his
mom and his aunt. Carley had come over to help her finish
unpacking, and they'd just settled on the porch with the
plate of welcome brownies Bryn had dropped off that morning and some big glasses of iced tea.

Milo had been in the barn, and his hair was tousled and damp
with sweat. The puppy, who seemed to tag along wherever the
boy went, plopped down on top of Milo's sneakers. "I think this
is the coolest place we've ever lived." He ducked his head toward
his aunt. "No offense, Aunt Carley. I liked your place too."

Carley chuckled and handed him a brownie. "None
taken. I love it here too."

"Me too," Jillian agreed. "It just feels good being here."
She took a sip of tea and glanced at her watch, again, as she
leaned back in her chair. "What have you been doing in the
barn?" she asked her son.

"Hanging out with Zane," he said around a mouthful of
brownie. "He let me help him brush and feed all the new rescues, and he's even gonna let me name one."

"Wow. That is cool."

"He said we're like their sponsors or something because

us living out here is what's gonna give them enough money to feed and take care of all five of them."

"That's true."

His face broke into a grin. "I like that. We never did anything like this in California." He gestured to the pan of brownies. "Okay if I take one of those for Zane? I just came back to get us some water."

"Of course." She couldn't help but smile at her son as he grabbed some water and another couple of brownies, then raced back toward the barn, Gus loping along in his wake. "He's really happy here," she told her sister. "Thanks for the push to move to Colorado."

"I did it as much for me as for you. I love having you here. I did kind of miss you guys last night though. My apartment seemed too quiet."

"Enjoy it while it lasts. Once you move out here, I'm sure we'll be in and out of each other's places all the time."

"I hope so. Although it will be nice to have our own spaces too." She nodded at her sister's wrist. "Why do you keep checking your watch? I thought you had the weekend off. Do you have to go in to work or something?"

Jillian shook her head and tried to hold back a frown. "No, sorry. I just…it's just…well, it's silly, but Ethan said he was going to stop by around lunchtime, and it's almost three, and it's just not like him to not show up, or to even text or call with an excuse."

"Maybe he had to do some campaign stuff. Or had a police emergency."

"In Creedence? Not likely." She chewed at a loose cuticle

on her thumb. "It's no big deal. I mean, he was just going to stop by. It doesn't really matter."

"Oh. I know that look," her sister said. "There's something else going on. What is it?"

"It's nothing."

"It's not nothing. Come on, I'm your sister. I know you. And you don't usually get so worked up over a guy. You like this one."

She sighed. "Yeah. I do like him."

"Is that why you're wigging out about him not showing?"

"That…and…it's just that I told him about Rad yesterday."

"So? I'm sure he figured out Milo has a dad out there somewhere. He *is* a law enforcement officer."

"No—I mean I *told* him about Rad. About the bank robbery and Rad going to prison and me taking his stuff and starting over."

"Wow. I didn't think you told *anybody* about that stuff."

"I don't."

"Wow. Jillie—I knew you liked him, but you must *really* like him."

She groaned. "I do, dang it. Which is why I'm freaking out a little. Because what if that's the reason he isn't here? Because I scared him off with all my crazy talk about being involved with a felon and an armed robbery."

"You weren't *involved* with the robbery. You got out of there as soon as you found out about it *and* you turned the guys in. Ethan's a pretty tough guy. I'm sure you didn't frighten him off."

"Doesn't matter how tough he is. He's still a deputy

sheriff—which means he's probably not super-interested in someone with such a criminal past."

"We've all got a past of some kind." Carley shook her head. "Quit trying to borrow trouble. Just because he didn't show up for lunch doesn't mean he isn't interested anymore. Jeez. Give the guy a chance before you automatically assume the worst."

As if talking about him had made him appear, Ethan's truck turned down Bryn's driveway and parked in front of the barn. He was pulling a horse trailer, but it looked empty.

Jillian could see Ethan in the driver's seat, and she knew something was wrong. His hands gripped the steering wheel as he leaned forward and pressed his forehead into it. His hat was on the dash, and he scrubbed a hand through his already mussed hair as he sat back and pushed open his door.

His shoulders were slumped as he looked around the ranch, then spotted her on the porch. She was out of her chair and running to him before she even stopped to think about it. She didn't know what'd happened, but she knew something had and that it wasn't good. As she got closer, he opened his arms and she threw herself into them, wrapping him in a hug. He pulled her against him, holding her tightly as he bent his head into the crook of her neck.

They stood there like that for several moments, just holding onto each other. Jillian was anxious to know what happened, was already imagining the worst-case scenarios, but she stayed quiet, giving him the time and space he needed, knowing he'd speak when he was ready.

He finally pulled away and wiped at the corners of his eyes with the back of his hand. "Thanks. I needed that."

"What happened?"

He inhaled a deep breath, then slowly blew it out. "I was on my way over here after lunch, but I wanted to stop and check in on Miss Miriam on my way. I just had a funny feeling about the way she was acting the other day. She said she just wasn't feeling right, and something was niggling me and told me I needed to stop in and check on her."

"Was she okay?"

He shook his head, and the look of despair in his eyes tore at Jillian's heart.

She let out a tiny gasp. "Oh no."

He nodded. "She was already gone when I got there. The doctor said she passed away sometime the night before. She looked at peace when I found her—like she'd just fallen asleep tucked into her favorite chair in the kitchen. The cat was curled on her lap as if keeping an eye on her until someone came."

"Oh. Sweet kitty."

"I knew something was wrong when I got out of the truck. I could just feel it. Then Applejack came out of the house and stood on the porch, whinnying and fussing up a storm until I got to him. Then he let me back into the house, and that's when I found her."

"Poor you. And those poor animals." Jillian's heart ached for all of them. "What's going to happen to them?"

"I promised her I'd take care of them."

"You?"

"Yes. She was like a grandma to me, and every time I stopped to see her, she reminded me that I promised to take care of them if anything happened to her. And that's what I'm going to do. At least until I can find a suitable home for them. But Applejack is practically despondent. I never knew a horse could seem so sad. I didn't know what to do. I couldn't even get him in the trailer. But he responded so well to Milo the other day, I thought maybe…"

He took a step back and opened the back door of his truck. The seat was up, and the mini-horse was lying on the floor, his front hooves tucked under his chest. Ethan lifted him out and set him on the ground. His legs were a little wobbly, and his head hung down as if he didn't have the energy to stand up. But he lifted his head at the sound of the barn door opening and Milo's voice calling to them.

"Hey, Ethan," he said, running toward them, the puppy loping along at his heels. His eyes lit at the sight of the little horse. "Cool. You brought Applejack."

The mini-horse seemed to recognize him and trotted toward the boy. He nudged Milo's side, then lifted his head and rested his chin on the boy's shoulder as if giving him a hug.

"Ohh," Jillian said on a soft breath, lifting her hand to press it to her mouth. The tears that had been threatening since Ethan's announcement fell freely as her son wrapped his arms around the horse's neck and pressed his cheek to Applejack's.

"What's wrong?" Milo said, peering at the horse. "Why does he seem sad?"

"He is sad," Jillian told him. "We all are. Miss Miriam passed away last night."

"Oh no." Milo hugged the horse again, offering his comfort. "I'm sorry, buddy."

A meow sounded, and Jillian looked back at the truck to where Shadow, Miss Miriam's black tabby cat, sat on top of the seat, her tail flicking around the headrest. She jumped to the floor of the cab, then down to the ground, then followed Applejack to Milo. Ignoring the puppy seated by his feet, she circled the boy's legs, brushing up against his ankle, then sat down next to his foot.

It looked like she had found someone new to shadow now.

Later that night, Jillian heard a scuffling then a shushing sound coming from Milo's room when she came into the bunkhouse after a visit to Bryn's.

His door was closed, and she knocked softly. "Milo? You okay in there?"

More shushing sounds. She leaned her ear closer, cocking her head to try to hear better.

"Yeah. I'm fine, Mom. I was almost asleep. See you in the morning."

Something about his voice told her he was *not* fine and her *mom* alarm bells went off. She pushed open the door and peered in. Milo was really in bed. Shadow the cat was curled on his pillow by his shoulder, and Gus the puppy was stretched out next to his belly.

He sleepily opened his eyes. "Good night, Mom."

She frowned. Something was off, but she couldn't quite

put her finger on it. It was obvious he was faking being almost asleep—she knew his true sleepy voice well enough to recognize that wasn't it. She could also usually tell when he was hiding something—and he was definitely hiding something. Hopefully it was just a book he was reading under the covers.

She took another look around the room but didn't see anything amiss. "Good night, Son. Love you."

"Love you too," he murmured, keeping up the ruse. "Hey, Mom," he said as she started to back out of the room. "Will you close the door behind you? I don't want Shadow to get out."

"Sure." It seemed like a reasonable request. Although the cat appeared to be quite content snuggled on the pillow. True to her name, she hadn't left Milo's side all day. Neither had Applejack. In fact, the mini-horse had been quite upset when they'd left him alone in the barn earlier. Maybe she should go check on him.

She started to pull the door closed when she caught the soft sound of a tiny huff of breath. "What was that?" she asked, stepping back into the room.

"Oh, that was me." Milo coughed into his elbow. "Might be coming down with something."

She narrowed her eyes. Who did this kid think he was fooling? Another huff sounded, followed by a snuffle. Turning her head, she did another slow perusal of the room. It sounded like it was coming from the closet. She crossed the room and reached for the door handle.

"Mom, no," Milo said, sitting up in bed as she pulled open the closet door.

"I had a feeling I'd find you in here," she told the mini-horse who was standing inside the closet, a pile of hay spread out around his hooves.

The mini-horse peered innocently up at her, then casually walked out of the closet, pausing to snuffle into her side, then crossed the room and climbed up on the bed next to Milo. He laid his head on the pillow by Shadow, and the cat snuggled against his neck.

"Oh no you don't, mister," she told her son. "You can't have that horse sleeping in your bed."

"But Mom, you didn't hear him before. He was so sad in the barn by himself. He was whinnying and neighing, and he sounded so miserable. It was breaking my heart. I *had* to bring him inside. And look how much happier he is." He stroked a hand down the horse's back.

His words almost broke her. She knew what it was like to lose someone, and it had been hard enough leaving him out in the barn earlier. But she was the adult here. And this was about more than just a sad horse. "Milo, I'm sorry. I really am. But I still can't let a horse spend the night in the house."

"Why not? He's housetrained."

"I understand that. Ethan told me he spent most of the day in the house with Miss Miriam, but he had access to go outside if he needed to. And he slept outside at night." She peered down at the polished wood floor. "And what if he has an accident? It's not like a puppy. Do you have any idea how much a horse can pee? I'd never get that out of the flooring. And besides that, this isn't even our house. We're *renting*, and

I don't recall seeing anything in the rental agreement about a pet horse."

"He's not just a pet. He's more like part of the family. And Bryn wouldn't mind. She loves horses."

"Yes, she does. But I don't know that she loves them in her house."

"Can't we just call and ask her?"

"No, Milo. I just left her house, and she was going to bed. She just finished a double shift and she looked dead on her feet. I'm not waking her up to see if you can invite your new horse inside for a sleepover."

"But Mom..."

"I'm sorry, Son. He has to go back to the barn. At least for tonight. Then we'll talk to Bryn tomorrow and see if we can figure something out." She slipped her hand under Applejack's halter and eased him off the bed. "Sorry, buddy."

"It's not fair."

"I know. I'm sorry to both of you." She led the horse out of the bunkhouse and back to his stall in the barn. He followed her willingly but looked so dejected and sad when she tried to close the gate, she almost gave in and brought him back inside.

No. No horses in the house.

Steeling herself, she turned to go and found Milo standing behind her. He had Gus, a pillow, and his comforter clutched in his arms. Shadow sat at his feet, her tail swishing around his ankles. "You said *he* couldn't sleep in the house, but you never said *I* couldn't sleep out here with him." He lifted his chin. "He just lost his best friend. I'm not leaving him alone tonight."

She stepped forward and pulled her son into her arms. "I love you so much, kid," she said, pressing a kiss to the top of his head. The puppy wiggled in his arms, stretching up to try to lick her cheek.

Milo smiled up at her. "Does that mean I can sleep in the barn with Applejack?"

She let out a sigh. "Sure."

Applejack's stall seemed huge, especially for such a small horse, and Jillian helped get Milo settled into the corner, laying out more straw and a horse blanket below his comforter. The boy and the puppy curled up on the blanket, and Applejack trotted over and laid down next to him as Shadow stretched and pawed a place for herself next to his head.

"You've got your phone with you?" she asked, peering down at the cozy group.

Milo nodded. "In my pajama pocket. And yes, I will call you if I need you." He offered her an encouraging smile. "Mom, I'll be fine. I'm basically sleeping in the backyard."

"I know. You're right. Good night." She took one last look before backing out of the barn.

Ten minutes later, she was back—hauling her pillow, a flashlight, a few bottles of water, and a couple of old blankets.

"What are you doing?" Milo asked, pushing up on one elbow.

"I couldn't let you sleep out here alone."

"Mom, I'm not a baby."

"I wasn't talking to you. I was talking to Applejack," she said, squatting down to scratch the mini-horse's neck.

Her phone buzzed as she was spreading out the

blankets. Apprehension filled her as she pulled it from her pajama pants pocket. It was after ten, and she didn't usually get good news when her phone rang that late. Maybe it was Bryn or Zane wondering what they were doing in the barn.

Her uneasiness increased as she saw Ethan's name on the screen. She held the phone to her ear. "Hey you," she quietly answered, not wanting to disturb the animals.

"Hey" was all he said, but she heard a sadness in his voice. It hurt her heart. He was always so positive, so upbeat. She'd never heard him sound so weary.

"You okay?"

"I'm hanging in there. But I couldn't sleep. I tried working on a campaign speech I'm supposed to be presenting to the Kiwanis Club next week, but my mind kept thinking about Miss Miriam and Applejack and worrying about how all of you were getting along tonight. How are you?"

"I'm setting up blankets and prepping for a campout in the barn."

"In the barn?"

"Yeah. Apparently we're doing a sleepover at Applejack's new place." She smiled down at the little horse. His head was resting across Milo's side. "We were worried about him too. And he didn't seem to want to be by himself tonight."

"Neither do I." His voice was practically a whisper as he uttered the words. She heard him take a deep breath and then clear his throat. "Listen, I gotta go."

"Oh. Okay." She lowered her voice and tried to infuse it with the affection and caring she felt for the man on the other end of the line. "I'm here if you need me. Call me back. Whenever."

"I will." He clicked off, leaving Jillian feeling cold and somehow even more alone, even though she was surrounded by pets and her boy.

Fifteen minutes later, Milo was almost asleep when Jillian heard an engine coming down the driveway, then a truck door slam. The door of the barn opened, and Frankie the goldendoodle came racing in, shimmied under the slats of Applejack's stall, and launched herself into Jillian's lap.

She ruffled the dog's neck, then looked up to see Ethan a few steps behind her. Jillian's throat tightened at the sight of him carrying a camping lantern, a couple of sleeping bags, and his pillow.

CHAPTER 14

"What are you doing here?" Jillian whispered, her heart racing, as Ethan let himself into the stall and dropped his stuff next to her.

"Same as Applejack. I didn't want to be alone." He offered her a crooked grin. "I mean, I didn't want the horse to be alone." He bent down to stroke Applejack's neck, and the horse nuzzled into his hand.

Milo smiled sleepily up at him. "Hey, Ethan."

"Hey, kid. How's Applejack holdin' up?"

"He's sad. But I think it's going to help him to have all of us here so he's not by himself tonight. Mom said she's going to talk to Bryn tomorrow about him sleeping in the house."

He shot a quick glance at Jillian, who shook her head no. "Well, thanks for taking such good care of him. And of Shadow."

"I love them both already." He snuggled deeper into his pillow and closed his eyes. "Thanks for coming. I'm glad you're here."

"Me too, buddy." He gave Shadow a chin scratch, and the cat let out a contented purr.

Jillian knew the feeling. She wanted to purr as well, as Ethan rolled out one of the sleeping bags and put his pillow next to hers. He hung his hat from the latch of the stall, then sat down next to her to pull off his boots. Frankie wriggled into a spot by their feet and rested her chin on Jillian's leg. "It seems everyone's glad you're here," she said.

He stretched out next to her, then turned on his side to face her. "Everyone?" he asked, with what sounded like a hopeful tone in his voice.

His hand was next to her hip, and she picked it up and laced her fingers with his. "Yeah. Everyone."

He smiled, but she still caught the sadness in it.

"You okay?" she asked softly.

He let out a breath as he slowly nodded. "I will be. I know Miss Miriam lived a good life and she's at peace now. And I can imagine she had a heck of a reunion with her husband in Heaven, but I'm still gonna miss her. I've known her since I was a kid. She was kind of like a second grandma to me."

She scooted a little closer and bent her head toward his, keeping her voice low so as not to wake Milo. "She seemed so spunky and was always laughing or trying to get you to laugh at something with her. I only met her a couple of times when I delivered some books out to her. But both times, I stayed to visit for a bit, and I really liked her."

"Everybody did. She was a real spitfire." He nudged her arm. "Kinda like you."

She smiled at the comparison.

"I am worried about Applejack though," he said, his tone switching to a more somber one. "That little horse really loved her, and she doted on him. I'm not sure I'll be able to find anyone else who will treat him as well."

She squeezed his hand again. "Don't worry about that. We'll keep Applejack for now. And Shadow too. And as far as finding someone to spoil him—look at where we are. Adorable little horse has the whole lot of us sleeping in the stall with him in the barn. And that's just because I wouldn't let him sleep in Milo's bed. And believe me, he tried."

Ethan chuckled, and the low rumble of it sent a dart of heat surging through her. Which was a totally awkward feeling in their current circumstance. "Thanks," Ethan told her. "This all means a lot to me. And it would to Miss Miriam too. She only met Milo the one time, but she commented on how much Applejack seemed to like him. She'd be glad that he's here with him." He raised his free hand and touched the backs of his fingers to her cheek. "I'm glad to be here too."

She swallowed, wanting to kiss him but knowing this was the worst possible time to be considering kissing. "Me too," she whispered.

Then they didn't say anything more for a while. They just looked at each other as the sound of Milo's breathing evened out and blended with the soft exhales of the mini-horse and the slightly louder ones of the goldendoodle.

"Your dog snores," Jillian said.

"You're telling me. And she always wants to curl up in my bed with me."

"She's not the only one," Jillian said with a coy grin, then turned on her side away from him. Still holding his hand, she scooted back to spoon against him as she wrapped their joined hands around her waist.

He pressed a kiss to the back of her head and pulled her

closer. His breath was warm on her neck, and she sighed contentedly.

A year ago, she couldn't have imagined spending the night on the floor in a barn wrapped in the arms of a handsome cowboy and in a big cuddle-puddle of her son and an assortment of animals, but for tonight, there was no other place she'd rather be.

———

The last two days had gone by in a blur for Ethan. Between the campaign stuff, his deputy duties, and helping with the arrangements for Miss Miriam's funeral, Ethan's brain was in a tailspin. The oddest part was that the one person who'd been making his mind spin for the last several months now seemed to be the one who was keeping him grounded. Not that a text from Jillian didn't still make his palms a little sweaty, but knowing she was in his corner and being able to call and talk things over with her somehow settled the craziness around him.

He hadn't seen her since the morning before when they'd woken up next to each other in the barn. Unfortunately, it was Otis the goat who woke him by nibbling his ear instead of Jillian, but it still felt pretty great waking up with her in his arms.

Apparently she'd borrowed a cot from Bryn and she and Milo had spent last night out there too, but Ethan had been on duty so he'd spent most of his night at the station and hadn't wanted to wake them when he got off. Jillian had told

Milo they couldn't keep this up, and Ethan had come up with a new idea and planned to implement it tonight.

His truck smelled like pepperoni from the two large pizzas stacked in his front seat, and his tool belt clanked against the floor as he turned in to the horse rescue ranch. Zane and Cade had offered to meet him there since the women would be gabbing it up inside the farmhouse for Taco Tuesday.

Zane, Milo, and Cade were hauling lumber to the side of the bunkhouse as he pulled up to the porch. "Hey, guys. Pizza's here," he called as he grabbed his tools and the pizza boxes.

Even though it was supposed to be girls' night, Bryn and Jillian had set up the porch for them, assembling paper plates, napkins, and Parmesan on the table and filling a cooler with ice and bottles of water, beer, and cream soda.

The guys joined him on the porch, grabbing drinks as Ethan slid the boxes onto the table. They all grabbed slices, ignoring the plates and using their jeans as napkins.

"So when are you guys going to tell me what we're building?" Milo asked as he struggled to twist the top off a cream soda.

"It's kind of a surprise for you and Applejack," Ethan said, taking the bottle, twisting the cap off, then handing it back to him. "He's used to sleeping in a little corral outside of Miss Miriam's house so we thought we'd build him sort of the same thing here."

"But he doesn't like to sleep by himself," Milo protested. "He still gets really sad if we try to leave him alone."

"That's why we're going to build the corral right outside your room. Then you can sleep in your own bed, but open the window, and Applejack can poke his head in to see you whenever he wants."

The boy's eyes widened, then a smile creased his face. "Cool."

"It's a temporary solution," Zane said, already reaching for his second slice. "Because once summer ends and it gets too cold, you'll have to shut the window. But hopefully he'll be acclimated enough by then to be able to sleep outside or in the barn on his own without getting so upset."

"Man, you guys are the greatest," Milo said. "Thanks for doing this."

"We are pretty great," Cade said, holding up his bottle of beer. "Here's to us, the makers of mini-horse stalls."

They all laughed as they clinked their bottles to his.

After they demolished the pizzas, they set to work under Zane's direction, and it didn't take more than a few hours to erect the structure. They enclosed three sides, using the wall of the bunkhouse as one side, and then left the front section more open with only the bottom half built up with wooden slats. Zane had found an old garden gate to use for the corral door, and Cade had built a small feeding trough that he nailed to the top of the slats. The area they built it on was already covered in grass, but they spread out a nice bed of hay for Applejack to sleep on right under Milo's window.

"It's so small, it looks like it's built for a hobbit," Cade said, leaning forward on his shovel to study the corral.

"Applejack would be a perfect horse for a hobbit," Milo said, leading the mini-horse into his new home. "What do you think, buddy?" he asked.

The horse wandered around the corral, sniffing the slats and the trough as Milo raced inside and lifted the window next to his bed. He poked his head out, and Applejack trotted over and nuzzled his neck.

"He likes it," Milo said, laughing. "I think he really likes it."

Cade, Zane, and Ethan grinned as they high-fived each other. Milo helped them clean up the work site and put the tools away before Cade went home and Zane left to do his nightly chores.

"I brought something else for you," Ethan told the boy as he dragged a long box out of the bed of his pickup. "But I'm going to need you to help me put it together."

"Okay," Milo said, following him into the bunkhouse and down the hall to his room. The puppy and Applejack trailed in behind them as Ethan set the box down in the middle of the floor. Shadow was curled up on Milo's pillow and stretched out a paw toward them as if in greeting. "What is it?"

"Your mom said you need a bookcase." Ethan split the box open to reveal a stack of wooden shelves. He pulled out the instruction sheet. "I'll bet you a cream soda we can have this thing put together and up in under thirty minutes."

Milo eyed the boards, then looked back at Ethan. "I'll bet *you* a cream soda we can do it in twenty."

Ethan laughed. "You're on. I like your style, kid."

Twenty-five minutes later, they clinked their cream soda bottles together in a toast to the new bookcase. It fit perfectly on the wall next to the dresser. Milo pulled a large plastic tub of books out of the closet, and they worked together stacking them all on the shelves.

At the bottom of the tub was a worn shoebox. Ethan lifted it out and set it on the bottom shelf.

"Oh, I usually put that one in my drawer," Milo said, reaching for the box. The puppy scrambled over his arm at the same time, knocking the lid of the shoebox to the floor and revealing stacks of white envelopes lined up inside.

The boy hurried to put the lid back on, but Ethan had already figured out what the box held. Milo tried to act casual as he told him, "They're letters from my dad. He's in...uh..."

"It's okay, Milo," Ethan assured him. "Remember? I know about Radley. Your mom told me all about him serving time in prison in California."

"Oh, yeah." He clutched the box to his chest, a furrow creasing his forehead. He stared at the box, then looked over at the bookcase, then back at Ethan. "So...um...actually... these aren't really from my dad."

Ethan kept his expression neutral. "No?"

"Nah." The boy shook his head as he ran his finger over the edge of the cardboard side.

"Then who are they from?"

He peered up at Ethan as if studying his worthiness. "You promise you won't say anything if I tell you? I mean, to *anyone*."

Ethan nodded. "I promise." He already knew who the letters were from, but he was curious as to who Milo thought had written them.

The boy took a deep breath, then let it out slowly. "My mom writes them. She thinks I don't know. But I do."

Oh. So he was just as smart as Jillian feared. Ethan

continued to wear his poker face. "Are you sure? How do you know?"

Milo lifted out a stack of letters and pulled a yellowed envelope from the bottom of the box. The name and address were written in block letters, but the stamp on the front looked similar to the one Jillian had ordered. "Because this one *is* an actual letter from my dad. And it's nothing like the others."

Ethan frowned. "How do you know that one is from him then?"

"For one thing, it has way more spelling errors. And also because it starts out all nice, then it ends with him asking me to send him some money."

"Oh." That Radley Mullins was a real bastard. He was glad they hadn't had to deal with having that jerk in their lives. But it wasn't Ethan's place to say any of that. It just seemed important that he listen. He waited for Milo to say something more, but the boy already seemed self-conscious. "So, did you? Send him money, I mean."

The boy shook his head. "No. I never even wrote him back."

"Does your mom know that he wrote you?"

Milo stared down at the envelope. "No."

"Why not?"

"For one thing, she's always told me he wasn't a really good guy and that we're better off without him. And I believe her. And also…" He lifted his shoulders in a shrug. "I like her letters and the stuff she writes to me. And I think it makes her feel better too. Like maybe it's a way for her to make up for me having such a cruddy guy for a dad."

Dang. Jillian wasn't kidding. Her boy was smart. And insightful.

"If I told her about the real letter from my dad, then I would have to admit that I knew she'd written the other ones. And then the letters would stop. And I don't want them to stop. They say the kind of stuff I wish my dad would say to me. But so far, no guy in our lives has ever lived up to the great dad that my mom is in those letters."

———

Ethan was crashed out on the sofa when Jillian let herself into the bunkhouse later that night. She'd been surprised when he'd called and offered to hang out with Milo while she'd been at her weekly girls' night. She'd been thrilled with his idea for the corral for Applejack—they could only spend so many nights sleeping in the barn—but hadn't anticipated his text saying he and Milo were having fun and that he'd planned to stay until she got home.

If she were being honest, she'd have to admit how much she liked the idea of the two of them hanging out. Milo had never had a good man as a role model in his life before. And now he had several. Getting to spend time with Brody, who was not just a good man but also a great father, was an extra bonus to his friendship with Mandy. And Zane and Cade had both taken Milo under their wings and taught him so much about ranching and being a cowboy. But it was different with Ethan—him taking the time and making the effort to hang out with Milo meant something more.

And Ethan being in her house, waiting up for her—sort of—after spending the last few hours palling around with her son had this little thing blooming in her chest that felt suspiciously like hope. And in her world of worst-case scenarios, there was no place for that particular blossom.

Still, her heart tumbled in her chest at the sight of Ethan sacked out on her couch, a lock of his dark hair falling across his forehead and a paperback open and tented on his chest. She stood in the doorway just looking at him and making believe for just a moment that this could be her life. That she could come home to a man waiting for her on the sofa while her son, and his horse, slept in the bedroom down the hall.

Ethan stirred and held out his hand as he blinked at her. "Hey there. Have a good night?"

She went to him, taking his hand and letting him pull her down on the sofa next to him. "Yeah, it was fun," she said, snuggling into the crook of his arm.

"I was just dreaming about a gorgeous brunette who wore superhero undies and was an amazing kisser." His voice was low and still a little sleep-filled, rumbling in her ear as he nuzzled her neck, then pressed a kiss to the spot she liked right behind her earlobe. "She looked a lot like you, but I'd have to test your kissing skills to make sure."

"Test my kissing skills?" She turned her head to face him, trying not to shiver at the delicious tingles his lips on her neck were sending through her. "Come on. Did you really think that line would work?"

He offered her a sleepy roguish grin. "It did on the

woman in my dream. In fact, it had her stripping her clothes off, superhero underwear and all."

A hearty laugh burst from her, and she covered her mouth. "Wow. That must've been some dream. But I'll bet the woman in it didn't have her son and his horse sleeping in the room down the hall. So, I'm sorry to tell you, this woman's blue-and-red Amazing Arachnid-Man undies are staying put tonight."

He groaned. "Oh man. Now I'm even sorrier, too." He peered down at her lap, then raised a devilish eyebrow. "Really? I'm missing out on the Amazing Arachnid-Man?"

She laughed again, a laugh that sounded almost like a giggle as she kicked off her sandals, then straddled his lap. "Maybe you don't have to miss out on everything," she murmured as she bent forward to press her lips to his.

He pulled her closer, his hands cupping her butt then sliding over the slick fabric of her leggings and under her tank top. The kiss deepened and it was taking all her willpower not to drag him back to her bedroom and have her way with him.

She heard a noise and felt a huff of breath on her neck—which shouldn't be happening since Ethan's mouth was currently locked on hers. She pulled away to see a big pair of curious chocolate-brown eyes staring at her over the back of the sofa.

"Oh gosh, you scared me," she told the little horse as he rounded the sofa and came over to nudge her side. She straightened her top before giving the horse a scratch behind his ears. "You must be ready to go out for the night," she told him.

"Either that or he heard the rumor about your amazing kissing skills," Ethan teased her, but straddling his lap left no doubt about his appreciation for her mad skills.

She pushed off him and together they walked outside to shepherd the mini-horse into his new corral. Applejack trotted over to the window and poked his head in to check on Milo, then as though satisfied that the boy was still close, he laid down in the thick pile of hay beneath the windowsill.

Confident that the mini-horse was okay in his new home, Jillian followed Ethan back into the bunkhouse.

"Hey, I want to show you what Milo and I worked on tonight. I bought him something, and we put it together and got it all set up." He started down the hallway and waved for her to follow. "I think you're gonna like it."

He stopped outside the door, and she peered into her son's room, her gaze going first to his sleeping form curled up in his bed with Shadow at his shoulder and Gus at his feet. His even breathing settled her as she looked around the room for some kind of project, expecting to see a Lego kit or maybe a model airplane.

She blinked at the tall wooden bookshelf already loaded with Milo's books that stood against the wall. Her first thought was one of gratitude at the perfect gift, then her brain shifted into thinking about how much it must have cost and what she might owe him in return. "You bought him a bookcase? Why?"

He looked confused. "Because you said he needed one."

"Yeah, but I meant that I'd planned to pop into the thrift store and see if I could find a cheap used one."

A sense of pride shone through his smile. "Well, now you don't have to. And we had fun putting it together. Even when Gus and Applejack tried to help." A furrow creased his brow. "What's wrong? Don't you like it? Did I get the wrong size or something? I kind of eye-balled the measurements, but I thought I got it pretty close."

"No, it's great. It's the perfect size." She shook her head and wrapped her arms around her stomach. "It just seems like a lot. And I guess I'm not used to anyone doing something like that for us."

He took her arms and pulled them away from her stomach and wrapped them around his waist. Cupping her face in his hands, he peered down at her. "Well, get used to it. Because you and that amazing kid of yours are worth it." He leaned in and pressed a tender kiss to her lips.

The sentiment, combined with the gesture of the gift and the emotion behind that kiss, tightened her throat. "Well, that was really thoughtful. And unexpected. And appreciated." She blew out a breath. "What I'm trying to say, although I'm not doing a very good job of it, is...thank you."

His smile returned, then turned mischievous. "I'll bet you're reconsidering my marriage proposal now."

She laughed and rolled her eyes. "No, I'm not. But I will give you a tip. Anything to do with books is like catnip for librarians, so you should have led with the bookcase." She offered her own playful grin. "If I would've known earlier that you gave my son a bookshelf *and* helped him put it together, you might've gotten into my undies after all."

CHAPTER 15

ETHAN SAT ALONE IN THE FRONT PEW OF THE CHURCH that Thursday, the scent of roses swirling around him as he waited for the service to start. He was the closest thing Miss Miriam had to family.

It had been her wish to be cremated and to have her ashes spread in the mountains above her farm, but for now, the women in their church had put together a simple service to honor her memory. There weren't a lot of people in attendance, but enough that it would have pleased her.

Ethan just wanted to get it over with.

A rustling next to him drew his attention, and the tightness he hadn't realized was in his chest eased as Jillian scooted into the pew and sat down next to him.

"Sorry I'm late," she whispered as she smoothed out her dress. She smelled like spearmint and vanilla and the lush floral scent of her usual perfume, and he just wanted to pull her onto his lap and bury her head in his shoulder.

"I didn't even know you were coming," he whispered back. He'd told her he was going to the funeral but he hadn't expected her to show up. It surprised him how bone-deep glad he was that she was there.

She picked up his hand and laced her fingers with hers.

"Of course I was coming. You're my friend. I wouldn't let you do this on your own."

Maybe that was it. No matter how strong his feelings for her were becoming or whatever silly "friends with benefits" label she wanted to put on it, when it came down to it, they had, at the very least, become good friends.

The first note of the organ resounded through the church as the organist began to play, drowning out any further conversation. But he didn't need to say anything. He squeezed her hand as he settled back against the cushiony velvet of the pew. He was just glad she was there.

━━━━━━━

Because there hadn't been that many in attendance, the service and the reception after finished in just over an hour. Ethan pulled at the knot of his tie as he stepped out of the church and into the late-afternoon sun.

"It's a gorgeous day," Jillian said, coming down the stairs behind him. "Feel like taking a walk?"

"Yeah. Actually, I do." He had yard signs to deliver to campaign headquarters, and he should start preparing for the radio interview he had coming up, but right now some time spent in the sunshine walking with this gorgeous woman was an offer he couldn't turn down. He dropped his suit jacket off in his truck, then the two of them headed for the park a few blocks away from the church. The park was set back against the mountains and had a great walking trail that meandered through a woody section, then looped around a small pond and back.

Jillian wore a sleeveless black flowy dress and flat sandals, and she pulled an elastic holder from the small black cross-body purse draped across her shoulder and wrangled her hair into a loose ponytail. "Ahh, that feels better," she said, falling into step beside him. "You have no idea how hot this mess of hair can get sittin' on my neck."

He reached to gently tug a loose curl that fell next to her ear. "I love your hair. You look great, by the way."

"Thanks. So do you. I've never seen you in a coat and tie." Her gaze raked over his light-blue Oxford and khakis, then she smiled at his boots. "You look great but I don't know that I've often seen khakis paired with cowboy boots."

He shrugged. "These *aren't* my cowboy boots. These are my church boots. Not to be mistaken for my work boots."

She laughed. "Got it."

"Thanks for coming to the service," he said. "It meant a lot to have you there. And it helped ease something in me." He stopped and looked down at her. "You're a good friend. You know I want something more, but for now, I want you to know I'm awful glad to have you as my friend." He wrapped an arm around her shoulders and pulled her to his side. Dipping his head toward her ear, he said, "That doesn't mean I don't still think about kissing you all the time. And in *all* the places."

She playfully elbowed his side. "And by places, do you mean the library and the ranch and in the truck?"

He grinned. "Sure. Those places too."

She shook her head. "You're crazy. But also pretty dang cute. Why hasn't somebody snatched you up already, Ethan Rayburn?"

He let out a sigh, the sudden memory of Tina hitting him like a brick to the chest. "Someone almost did. Once."

"Ooh, this sounds good. Tell me about her." She turned and resumed their walk along the path.

"There's not much to tell. She didn't end up being the person I originally thought she was."

"Oh, there's definitely a story there. Spill it."

"I met her at the Creed, you know, the Creedence Tavern, that restaurant and pub out by the highway."

"Yes, I love their burgers. And Milo loves the way they cut their hot dogs open and serve them on a hamburger bun."

"Oh yeah, they've done that forever. My favorite is their rib eye."

"Okay, now you're just stalling."

He sighed. "Yeah, I guess I am. That's because I'm not real anxious to tell you this story."

"Why not?"

"Because it doesn't paint me in a very favorable light."

She raised an eyebrow. "Now I'm really intrigued. I can't wait to hear the *unfavorable* side of Ethan Rayburn."

"Her name was Tina, and we met right after I'd graduated from the academy and come back home to Creedence. I wasn't really looking for anything, but we talked some that first night and seemed to hit it off, and then she called several times and stopped by the station, bringing me coffee and donuts, and I finally asked her out."

"Ahh," Jillian said. "I know what a sucker you are for a donut."

He chuckled, but it didn't hold much amusement. "We

started dating, and she seemed like she was really into me. I'd never had someone act so enamored of me before, and I can admit that I liked it. I was flattered, you know? But our relationship moved really fast. I mean, we got along well, at least I thought we did, then somehow within a few months of us starting dating, we were engaged and planning a wedding. The ceremony was only a few months out when she told me she was pregnant."

"Pregnant?"

He nodded. "It was a shock at first, but then I was happy about it. I thought I was going to get a wife and a child all at once—a whole family. And I was ready. Excited, even. But it was all a lie."

"A lie?"

"Yeah. Because the baby wasn't mine. Even though she treated me like I could do no wrong, she'd been seeing someone else for months behind my back. And it turned out her being so great to me was all a bunch of BS, just bait for the trap she was setting. Apparently, she was tricking me into marrying her because I was the better bet of the two of us. I had a good job and a promising future, whereas the baby daddy was a total loser."

She grimaced. "Oh no. That's bad. How'd you find out?"

"The usual. Caught 'em together. They were at her place. I thought I'd surprise her and stop by on my lunch break, but I was the one who got the surprise. Then that asshole tried to pick a fight with *me*. Can you believe that? I guess she'd just told him the baby was his, and he went all ballistic, claiming he wanted to marry her instead."

"What did you do? Did you fight him?"

He huffed. "Heck no. She wasn't worth skinning my knuckles for. I told him he could have her."

"What happened to them?"

"They got married and moved to Missouri. I guess that's where his family was from. Had a little girl from what I heard."

"What did you do?"

"What most anyone would do in that situation—holed up for a few days, licked my wounds, got drunk and into a little trouble with a friend, then threw myself into my work and vowed never to trust a woman again."

"Sounds reasonable."

"I was doing a fine job of it, too, until this gorgeous librarian moved to town. And now she has me rethinking my whole strategy."

She smiled over at him, and the sight of her smile wrapped around his heart like a warm blanket. "It seems to me like you dodged a bullet. She sounds terrible. I think you should be thankful you didn't get stuck with her. But I'm confused about one thing. You said this story didn't paint you in a very favorable light. What in that story made *you* look bad?"

"All of it. But mainly the part where I was just a dumbass dope who bought into her lies and believed her when she said she had real feelings for me." *Believed that she loved me.* He kicked a rock out of the path in front of them. "I got so caught up in this woman who treated me like I was a king that I never stopped to think about why she would do that or why it was all happening so fast."

"So what you're saying is you don't want me to treat you

like a king? What about a prince?" She grinned as she teased him. "Actually, you seem way more like a knight to me."

He chuckled. He couldn't believe it. He'd just told her this terrible story and she was taking it all in stride and teasing him about it. Dang—that only made him like her more. "A knight in shining armor who rescues skirtless damsels from barn lofts after they've gone to battle with cantankerous goats?"

"Yes, exactly." She laughed again, and he loved the sound of her laughter. It was at times soft and light but could also be hearty and bawdy. It was infectious to him and hearing it seemed to always draw out his smile.

He wouldn't have thought it, but he felt better after telling her about Tina. Although he hadn't told her the whole story. Not all of it. Not the stuff that had happened afterward with Brian. But those things could wait for another day. They were laughing and having fun again, and he'd had enough sharing and downer topics for one afternoon.

He wrapped an arm around her and pulled her to his side. "So do you want to come over this Saturday night? I think Nudge and Buddy miss you. You could bring Milo, and we could barbecue and take the horses out for a trail ride."

"That sounds fun, but I can't."

His shoulders tightened. "Because of what I just told you?"

"No, of course not. Because Bryn and Zane are going out of town this weekend. They found someone to adopt a couple of those horses we rescued so they're hauling them down to Durango, and I promised to keep an eye on things and feed the animals while they're gone." She stopped and turned to him, sliding her arms around his neck and batting her eyelashes at him. "So maybe you could come to my place on Saturday? And I might even cook you dinner."

"Sounds good to me. But I don't get why you're doing that goofy thing with your eyelashes."

She tilted her head and offered him a coy grin. "Because in exchange for me cooking you dinner, I was hoping you'd…"

It was his turn to grin. "Do that thing with my tongue that makes you call my name and compare me to a Greek god?"

Her eyes widened, and a laugh burst from her. "No." She swatted at his arm. "A Greek god? Really?"

He lifted one shoulder in a shrug. "It sounded that way to me."

She shook her head. "I was going to say I was hoping you'd help me feed and take care of the horses."

"Oh, well, sure. I can do that. I'd be glad to. You don't even have to bribe me with a home-cooked meal."

"Oh great. Then could you pick up a pizza on your way over?"

He laughed. "Yeah, I could do that. Pepperoni, right?"

"Yes, thank you. You're the best." She leaned in, going up on her toes to press a quick kiss to his cheek, then spoke softly into his ear. "And also, Milo is spending the night at Mandy's on Saturday, so that tongue thing you were talking about is definitely still up for discussion."

"Before or after the pizza?"

"Depends on how hungry we get."

"I'm feeling pretty famished right now." He pulled her closer and kissed her.

Her body pressed to his as she deepened the kiss. Heat surged through his veins. He could tell her ten ways from Sunday how much he liked being her friend, but he wanted more. He wanted all of her.

Thoughts of Tina tried to slither their way into his mind like the snaking tendrils of a parasitic vine. He'd let himself fall in love once before, had let himself imagine a life with a wife and a child, a family. And that had blown up in his face. He'd made a vow never to let himself get that close to another woman, but meeting Jillian had him questioning that vow. Hell, he'd proposed to her twice already.

He was in way over his head with this woman. He was at a crossroads in his job and in a race for sheriff—the results of this election could change his whole career. That's where his mind, his focus should be. Not on sharing a slice of pepperoni pizza and possibly a pillow with Jillian Bennett. But he couldn't help it. He was consumed with her. Everything about this woman turned him on, from the flirty way she teased him to the lush curves of her body that kept him up at night fantasizing about moments like these. He couldn't keep his hands, or his lips, off her.

Her skin was so soft, and she smelled so good and *felt* so good. All the other stuff in his life just seemed to fade away. Standing on the trail with the leaves of the trees rustling around them, it felt like they were all alone, as if they were the only ones in the world.

His hand was skimming over her hip, inching toward the hem of her dress, the smooth skin of her leg too dang enticing, when they heard someone clear his throat. *Shoot.* Definitely *not* alone.

They pulled apart, smoothing their clothes as they turned toward a man standing on the trail behind them. He was in his mid-forties and wearing jogging clothes, although his thick chin and paunchy middle suggested he was fairly new to the sport.

Ethan held back a groan. Barely.

"Hey, Con," Ethan said, tipping his head in the man's direction. "I didn't realize you were a runner."

"Oh yeah, I'm an avid jogger." The man ran a few steps in place, then patted his substantial belly. "You know, gotta keep in fightin' shape."

Jillian tried to discreetly take another small step back, but it was too late. Ethan was sure the other man had already gotten an eyeful. Thank goodness they'd heard him when they did.

"Jillian, have you met my esteemed opponent in the race for sheriff?" Ethan asked, gesturing to the man who wore a smirk on his face that he sorely wanted to knock off. "This is Deputy Sheriff Conway Peel," he said after she shook her head. "Con, this is Jillian Bennett, the new head librarian in town."

Conway smiled as he held out his hand, but Ethan caught the leering way his gaze traveled down Jillian's body then back up again to meet her eyes. And from the way her jaw was clenching, he guessed Jillian saw it too.

"So good to meet you," Conway said, his voice dripping with pretentious charm.

"Good to meet you too. I don't think I've seen you at the library. Are you a big reader?"

He shook his head. "Who has time for books these days? Although if I would have known more about the new hire, I might have stopped in to 'check something out.'" He made air quotes around the words and chuckled at his own pun. Then he changed his tone, lowering his voice like they were sharing an inside joke. "Is it true what they say about librarians?"

Ethan drew his fingers into a fist at his side. Seriously? It was not going to help his campaign if he throat-punched his opponent, but he was fairly certain it would be worth it.

Thankfully, he was saved from starting a brawl with his rival by Jillian's cutting comeback.

"You mean that we're super smart, can manage stingy budgets from state governments, and that we get annoyed by incorrectly shelved books and small patrons running amok in our libraries without proper adult supervision? Yeah, that's pretty much all true."

He raised an eyebrow, then gave her another once-over with his eyes, his gaze a little steelier this time. "What brought you to our fair city, Miss Bennett? You're a long way from California."

"My sister lives here."

"Ahhh," he said, still studying her. "And you're a single mom? Is that what I heard?"

"That's correct." She lifted her chin just the barest degree. "For someone who doesn't frequent the library, you sure seem to know a lot about me."

"I guess when someone new comes to town, I make it my business to know. Part of the job and all." He glanced at

Ethan. "But I didn't realize you all knew each other…quite so well."

Ethan didn't like the tone in his voice. "We've been friends for a while now."

Conway lifted an eyebrow. "Friends, huh?"

"Yep. Friends." He hoped his curt tone would *curt*ail the conversation. "We happened to run into each other at Miss Miriam's funeral."

Conway peered back down the trail. "You're a long way from the church."

"It was a nice day. We decided to take a walk. Which we should probably get back to." He tipped his head again. "So, if you'll excuse us."

He lifted his hand. "Oh, yeah, by all means, you all should get back to your *walk*. We'll have time to catch up later." He gave Ethan a knowing grin, then waved as he took off down the path. "Nice to meet you, Miss Bennett. I'm sure we'll be seeing each other around," he called over his shoulder.

"Not if I can help it," Jillian murmured, not quite under her breath. She turned and continued walking down the path at a brisk pace.

Ethan caught up to her but the easy affection they'd shared before Conway interrupted them was gone. Jillian's arms were crossed over her chest, a clear sign to him that she was closing herself off and had no interest in holding his hand.

What had happened? A few minutes ago they were laughing and making out like a couple of teenagers. Now she couldn't even look at him.

"Hey, you okay?" he asked.

"I'm fine," she said, her tone and demeanor telling him she was anything but fine.

"I'm sorry about that. I know Con is a jerk, but I thought you totally put him in his place."

"He is a jerk. And a dangerous one," she said as they left the trail and started back down the sidewalk toward the church. Her car was parked next to his truck on the other side of the street, and she stepped off the curb then hurried across the road, already digging in her purse for her keys.

"*Dangerous?*" He kept pace with her, but it was obvious by the way her long legs were eating up the asphalt that she was in a hurry to get away from him. "Look, Conway's an idiot, but he wouldn't hurt anyone."

She beeped the key fob toward her car and yanked the door open before turning back to face him. Her friendly smile was gone, and she had an edge of hardness to her eyes. "That's where you're wrong, Ethan. That guy could not just hurt us but he could destroy both you *and* me."

"Listen, Jillian—" he started to say, but she raised her hand and cut him off.

"No, you listen. This is exactly what I was worried about. I just want to live a quiet life, do my job, and raise my son and be the best mom I can be. I don't want or need trouble for me or for you." She pressed her palm to her mouth as her shoulders curved in, then she pulled in a shaky breath and straightened her shoulders.

Her eyes still held a pained expression as she raised her chin, and dread shot through him. What was happening? How had everything changed in what felt like the blink of an eye? And make no mistake, something had changed. She had changed. Everything about her, from the flat press of her lips to the way she held one arm across her stomach as if trying to hold herself together.

"I like you, Ethan. I do," she said, and the tremble in her voice almost broke him. "But I think we need to back off a little bit and not see each other for a while. I'm sorry." She held his gaze for one second, then ducked into her car and pulled the door shut. The engine started, and she pulled away before he even had a chance to stop her. Although what was he going to do—jump in front of her car?

Yeah, maybe. He should have done something. Instead, he'd just stood there like a dope, with his mouth hanging open and what he was sure was a mystified expression on his face.

What the hell had just happened? What did *a while* mean? Like, for the next few days, or the next few months?

He felt numb as he sagged against his truck. How had seeing Con screwed everything up? She'd said he was dangerous, but he had no idea what she was talking about.

There was nothing Conway Peel could do to hurt *him*.

Except win the election.

CHAPTER 16

Jillian maneuvered the book cart into Amos's room that Saturday morning and was pleased to see him sitting up in the chair and with a healthy bit of color to his cheeks. "Hi, handsome," she said. "You're looking good today."

"Thanks. I'm feeling pretty good. I just had a great visit from my grandson. You just missed him. I was hoping to introduce you two—I think he'd be perfect for you. Unless you've figured out your man troubles and decided to give your guy another chance."

"If I only had a nickel for every sweet old person who had a grandson who would be just *perfect* for me, then I wouldn't be spending my Saturday mornings pushing books around or driving a ten-year-old car." Although she did love her car.

"That may be true, but *my* grandson takes after me—so he's a pretty handsome guy."

She arched an eyebrow. "That's what they all say."

He chuckled. "So, tell me what's new."

"I've got a couple of the latest mysteries, and I found a book that has a bunch of tales of the Old West that I thought you'd like."

"Who cares about the books? Although that Old West one does sound kind of good. But I'm asking about what's new with you. If you're not gonna take a chance on my grandson, you might as well tell me what's happening with your fella."

She perched on the end of the bed. *Nothing*. That's what was happening with her fella. She hadn't talked to Ethan since the funeral on Thursday. He'd tried to call a couple of times, but she'd let her phone go to voicemail and hadn't had the courage to listen to his messages. She was afraid if she did, her resolve would crumble and she'd race right back into his strong, muscled arms. "First of all, he's not *my* fella. He's just *a* fella."

"Well he's *a* fella who just made your cheeks go rosy pink."

"That's because I like him, but we're in a weird place."

"What does that mean?"

"I don't know. It means that I want to be with him, but there are a lot of extenuating circumstances. It's tough. My focus has always been on my son and trying to be a good mom *and* dad to him."

"That's a lot of pressure for one mom."

"Maybe, but I'm all he has. I've always tried to raise him so he feels like he's loved and to think of his dad as a decent guy. Which he absolutely is *not*. But that's part of why I've never let myself get involved with another man."

"Sounds lonely."

She shrugged. "Sometimes it is. But I've kept myself so busy with life and putting all my focus on my boy that I've tried not to notice." Although there had been times— especially since she'd met Ethan—when she'd started to notice that loneliness more. "I haven't done a lot of dating, but something about this new guy feels different. Like maybe we have a chance." She let out a soft sigh. "I've kept my guard up for so long, it's hard to let it down. After everything that's happened in my life, I just have a hard time trusting men. Present company excluded."

Which was true. For some reason, she'd really bonded with the old guy, and she did feel like she could trust him. She gave him the abbreviated version of what had happened with Rad.

"That's some story," he said, when she'd finally wound down.

She picked at a loose thread on his bedspread. "Now you can see why I'm cautious about getting involved with someone new. I've only trusted my heart to one guy, and he didn't even care what happened to me. So maybe some of it is that I also don't trust myself. I made some bad decisions back then. I got in with the wrong kind of people, and those decisions still haunt me. And it's not like Rad is totally gone from my life. He's my son's father, and that's a lot to ask a new guy to understand. Especially if my past can come back to bite us both."

Amos steepled his fingers in front of his chin, then pointed them at her. "You know, your story sounds a lot like what happened to my Trudy. Not the armed robbery business, of course, but some of the other stuff."

"What do you mean? Last I heard, you'd fallen head over heels for Trudy and the two of you were starting a grand summer romance."

He sighed as his gaze turned wistful. "Oh, we did have a grand romance. I fell so hard for that woman I could barely think straight. I asked her to marry me on our first date."

"You did?" She tried to laugh, even though her heart hurt at the similarity of Ethan proposing to her.

"Oh yeah, I did. She turned me down, of course. But I asked her again at the end of the summer, after we'd fallen in love and I thought I had a better chance of her accepting. I bought a ring and everything."

"And?"

"And she turned me down again. Just about tore my heart out. I'd had big dreams of us getting married and buying a little farm. But apparently she'd had big dreams too. But hers involved moving to New York to become a model or a movie star or some such thing."

"Oh no. What did you do?"

"What could I do? I let her go. I loved her so much that I wanted her to be happy. Then I moped around and made everyone crazy with how dang moony I was. My parents especially. They never liked her anyway—always said she was too wild. And she was. She had this fearlessness about her, this zest for life. I think it scared them. After she was gone, everyone said they'd known she was going to break my heart. They'd always thought I was too nice for someone like her. But that was only because they didn't know her like I did. Underneath that fearlessness was about the biggest heart of anyone I knew—she'd give anyone the shirt off her back if they needed it."

"She sounds great. So what happened? Did she become an actress?"

He shook his head. "Nah. She had some auditions and a few small parts. But nothing panned out like she'd hoped.

That's how I think her story sounds like yours. You went to California and Trudy went to New York, each of you thinking you were going to start this exciting new life but nothing turned out like you hoped. And like you, Trudy had gotten herself into some trouble and mixed up with the wrong people and she didn't know how to get herself out. She was sharing some crappy apartment with I don't know how many other people, and it was the seventies so people were experimenting with all sorts of drugs, and they were abundant with the crowd she was in.

"I hadn't heard from her in months, then she called me one night—sounded like she was already drunk or high on something—I could hear a party going on behind her. She was crying and sounded so miserable, it just about ripped my heart out all over again. She told me she was in way over her head and that she wished she'd never left home. I'd never felt so dang helpless. So I asked her if I came to get her, would she come back home and marry me. And without skipping a beat, she said 'in a New York minute.' So I walked out the front door, got in my truck, drove all through the night, all the next day, and into the next night."

"To New York?"

He nodded. "You're darn tootin'. I'd already thought about driving out there to visit her, so I'd checked the map and knew all I had to do was get on I-70 and drive for twenty-nine hours or so. So that's what I did. I only stopped for gas, cheeseburgers, and coffee along the way. I drove an old truck back then, and I wasn't entirely sure it would make it, but I didn't care. I'd have walked to her if I'd had to.

"I'll tell ya, when I walked into that apartment, I've never seen anything like it before or ever since. The place was a shithole, if you'll pardon the expression. I stood in the doorway, trying to find her through all the people and the smoke, and a gall-durn cockroach crawled across my boot. The place stunk like rotten food and body odor and there was trash and drug paraphernalia everywhere. It was dark, but I'll still swear I saw a rat in there.

"You should've seen Trudy's face. She walked out of the kitchen holding a bag of potato chips, and her mouth fell open when she saw me, and she kind of blinked like she couldn't quite believe it. For just one second, I started to doubt if I'd made an error in judgment, then she dropped the chips and ran across the room and into my arms. And I gave that woman a kiss like my life depended on it."

"Aww, Amos, you old romantic," Jillian said, completely engrossed in the story. "So then what happened?"

"The kiss must've worked because she threw her stuff in a bag and left with me right then. We stopped to see the Statue of Liberty and the Empire State Building, then we drove straight back to Colorado and got married two weeks later. She trusted me to get her out of there, and I spent the rest of my life trying to make sure she never regretted the decision to get in that old blue truck and drive away from that life with me."

"And what about your parents and all the people who thought you two shouldn't have been together or that she wasn't worthy of you?" Jillian cringed at the words. She knew that crushing deep belief of not feeling worthy of another person.

Amos waved his hand through the air. "Anyone who mattered knew I was the one who wasn't worthy of her. And eventually she won 'em all over. She never lost that spirit of adventure, we just incorporated it into our life. My parents grew to love her, in fact she and my mom ended up great friends."

Jillian smiled. "I love that."

"My point is that you'll never know what could happen unless you try. If I wouldn't have driven to New York that night, I would have missed out on the best thing that ever happened to me. And if you don't at least give this thing with this fella a chance, you could be missing out on one of the greatest stories of your life."

She sighed. "That's easy to say, but it's hard for me to take that leap."

"I know I'm just an old beat-up cowboy, but I've still got a little good advice in me. And I'm tellin' ya, don't let the bad choices you made in your past dictate all the new decisions you make in the future." He leaned back in his chair and flashed her an impish smile followed by a wink. "And if it doesn't work out, there's always my grandson."

———

Jillian was sitting on the porch later that night sharing a bowl of cantaloupe with Tiny when she spotted an old blue pickup coming down the driveway. Tiny, whose snout was practically touching the bowl as her head rested in Jillian's lap, snuffled for another square of melon. Jillian frowned at the truck as she passed the pig the last bite, then set the bowl on the table and stood to greet the visitor. She hoped it wasn't someone with questions about the horse rescue.

No, she thought, gulping at the sight of the handsome cowboy stepping out of the truck with a pizza box in his hand. He wasn't here *about* a rescue; he was apparently here to do the rescuing.

"Ethan," she said, smoothing her hair with one hand and wishing she were wearing something besides cut-off jean shorts and an old T-shirt that said THAT'S WHAT I DO—I READ AND I KNOW THINGS.

Tiny squealed with enthusiasm and took off down the porch steps, probably more eager to greet the pizza than the hunky deputy.

"Hey," he said, his grin sheepish as he stepped onto the porch.

"Hey," she answered. *Wow. So far so good. Totally casual.* She wiped her sticky cantaloupe-covered fingers on a napkin. "What are you doing here?"

"You invited me. Remember you asked me to help you take care of the animals and bring a pizza?" He lifted the lid of the box and the scent of garlic and cheese wafted toward her. "I even got extra pepperoni."

"I know," she said, almost caving at the scent. Her stomach growled, and she pressed her nonsticky hand against it. "But that was before…"

"Before you said we should back off a little and not see each other for a while?"

She nodded, pulling the edge of her bottom lip under her front teeth as she tried to regain her resolve *and* remember why she'd said something so crazy. Why did the man have to look so dang good?

He tipped his Stetson back off his forehead as he leaned against the porch railing. "Well, you see, the way I figure it, 'a while' could mean all sorts of things. And since I haven't seen you or talked to you or got you to answer any of my calls for the last few days, it sure feels like it's been 'a while' to me."

"Ethan," she said, without much bluster.

"Look, I've got pizza and I can hear your stomach growling all the way over here, so what do you say we grab a slice, have a little supper, then I'll help you with the animals. Okay?"

She shifted from one foot to the other.

"You *do* still need help with the animals, don't you?"

"Yeah."

"Well then, I'm your guy. And this pizza is getting cold."

I'm your guy?

She wished that were true. Then she wished that that wish was even a possibility. But she knew it wasn't.

But the man did have a point about her needing help with the animals and being hungry. She'd only had a few squares of cantaloupe. She'd given most of it to Tiny, who'd seemed to be enjoying it much more than she had. "Wellll, I hate to see a good pizza go to waste, so you'd better come in."

"That's my girl," he said as he followed her inside.

"Not you," she said to the pig, who trotted in on his heels. Jillian turned to open the screen door to let the pig out and was surprised to find Otis on the porch, his neck outstretched as he peered through the screen. He snuck through the door before she had a chance to close it, and his hooves clicked on the hardwood as he scampered across the floor toward Ethan. "That dang goat can smell a pepperoni from a mile away," she muttered. "Don't give them any pizza," she told Ethan, who was now cornered in the kitchen between the ornery goat and the massive pig.

He laughed as he pulled paper plates from the pantry. "But they're being so good. Frankie would have already found a way to leap to the counter by now. These guys are just sniffing the box."

"Yeah, well, watch out for Otis. He's so wily, he might just grab the corner of that thing and take off with it. Then none of us will have pizza."

Ethan wisely pushed the box farther back on the counter before opening the lid.

"Come on, you two. Get out of here." She opened the door again to find Shamus, the mini-horse, trotting up the porch steps and trying to muscle his way inside. "What are you doing here?" Jillian asked the horse, trying to block his path. "Did Otis let you out?"

The goat answered with an affronted bleat, as if to say it was the other way around.

"You sure they can't have some?" Ethan asked, holding up a slice of pizza. "I did get a large."

"Yes, I'm sure. I may not know a lot about animals, but I'm sure pepperoni pizza is not on the approved food list."

He set the slice back in the box, then opened the refrigerator and pulled out a small bag of baby carrots. "I'm not saying carrots are in the same league as pizza, but do you think we can lure them back outside with these?"

"It wouldn't work for me. I'd never choose a carrot over a pizza. But let's try it anyway."

He passed her a couple of carrots and between the two of them they got the pig, the goat, and the mini-horse out onto the front porch. Then Ethan tossed them the rest of the carrots and Jillian quickly shut the door.

Otis let out another insulted bleat and head-butted the screen door.

Jillian ignored the goat, crossing the room to peer carefully out the corner of the window as if she were a nosy neighbor spying on the house across the street. "They're eating the carrots," she whispered. "Even Otis. He must have gotten worried that they'd eat them all without him, because he's happily munching one. Now they're leaving," she said, giving Ethan a play-by-play.

"Are they allowed to just roam free around the farm?" Ethan asked from right behind her.

She let out a squeal to rival one of Tiny's. "Holy cow. I didn't know you were behind me." But she knew now. Especially because her skin just got goose-pimply and the room suddenly seemed too warm. She'd told him they needed to back off, but holy hot cowboy, she had missed him. It had only been a few days, but she'd missed his texts and talking to him on the phone. She'd gotten used to the rich timbre of his voice in her ear as he laughed or asked her about her day.

He peered down at her, his expression changing from the

amusement of watching the animals to something more serious. Reaching up, he brushed a lock of her bangs from her
forehead, and she shivered. His voice was low, almost a whisper, and holding a depth of emotion as he said, "I've missed
you too."

She blinked and swallowed at the sudden dryness in her
mouth. "I didn't think I said that out loud."

His fingers softly caressed the side of her cheek as he kept
her gaze locked in his. "You didn't. But I could tell you were
thinking it."

She huffed out a small laugh. "So you're a mind reader?"
She planted a hand on her hip. "What am I thinking now?"

He narrowed his eyes and studied her. "I'm getting a bit
of a mixed signal. You *are* thinking about the pizza—but I'm
not sure if you're thinking we should go eat it, or if you're
wishing we'd forget about it and that instead I'd lean in and
kiss you senseless, then pick you up and carry you into the
bedroom."

"Wow. You got all that just from staring into my eyes."

He nodded as he tried to hold back a smile. "Pretty
impressive, huh?"

She shook her head. "That was definitely *not* what I just
thought."

He slid his arm around her waist and pulled her close.
"How about the other stuff? I'm feeling like that was spot-on."

His conjecture had been pretty dang close, except she
hadn't been thinking about eating the pizza. What was it
about this man that had her throwing all intelligent thought
out the window? She touched her finger to the corner of his

mouth, then lightly brushed it over his bottom lip. Her pulse quickened at his instant reaction—his eyes closed as his lips parted and he pulled in a quick breath.

"You were half right," she told him.

He opened his eyes and grinned wickedly down at her. "Which half?"

"The part about wishing you'd kiss me senseless, then carry me into the bedroom." She pressed against his lips with her finger as he pulled her closer and leaned in. "But I was also thinking that if we went there, we wouldn't want to leave, and we have animals to feed and chores to see to before it gets dark."

He groaned. "Dang, I hate it when we have to be all responsible. But you're still pretty sexy even when you're being sensible." He took her hand away from his lips and pressed a soft kiss to her open palm. A thrill ran down her spine. "I'll bet we can manage to fit in at least one kiss before I let you go."

Still holding her hand, he leaned closer and pressed a soft kiss to her lips. Then another, firmer this time, then another and another. And then she was lost.

Minutes, or hours, or possibly days later—she seemed to have lost the ability to calculate time—she pulled away and tried to catch her breath.

His lips curved into a slow grin. "How did I do? Do you have any senses left?"

"Barely," she whispered. She'd thought kissing her senseless was a figure of speech, but he'd made good on the idea. She could scarcely string two thoughts together. Well, two thoughts that didn't involve dragging him into her bedroom and getting him naked.

"Me too. But I've got enough to know that if I don't stop now, I'm not sure I'll be able to keep from picking you up and tossing you into bed."

"You might be a better mind reader than I thought."

He laughed and let her go. "Why don't you grab some plates for the pizza while I take a cold shower? Any chance there's any beer left from last weekend?"

"No. But I think there's still some cream soda in the fridge."

"Sold."

Four slices of pizza and two cream sodas later, they headed out to feed the animals.

"Where's Applejack?" Ethan asked as they walked into the barn.

"Milo took him with him."

"To Mandy's house?"

Jillian laughed. "Yeah. Isn't that a hoot? Only in Creedence can you take your horse with you to a sleepover."

"It helps when your friend's dad is a veterinarian. But still, that *is* funny."

"The good thing is the horse seems to be adjusting better. He doesn't seem quite as sad. That corral idea you had was genius. Although it does still freak me out to go into Milo's room and see a horse's head stuck through the window."

"More than it freaked you out to see a horse in the closet?"

"No. That one was the definite winner."

They measured and dispensed feed and hay, changed and refilled water buckets, and gave the new horses each a quick brushing. Bryn and Zane had been grooming them a couple of times a day to help socialize them and earn their trust before releasing them in with the other horses.

Jillian was aware of every one of Ethan's movements—every time he brushed past her or she caught a whiff of his cologne. He wore his standard jeans and square-toed cowboy boots, but tonight he had on a light-blue T-shirt and a straw cowboy hat instead of his usual brown felt one. The muscles corded in his arms as he tossed hay bales into the stalls and carried them out to fill the back of his pickup.

"I don't remember seeing this truck," she said, as they walked toward it. It reminded her of Amos's story of driving all night in an old pickup to get to his Trudy, and she had to wonder if her dream cowboy had just arrived in an old truck too. "Is it new? Well, obviously it's not new, but new to you, I mean." Oh geez. It was as if her mouth suddenly failed to remember how to talk.

Ethan chuckled. "No—it's not new. It's old. I've had it forever. It was my first truck. And I guess I'm kind of sentimental because I kept it around even when I upgraded to a new one. The thing still runs great, so I use it around the ranch and when I'm off-duty. I drove it over here the other night."

"Oh, that would explain the sleeping bags still in here," she said as Ethan opened the passenger door for her and she saw the two rolled up bags on the floor of the cab. "We were already in the barn when you got here and then you left early, so I guess I never saw your truck."

Ugh. Stop babbling, she chided herself as Ethan circled around, then climbed into the driver side.

"Ready?" he asked, cranking the engine.

"Yep." She buckled into her seatbelt as they pulled out of the driveway and headed down the highway toward the west pasture. She'd done this route with Zane the other night in preparation for the weekend, so she knew when to jump out and help open and close the gates. Ethan had a classic country station on the radio, and the scents of pine trees and freshly mown fields wafted through their open windows as they bumped along the tire-worn path.

"I really do appreciate you helping me," Jillian said as they tossed the final bales out to the cattle several minutes later. "Zane showed me what to do and said I could use one of the farm trucks, but you sure made it easier."

He shrugged as they watched the cattle meander toward the hay bales. "It was nothing. I'm happy to help—and glad to have an excuse to see you." He nodded toward the mountain beyond the field. "There's an old dirt road up there that leads to Bryn's family's cabin. You ever been up there?"

"No."

"Well, there's this one spot on the way up, it's like a pull-off on the shoulder, and if you park in a certain way...well, you've just got to see it. But I promise it's really cool. You up for a little drive?"

"Gosh, with a build-up like that, how could I say no? I don't wanna miss out on something *really cool.*"

It had been just past dusk when they'd loaded the truck and headed toward the pasture, but the sun had now fully set behind the mountain and night settled in as Ethan maneuvered the old truck up the rocky path.

"Don't worry. I've been driving up here since we were

kids," he told her. "There's a lake on up past the cabin and we used to come up to go swimming. I can bring you up here sometime, if you want. You and Milo would love it."

"Um, sure. I guess. Maybe." She was doing the worst job of sticking to her guns as far as her plan to distance herself from Ethan and cool off the amount of time they were spending together. In fact, between taking a drive with him and casually planning a family outing, she would have to say she was doing the opposite of sticking to her guns. She wasn't even in the same room as the guns.

"This is it," Ethan said, pulling past a wide section of shoulder, then putting the truck into reverse and backing into the spot.

"Won't backing in make it a little hard to see anything?" Jillian asked, peering through the windshield at the wall of mountain in front of them.

"It's all in your perspective," he said, grabbing the two sleeping bags. "Come on." He got out, pulled the bags free and tossed them into the bed of the pickup. Dropping the tailgate, he climbed up and then held out his hand to help her.

Using one bag to lie on and the other as a back rest, he sat down with his back to the cab and stretched out his legs in front of him. He patted the spot next to him. "Best seat in the house."

"For what?" She was still facing the mountain, confused about what the big deal was as she lowered herself down, then gasped as she turned around to sit beside him. "Oh my gosh. Look at all the stars," she said, pointing to the sky in front of them. "It looks like we're up in the sky with them."

The combination of how high up the mountain they were, the truck being parked so close to the edge, and the tailgate being down, gave the illusion they were floating in the air. The rest of the mountain faded into the dark behind them, and it felt like they were part of the sky.

"I tried to tell you," Ethan said.

A laugh bubbled out of her. "You were right. This *is* really cool."

His face split into a boyish grin as if he'd just won a ribbon at the county fair. "I told you. It's all in your perspective."

———

Ethan scooched down until he was on his back. "If you look at it from this angle, it feels almost like you're floating in space."

He scrunched up the sleeping bag to form a pillow as she scooted down to lie next to him. "Wow. I don't think I've ever seen so many stars."

"It helps when you get out here away from all the city lights. Not that Creedence has a massive skyline, but they still make a difference." He rolled to his side to look at her. "Although it's kind of hard to pay attention to the stars with you lying so close to me."

"Do you want me to scoot over?" she asked as she pulled slightly away.

"No, but I'm kind of cold." He folded his arms over his chest as if he were shivering. "So I wouldn't mind if you scooted closer."

She gave him a small eye roll, as if to let him know she wasn't fooled by his ruse. "It is *not* cold out here. It's a gorgeous summer night. If anything, it's too warm."

"Oh, are you too warm? I could help you take a layer off."

She peered down at her tank top and jean shorts. "I'm only wearing one layer."

"Then you shouldn't need much help."

She swatted playfully at his arm. "Do those lines ever work?"

"I don't know. It's the first time I've tried them. But you've still got your clothes on, so I'm gonna go with 'not very well.'"

She shrugged. "Oh, I don't know. They might have worked better than you think." She pulled her tank top off and climbed over him to straddle his waist.

Sitting astride him in just her bra and jean shorts, she looked sexy as hell. He toyed with the top snap of her jeans. "So, what mock superhero are you channeling tonight?"

"None. I'm just wearing plain black bikinis. I didn't think I was going to see you tonight, or at all really, so I wasn't feeling very courageous or brave."

"That's when you need your superpowers the most," he told her. "You want to borrow mine?"

She leaned forward, giving him an even more amazing view. "You have superpowers?"

"Sure I do. They're all in here." He lifted off his cowboy hat and set it on her head. "Now you have the power to do whatever you want to me."

She straightened the hat on her head, and the friction of

her denim against his as she moved was making him crazy. "That's a lot of power to give me."

"Darlin', haven't you figured out by now that it doesn't matter if you're wearing my hat, your superhero undies, a down parka, or nothing at all, I am completely at your mercy."

CHAPTER 17

ETHAN COULDN'T HAVE SPOKEN TRUER WORDS AS HE lost all track of time, utterly at the mercy of Jillian. He loved that each time they were together, he discovered something new about her.

He'd thought the first time had been spectacular, but every time seemed to go to another level, drawing them closer together not just physically but emotionally as well. And he could feel it in her too, could sense her letting go a little more each time, her movements bolder and more brazen. And he loved it.

The vision of Jillian naked except for his cowboy hat, sitting astride him, her hair loose and curly around her shoulders, was an intoxicating image he would never forget. She relished the position of power, teasing and seducing as she rocked and rode him into delicious torment.

Afterward, he lay back, his arms flung out at his sides as she collapsed over his chest. "Dang, woman. Forget the fancy undies, I think you need to plan on wearing my cowboy hat every time from now on."

She laughed as she slid off him and nestled into the crook of his shoulder. "Who said there was going to *be* a next time?"

He groaned. "Come on now. If there's not, then I'm in for

a life of celibacy, because you have now ruined me for any other woman."

She let out a bawdy laugh. "Good." She snuggled against him.

He rolled onto his side so he was looking at her. Brushing the backs of his fingers against her cheek, he was overcome with a rush of emotion. He knew what it was and wanted to tell her how he felt but didn't want to scare her. "You are so beautiful. It makes my chest hurt just to look at you."

Her eyes widened, then her expression softened.

"Marry me." The words slipped out before he could stop them. And seemed just the right thing to say when he was trying *not* to scare her.

She shook her head. "You're crazy."

"Crazy about you."

She pushed up on her elbow, turning toward him as she studied his face. "I can't figure you out, Ethan Rayburn. Why in the world would you even consider marrying me?"

"Oh, I've more than considered it. I've already thought of a band to play at the wedding and figured out how to convert the spare room into a cool bedroom for Milo. I've imagined you in *and out* of the white dress, and I've even considered some possible names for Milo's future little brother or sister."

"Brother or sister?" she squeaked.

Wow. He went right from the frying pan to swan-diving into the fire. "Okay, pretend I didn't say all that. Sometimes I don't know when to keep my mouth shut. But I do think about the future."

"And I'm in it?"

"Darlin', you *are* it. You *and* Milo."

She swallowed, and blinked as tears sprang to her eyes. "Are you just trying to get lucky again?"

He pulled her closer to his side. "I already feel like the luckiest guy around. Jillian, I know all this feels sudden. And I should probably cool it with the marriage and the prospective children talk."

"Ya think?"

He let out a soft laugh. "It's just that from the moment I first met you, I knew you were somethin' special. It wasn't just that goofy book wizard T-shirt you had on. It was everything about you—the way you laugh, your quick wit, the way you are with your son. You're so smart and funny, but you're also thoughtful and kind."

She pressed a hand to his chest. "Stop it. You're making me blush." She peered up at him from under her lashes, a playful grin on her face. "Just kidding. Keep going."

He chuckled again. "See, this is what I'm talking about. You make me laugh. You're sarcastic but also sweet. Plus you're gorgeous and sexy as hell. You took my breath away the first time I saw you standing on Cade's porch. You remember? I could barely string two words together, I was so tongue-tied. And that doesn't happen to me very often. I felt something that day, and every day since. I think you feel it too."

She gave a small bob of her head.

"It's not just that I'm attracted you. Although make no mistake, I *am* attracted to you. I think about you and *this*..." He motioned to their entwined bodies. "...all the time. But it's more than *this*. It's like we just click. Am I making any sense?"

She nodded again.

"When I'm with you, I feel happy. And then all this stuff—I don't know—emotion or whatever, I guess, just wells up in me, and when I open my mouth, a proposal pops out."

"I've noticed."

He skimmed his fingers down the side of her arm. "I know I'm a total dork, but I'm not trying to scare you or push you into anything you're not ready for. I'm a very patient man, and I'm good with whatever time you want to give. Just don't shut me out."

Jillian touched his cheek. "I hear you. And I agree there's something really good between us. I've been telling you for weeks that I'm not going to sleep with you or get involved, yet somehow every time I'm around you, I fall into your arms and we end up naked."

He grinned. "I know. Isn't it awesome?"

She laughed and nudged his ribs. "You *are* a dork. But you're a cute dork. And I like you too. But—"

He pressed a finger to her lips. "No 'buts.' Not tonight. How about for tonight we just be together and worry about the 'buts' tomorrow, or the next day, or next year?"

"Okay," she whispered. "Just for tonight."

Ethan had one arm on the wheel and one arm around Jillian as he drove down the highway. They were stopping at his ranch to pick up Frankie, and Ethan's toothbrush, then heading back to Jillian's for the night.

"Did you really think of names for our future kids?" Jillian asked.

"Yeah, absolutely. I tried to think of something literary that still sounded cool and had a little cowboy to it."

"Okay, I'm dying to hear this. What did you come up with?"

"Huck or Finn if we have another boy and Darcy if it's a girl."

She tilted her head. "I can't believe I'm about to say this, especially since I'd never imagined naming a child Huckleberry before, but I think I actually love all of those names."

I think I actually love you.

He didn't say the words out loud. He'd spilled his guts enough for one night. But he was thinking it.

He pulled her closer and loved the way she nestled against him. "I had a feeling you would. I'd also considered Harry and Hermione, but thought those were just a little too cliché."

She barked out a laugh, and he loved the sound of it.

The window was down, and the radio was playing an old country song and he couldn't help but hum along. He felt great. Their time on the mountain had been about as close to perfect as it could get. Nothing could mess up this night.

Except maybe a strange truck and horse trailer parked in front of his barn.

"What the hell?" He peered through the windshield as he slowed the truck, a bad feeling settling in his gut. "I don't know what's going on, but I know it isn't good."

"Maybe it's just a neighbor," Jillian suggested.

"I can't think of any of my neighbors who'd show up to my house unannounced in the middle of the night hauling a horse trailer." He shook his head. "No, something feels very wrong." He cut the lights and the engine as he eased to the shoulder of the road before getting to his driveway. He hoped the combination of the tall grass and the dark color of his truck would conceal it enough to avoid notice if the owner of the truck happened to glance toward the highway. "I'm gonna go check it out."

Popping open the glove box, he pulled out a handgun secured in a holster.

"Do you really need a gun to check it out?"

"I'd rather have it and not need it than need it and not have it."

"Be careful," Jillian whispered.

"Stay here. Lock the doors. I'll be back." He opened the door and slipped out, pushing it quietly shut behind him. His boots made soft footfalls in the dirt as he crept up the driveway, trying to stay silent as he assessed the situation.

A frightened whinny rent the air as the barn door banged open. A beefy bald man emerged, dragging Buddy on a lead rope toward the trailer.

"Ethan, that's the tattooed guy from the illegal racetrack," Jillian whispered from behind him, causing him to jump what felt like a mile off the ground.

"Holy shit. You scared the crap out of me." He pressed his free hand to his chest. "I thought I told you to stay in the truck."

"Haven't you figured out by now that I'm not very good at following orders?"

"Well, I need you to follow these. If that *is* the guy from the racetrack, he's probably armed and we know he's dangerous."

"It *is* him. I'd recognize that guy anywhere."

"All the more reason for you to go back to the truck. Jillian, I can't stand the thought of you getting hurt."

"Well, I don't want you to get hurt either."

He scrubbed his hand across his head. "Okay, thank you, that's nice. But of the two of us, I'm the one who's got a gun. *And* police training."

"What's your point?"

"Jillian, please go back to the truck. This asshole is trying to steal our horses. I need my wits about me to take him down, and I can't do that if I'm also worried about you. So don't do it for me—do it for the horses. Plus I need you to call in and request some backup. Tattoo Guy's the only one we can see, but we don't know for sure that he's alone."

She let out a small huff. "Okay, fine. I'll do it for the horses. And to get you some backup." She turned and scurried back toward the truck.

Ethan stayed low and close to the brush along the edge as he stole down the rest of the driveway. He could hear the guy cussing as he snuck closer. Buddy was giving him hell about getting into the trailer, rearing back and stamping his hooves in the air.

Atta boy, Buddy, keep him distracted, he thought as he bent forward and ran toward the front of the truck.

"Get in there, you good-for-nothing piece of shit," the man snarled as the crack of a whip shot through the air.

Rage simmered just below the surface—Ethan hated the thought of his horse being abused. And even though Buddy and Nudge had only been at his ranch a few weeks, he already considered them his horses—his and Jillian's. But that was a box he'd have to unpack later. His training had taught him to keep his cool and separate emotion from a situation, and he called on those instincts now as he cautiously leaned forward to peer around the hood of the truck.

Jillian was right. Ethan positively ID'd the guy as the one from the racetrack as Buddy forced him back a few feet and into the circle of illumination cast from the beam of the yard light next to the barn. They hadn't taken him in the day of the horse rescue raid, but his name, Darryl Kemp, had been logged in the file. After his altercation with Milo and Jillian, Ethan had run a check on him and wasn't surprised to see he had a record. It was a bunch of petty stuff, disorderly conduct, petty theft, possession, reckless driving—but the assault charges told him the guy liked to use his fists and whatever weapons he could find. His last charge had been a bar fight and he'd clocked a guy with a platter of wings.

From this vantage point, Ethan could see into the barn and confirm Nudge was still in her stall. And it didn't look like he had anyone else with him. That would help. Especially since Ethan was off-duty so he had no handcuffs or any way to restrain the guy. *Where is that backup?* He prayed Jillian had already called and that they were on their way. Until then, he'd have to improvise.

"Drop the rope and back away from my horse, Kemp," Ethan said, stepping out from behind the truck, his weapon raised and aimed.

The man's eyes went wide for a split second, then they narrowed into beady slits as he tightened his grip on Buddy's halter. "This ain't *your* horse."

"Then why are you trying to steal him out of *my* barn?"

"You stole them from us first."

"I *rescued* them from you. What do you even want them for? We already closed down the racetrack, so they're worth nothing to you." *Keep him talking.* He might tip Ethan off to another illegal betting track.

"They're worth something to the slaughterhouse that'll give me cash for 'em. And they pay by the pound, so thanks to you fattening 'em up the past few weeks, they'll be worth even more."

Bile rose in his throat. Ethan felt sick to his stomach. This guy was stealing these horses just to sell them to a slaughterhouse? "It doesn't matter how much they weigh because you're not taking them with you. They belong to me now. And possession is nine-tenths of the law." That wasn't really a law, but this guy probably didn't know that.

The man's lips curved into an evil smile. "Yeah, well, that works out pretty well for me since I've got this one in my possession." He raised the lead rope.

Buddy took a frightened step back, rearing up his head, then leaned down and bit the man's arm.

Kemp let out a yelp as he dropped the rope. He bent forward, clutching his arm.

"Not anymore," Ethan said, tucking his gun into the waistband at the back of his pants and charging toward the guy. He bent low as he tackled him, knocking him to the ground. Ethan had the element of surprise, but Kemp was strong and he wasn't going down without a fight.

Swinging wildly, one of Kemp's fists caught Ethan in the face as they wrestled. A burst of pain exploded in his cheek. Ethan ignored it, adrenaline surging through him as he tried to get the scumbag onto his stomach.

Kemp's arms were flailing and he was bucking Ethan, trying to get out from under him. Ethan got ahold of one of his arms and tried to pull it behind the assailant's back, but Kemp reared back like a caged animal. The motion knocked the gun loose, and it went skidding across the dirt.

Both men froze at the sound, their heads whipping toward the weapon before Kemp let out a roar and pushed up, trying to belly-crawl toward the gun. Ethan doubled his efforts, knowing he had to get the guy under control and not give him a chance to reach the weapon. Darryl's hand shot out toward the gun, and Ethan clamped his fingers around his forearm.

Before either man could reach it, the gun was snatched up by Jillian.

"Don't move, asshole," she said, her voice hard as steel.

Kemp sneered up at her, but he stopped struggling for the moment. "What are you going to do? Shoot me?"

Instead of being intimidated, which Ethan assumed was how Kemp thought she would react, Jillian took another step closer. Her tone dropped to an even harder place as she replied, speaking the words slowly: "Just give me a reason."

Ethan felt Kemp go still, as if her statement actually frightened him. He took full advantage of the moment, yanking the guy's arm behind him and pinning him down as he called out to Jillian, "Grab me some of that baling twine from the barn. There's a bunch of it hanging from a nail right inside the door."

She kept the gun trained on Kemp as she took several steps backward and grabbed a handful of the twine from inside the barn door. Hurrying back, she stopped several feet away, enough that the horse thief couldn't get a hand out to reach her, and tossed the twine to Ethan.

He grabbed it and quickly secured Kemp's hands behind his back, wrapping them up like he was calf-roping at a rodeo. He'd just finished tying the knot when the sound of sirens wailed through the air as three deputy cruisers sped down the highway and turned into Ethan's driveway.

"I'd better take that now." Ethan held out his hand toward Jillian, and she passed him the gun. He fit it back into his waistband as the cruisers pulled up in front of the barn. Gravel flew as they braked to a stop. Then all three doors swung open, and three deputies came bursting out, all with their weapons drawn.

Now they showed up.

"You can put your weapons down," Ethan called to them. "I've got the perp secured, but I could use some handcuffs."

"What happened?" Deputy Knox Garrison asked, holstering his weapon and passing Ethan a pair of cuffs. He and Ethan had worked together since they'd graduated the academy and both had been hired by the county. He was a good man and a good deputy and someone Ethan trusted with his life.

"Caught this guy trying to steal my horses. He's one of the dirtbags involved in that illegal racetrack operation we broke up a few weeks back."

"Is he the only one out here?"

"Yeah. I wasn't sure how many guys were involved when I had Jillian call." Ethan nodded toward the three cruisers. "Probably didn't need quite this much backup."

Knox grinned. "Well, you know. It was a slow night. And we don't often get calls for backup. You should have seen me and Martinez racing toward our cruisers to be the first to respond. Ace was already out and caught up to us where County Road 9 meets the highway."

"I already called dibs on taking the guy in," the younger deputy, Martinez, said, pushing his shoulders back.

"Be my guest." Ethan lifted Kemp by the arms and passed him off to the waiting deputy. "Stick him in your cruiser and take him back to the station. I'll follow in a few minutes to give my statement."

Martinez towed Kemp toward his car and heaved him into the back seat.

"Looks like you've got this one handled," Ace, the third deputy, called. "You need anything else from me?"

"Nah," Ethan told him. "Thanks for coming out."

"Sure. It was fun," the deputy said as he opened his cruiser door. "See you back at the station." He followed Martinez's car out of the driveway and onto the highway.

Ethan dusted his jeans off, then held out a hand to Knox.

"Thanks for coming out. Appreciate it." Before he could shake, he turned at the sound of Jillian's alarmed cry.

"Ethan, oh my gosh, come over here," she said, standing at the back of the trailer. She had the door open and was holding her hand over her mouth and nose.

He and Knox hurried toward her, then both pulled back at the stench of the trailer.

Ethan peered in and his stomach convulsed at the sight of the gaunt mare tied inside, her hooves buried in inches of soiled hay and waste that Kemp had obviously neglected to clean out. "Bastard," he said through gritted teeth.

Holding his breath, he reached for the door, but Knox stopped him. "I feel for the horse too, but we need to photograph this before we touch anything."

"But look at her." Jillian's face contorted in pain.

Ethan wrapped an arm around her shoulders. "I know. And we're gonna help her. But Knox is right. As much as we want to get her out of there, we need to document this so we'll have it to use as evidence against that asshole."

Jillian lifted her chin as she nodded. "Okay. How can I help?"

"Just take a bunch of pictures, but don't touch anything."

"I already opened the door."

"That's fine. We can note that. But don't touch anything else."

They all pulled out their phones and spent the next several minutes photographing and documenting the contents of the truck and trailer. When they were finished, Ethan told them, "As much as I hate for her to be in there for even another second, I think it's best that I leave her where she is and drive her over to Bryn's. I know it means she'll be in that filth another five minutes, but I think that will be easier on her and less traumatic than taking her out and trying to put her back into one of my trailers."

"Why can't we take her out and just put her in your barn?" Jillian asked.

"It makes more sense to take her to Bryn's. She's better equipped to handle this type of situation, and if she's at the horse rescue, someone can monitor her recovery all the time. Plus I think it will be less stressful for her if we take her out and put her in a stall where she'll be able to stay."

"I agree with you," the other deputy said. "Why don't I drive this rig over to the Callahan place and help you get her unloaded, then I can take it on in to the impound lot and get one of the guys to bring me back to my cruiser."

"Good idea," Ethan said. "We'll be right behind you. Give me like two minutes to make sure he didn't do any other damage, then I need to grab my dog and get my horse put away."

"That's not gonna take long," Jillian said, pointing inside the barn to where Buddy had already gone back into his stall. Nudge stood as close as possible to him, her chin resting on the top edge of the wall connecting her stall to his.

"You're a good horse," Ethan told him, giving them each an extra scoop of feed before shutting the gate to Buddy's stall.

He let out a sigh of relief as they hurried toward his house. "That could have gone so much worse," he told Jillian. Everything seemed to be in its normal place around the porch. "It doesn't look like Kemp even came up to the house," he said, easing the door open just to be safe.

The sound of toenails clicking on hardwood met them as Frankie sprinted down the hall and launched herself at him. He was already on one knee and ruffled her neck as he caught her to him. "Good dog." He looked up at Jillian and tilted his head toward the kitchen. "Laundry room's off the kitchen and her food is in the canister next to the dryer. Would you mind tossing a few scoops into a baggie and grabbing her water dish and leash while I do a quick check around the house?"

"I'm on it," she said, already moving toward the kitchen and yanking open the drawer that held the baggies.

Frankie raced along at his heels as he flipped on lights and poked his head into each room. He grabbed his toothbrush and a clean set of clothes, then met Jillian back by the front door. She had a baggie full of food and the dog's things in her hands and was already hurrying down the porch steps as he closed and locked the door behind them.

"Come on," she said, practically running down the driveway toward the truck. "I don't want that poor horse to be in that disgusting trailer any longer than she has to be."

"I agree," he said, yanking open the door and whistling for the dog. Jillian was already climbing in the other side as Frankie jumped onto the seat. Turning the truck around, he floored it, making it to Bryn's in less than four minutes.

Knox had the trailer backed up to the barn and was just bringing the horse out when they pulled up. Ethan rolled down the windows and told Frankie to stay in the truck before getting out to help the other deputy.

"You have any trouble with her?" Ethan asked, pulling open the barn door.

"None at all. She seems like a sweet horse and really docile." The deputy gingerly stroked his hand over her dirt-caked neck.

"She's probably just so happy to get out of that filthy trailer. I can't believe how disgusting Kemp let it get." Fury rose in Ethan, and he fisted his hands at his sides. "It makes me want to toss Kemp in there for a few days and see how he likes it."

Knox grimaced. "I'll help you do it."

Ethan pushed the anger back. He needed to focus on the horse. "Give us a minute to get a stall set up for her."

Jillian had already opened a stall door and was dragging a bale of hay into it. Ethan helped her to spread it over the floor and fill the troughs with fresh food and water, then Knox led her in.

"She's so thin," Jillian said, a tremble in her voice. "And her poor coat is full of dirt and mud and…"

Ethan put an arm around her. "I know. I want to clean her up too, but I think she's been through enough tonight. She's got fresh water, and you gave her some sweet feed and some hay. Let's let her get settled tonight, then we'll get her all fixed up tomorrow."

Jillian nodded, then turned toward Knox. "Thanks so much. For all your help."

"Don't mention it. I only wish I could do more." He waved his hand toward the trailer. "I'm gonna take this over to the impound lot, then get Martinez to run me back out to my cruiser. I wouldn't worry about coming in tonight, Ethan. We can get your statement in the morning."

Ethan left Jillian in the barn and followed him back toward the truck. "Thanks again, Knox. I want to get this guy on everything we can. Not just the attempted robbery but the animal abuse and cruelty too."

"I'm with you, brother."

Ethan watched him pull away before heading back into the barn. He'd been out to Knox's ranch many times and knew the deputy had a soft spot for animals. Besides having a horse of his own, he had a dog he frequently brought into the station with him.

"How's she doing?" Ethan frowned at how stiff Jillian's shoulders were as she watched the horse greedily wolf down the feed.

"She's eating like her life depends on it. Which it looks like it does."

They'd only given her a small amount to start with. "Let's make sure she keeps this down, then I'll come out again in an hour or so and give her another few handfuls. Why don't we give her a little space for now, let her settle in while we get cleaned up." Between the scuffle with Kemp and help-ing with the horse and trailer, they'd both gotten covered in muck and dust.

"Yeah, okay," she said, her voice flat as she absently rubbed at a smudge of dirt on her arm.

"You all right?"

She walked past him and headed toward the bunkhouse. "Yes. No. I don't know." She wrapped her arms around her middle. "I just want to take a hot shower and wash the stink of that asshole off of me."

"Let me get Frankie, and I'll meet you in the house."

The shower was running by the time he grabbed the dog and her stuff, locked up his truck, and walked into the bunk-house. Frankie jumped onto the couch, pawed at the throw pillow, and settled into the corner as if she lived there.

Ethan could hear the water through the just-open crack in the bathroom door as he set Frankie's things on the counter and pulled off his boots. He left them next to Jillian's sneak-ers by the front door and padded down the hall. Leaning his head toward the door, he was getting ready to call out to ask her if she was okay again when he heard her sob.

Pushing open the door, his heart broke as he saw her leaning into the wall of the shower, her shoulders shaking as another hard sob stole through her.

Shucking his clothes, he stepped into the shower behind her, gathering her into his arms and holding her against him. Her arms went around his back and she clung to him, sob-bing into his shoulder. The warm water beat against them as he pressed a kiss to the side of her head. "It's okay, darlin'. I got you."

CHAPTER 18

"I was trying to be so strong," Jillian explained twenty minutes later. She was curled on the sofa clutching her brush, her hair in a towel and her body wrapped in a soft terry cloth robe. Ethan was in the kitchen preparing two cups of tea.

"I know," he said, gently taking her brush from her hands and replacing it with a warm mug.

She took a sip as he set his mug on the coffee table then sat down beside her. "But then I thought about you going after that guy and carrying a gun. And then I saw you on the ground, and then *I* was holding a gun on an actual person." Her body convulsed in a shudder. "Not that I would deem that guy much of a person. Part of me wishes I would have shot him, at least in the leg or something."

"I hear you. After the way he treated that horse, I wish I would have shot him too." He slid the towel from her head, tossed it on the table, then gently pulled the brush through her hair.

"How could someone be so cruel to an animal? He was trading her life for some cash." Her hand fluttered to her mouth as her heart started racing again. "And he was trying to steal Nudge and Buddy to sell them too. If we hadn't stopped by at just that exact time, he would have done it. Our horses might have already been dead by now."

Ethan wrapped an arm around her shoulders and touched his forehead to hers. "But we *did* get there at the right time. And our horses are safe. It all turned out okay."

"But what if it hadn't?" She touched his swollen cheek as her voice dropped to a whisper. "What if something had happened to you?"

"But it didn't. I'm fine. The horses are fine. We did a good thing tonight. Not only did we save Nudge and Buddy, we saved another horse. And put a bad guy behind bars."

"How do you do this every day?"

"I don't do *this* every day. Most days I deal with routine stuff like noise ordinances and traffic violations."

"So you're not constantly in danger?"

"Not unless you consider filling out a lot of forms dangerous. Although last week I did have to deal with a woman who'd had her shed broken into."

"By an armed criminal?"

"No, by a bear. That's where she kept her birdseed." He turned her back around and worked through a tangle in her hair. "Jillian, I'm a deputy sheriff. Sometimes my job is dangerous. But the majority of my time is spent helping people. Remember, you drove by me last week when I was helping old Doc Hunter after he'd accidentally driven his riding lawn mower into the side of the Tasty Freez."

She laughed. "Why did he even *have* his lawn mower at the Tasty Freez?"

"According to him, he'd just finished mowing his lawn and had a craving for a root beer float."

She closed her eyes and reveled in the delicious feeling of him stroking her brush through her hair. "I can't believe you're brushing my hair."

He set the brush on the coffee table, then leaned back against the sofa. "I know. I'm not sure why, but I was holding the brush and it seemed like the right thing to do."

"It was. It was perfect." She nestled into his shoulder. "You're kind of perfect," she said softly into his chest. Tilting her face up to his, she looked into his gorgeous blue eyes and saw such tenderness there, it hurt her chest. Emotion burned the back of her throat, and she feared she might start crying again. "I could really fall for you, you know?"

His lips curved into a roguish grin. "That's what I'm hoping for."

―――――――

The next morning, Frankie followed Jillian into the kitchen as she went in search of coffee for her and Ethan. Frankie was such a cute little dog, with her curly brown hair, expressive eyes, and her eagerness to please. Jillian tossed her one of Gus's dog treats from a canister on the counter.

"Coffee ready?" Ethan asked, coming down the hallway. His hair was still damp from the shower, and he smelled like soap and shampoo.

"Almost," Jillian said, turning to grab a couple of mugs

from the cupboard. She gripped the counter and let out a gasp as she looked out the window and saw an unfamiliar gray truck parked outside of the barn. "Ethan," she whispered pointing toward the truck. "Is that Kemp? Or someone else here to steal Bryn's horses?"

"Hey, it's okay," Ethan said, putting an arm around her shoulders. "That's Knox's rig. You know, the deputy you met last night."

"Yes, I remember who Knox is. I wasn't *that* freaked out. But what's he doing here? Do you think Kemp escaped last night and he came out to warn you?"

"The barn door's open, so it would be weird if he were trying to warn me from in there." He crossed to the front door and pulled on his boots and hat. "Best way to find out is to ask him."

"I'm coming with you." Forgetting about the coffee, she followed him toward the barn, thankful she'd already gotten dressed in shorts and a T-shirt. She rubbed the sides of her arms as if she were cold. "I don't know why I'm so jumpy. I'm normally pretty calm in stressful situations, and I'm usually the first one marching in to tackle tense stuff."

"Don't beat yourself up," Ethan told her. "That was more than just a stressful situation last night. There was a gun involved and that can mess with your emotions."

She let out her breath and tried to release the tension in her shoulders. "Thanks."

"Knox?" Ethan called out as they entered the barn.

"In here," the deputy answered from inside the rescued horse's stall. "Hey, guys. Hope it's okay I stopped by. I couldn't stop thinking about this horse last night and what bad shape she was in, and I wanted to check on her this morning."

"Sure, it's fine," Ethan told him.

"I brought her a couple of apples and some carrots," he said. "She loves them."

"Wow. That was so nice of you," Jillian told him, crossing to the stall and reaching out to pet the horse's neck.

The deputy shrugged. "I had the morning off anyway. And like I said, I couldn't stop thinking about her. I brought over my farrier tools and thought I'd clean up her hooves and see if she'd let me brush her. If that's okay with you all?"

Ethan glanced at Jillian first, then nodded in agreement. "Yeah, that's great. I noticed last night her hooves were in bad shape. She's gonna feel better just getting them cleaned up. But I think she's gonna need more than a brushing. I was thinking we'd hose her down this morning and try to wash some of that stink off her."

"Good idea," Jillian said. "I saw some animal shampoo in the tack room."

Knox grinned, and Jillian noticed what a good-looking guy he was. Almost as tall as Ethan, he was dressed similarly in jeans, cowboy boots, and a T-shirt, the sleeves hugging his substantial biceps. He had an easy smile and a smudge of whiskers that matched the dark hair showing under his Stetson. "Great. I'd like to stay and help if I can."

"Yeah, we'd be glad to have you," Ethan said. "We were just grabbing coffee, then we'd planned to come out and feed the horses and take care of the morning chores."

Knox held up his hand. "I don't want to get in the way of your coffee."

"I was going to make us something to eat," Jillian told them. "Why don't you start feeding the animals, and I'll run back to the bunkhouse. Give me fifteen minutes, and I'll bring out coffee and some breakfast burritos."

"That sounds great," Ethan said.

She turned to the other man. "Knox, can I interest you in one?"

Ethan jerked a thumb toward the other man. "I've never seen Deputy Garrison turn down an offer of food."

Knox tilted his hat toward Jillian. "I don't want you to go to any trouble, but I wouldn't say no if you're making them anyway."

Twenty minutes later, Jillian walked back into the barn carrying a small box holding three travel mugs of coffee and several foil-wrapped breakfast burritos. She wasn't a whiz in the kitchen, but she could do scrambled eggs with ham and cheese, and her breakfast burritos were one of Milo's favorite meals.

The radio in the tack room was tuned to a country station, and she laughed as she could hear both men singing along to an old Garth Brooks song. "Breakfast's ready," she called to Knox, who was gingerly running a brush over the new rescue's coat, and Ethan, who was breaking apart bales of hay and filling the troughs of the other two horses housed in the barn. "I didn't realize I was gonna get a concert with my meal. You two ever think about going on the road?"

"And give up our sweet government jobs for the fame and

fortune of being rock stars? No way," Ethan teased her as he brushed his hands off on his thighs. "Your timing is perfect though. I just finished feeding all the horses." He waved his hand toward the open side door of the barn that led into the corral. "I tossed a bunch of hay in the troughs out in the corral and that dang goat of Bryn's just jumped up in the trough and was standing there eating while the horses filed in and just ate around his skinny legs."

"Bryn said he does that all the time. We saw him do it a few days ago. It cracked Milo up." She passed Ethan a coffee. "I called Brody while I was up at the house and asked him if he'd have a few minutes to look in on the new horse when he drops Milo off this morning. He said he'd be glad to, and would bring her some dewormer and have some antibiotics on hand if she needs them."

"That's perfect," Knox said. "I got her hooves trimmed and cleaned up, and she's been letting me brush her. I think she'll be okay getting a bath. For everything she's been through, she's still a real sweetheart." He nodded his thanks to Jillian as he took a mug of coffee. "Now that I've brushed some of the dirt away, I can see her coat's a real pretty reddish brown, so I was thinking we could call her Sienna. Unless you all had something else in mind."

"I love it," Jillian said, passing each of the guys a foil-wrapped burrito. "I hadn't even thought about what we'd call her, but Sienna sounds perfect."

"I agree," Ethan said before biting off the end of his burrito. He groaned. "This is amazing."

They sat on stacks of hay bales to eat their breakfast, then brought Sienna out into the side corral and tied her to the fence. She stood docilely, calmly eating slices of apple from Jillian's palm as Ethan and Knox wet her down with the hose and soaped up her coat.

Jillian held her other hand up to block the sun from her eyes as she peered around the horse's neck. "She seems to be handling the bath okay. I don't think it's even making her nervous."

"She's doing great. It seems like she's loving the attention, *and* the apple slices, you're giving her," Ethan said, dropping his hat on Jillian's head as he crossed to the spigot on the side of the barn. "I think she can handle a little more water pressure now, and we'll get her cleaned off quicker."

"Yeah, she's good." Knox rubbed a hand down her soapy neck as he sprayed the hose over her coat.

Between the sounds of the radio playing and the water running, Jillian didn't know anyone had pulled up to the ranch until she saw her sister come walking around the corner of the barn. Carley must have stopped in on her way to the salon because she looked adorable in a short white sundress and thick wedge sandals. Her long blond-streaked hair shone in the sunlight, and she'd styled it in big soft spirally curls. Brody, Mandy, and Milo were a few steps behind her.

Jillian raised her hand to wave. Her sister raised her hand back just as Knox lifted the hose to wash off the horse's back. The water pressure kicked in at the same moment, and the spray shot over Sienna's back. Carley let out a shriek as the water hit her square in the chest.

"What the heck?" Knox's eyes went wide as he rounded the front of the horse to see Carley standing on the other side of the fence. Her soaked white dress had gone practically transparent and her red bra and matching bikini panties were clearly visible. His mouth dropped open, then he closed it, then opened it again, as if he couldn't remember how to form words.

"Oh, shoot," Jillian said, climbing over the fence to help her sister as her son burst out laughing. She'd caught the laughter on Ethan's face too but he had the good sense to stay on the other side of the horse.

"Oh my gosh, I'm so sorry," Knox finally managed to say. He passed the hose to Ethan and climbed over the fence after Jillian.

"It's just a little water," Brody said, walking up to Carley. Then he caught sight of her front and covered his eyes with his hand as he turned his head away. "Oh. My."

"You can totally see your underwear," Milo said, pointing at his aunt as he bent double with laughter.

Carley's mouth was open too as she stood frozen in place, her arms outstretched as if she'd been trying to ward off the water.

Mandy jumped in front of Carley, extending her arms out as if trying to block everyone's view.

Jillian finally reached her sister and put an arm around her, turning her away from the fence and the deputy who didn't seem to know what to do with his hands as he reached out, then pulled them back, then reached out again. "Let's go up to the bunkhouse and find you some dry clothes. You can borrow something of mine." She swatted at her son as she walked by him. "Quit laughing at your aunt."

"But…her underwear…" He fell into another fit of giggles.

"Why don't you guys focus on the horse? We'll be back in a few." Jillian led her sister across the yard and up the steps into the bunkhouse. "Sorry, sis. At least he didn't squirt your hair."

Her sister looked down at herself and pulled her clinging dress away from her skin. "No, this is much better than getting my hair wet. I'd so rather have my nephew, my veterinarian, my sister's new boyfriend, and some super-hot guy see my red lacy underwear than have to dry my hair again."

Jillian cringed. "Yeah, not an ideal situation. But your hair does look amazing today." Frankie jumped off the sofa and ran a circle around their legs, hoping for a pet. She leaned down and gave the dog a scratch as they walked down the hallway, even though it had been less than an hour since she'd seen her last. Opening the linen closet door, she grabbed a towel and passed it to her sister. "And also, Ethan is not my new boyfriend."

"Oh? You mean you've already moved him to *old* boyfriend status?" Carley smiled at her as she pressed the towel to her soaked dress.

"No, I mean he isn't my boyfriend at all."

"Oh, yeah, right. Keep telling yourself that. Or maybe you should tell Ethan that since he's the one who's asked you to marry him twelve times."

"Not twelve times. Only three."

"Wait, three? Last I heard it was only two." Carley peered

around the bunkhouse as if looking for evidence of a proposal. "What happened last night to make him propose again? Were you wearing the black-and-gold BatChick underwear? I told you they were sexy. To nerds anyway."

"Ethan isn't a nerd. And no, I wasn't wearing any of the superhero underwear." She turned her face to the side and tried, unsuccessfully, to hold back a smile. "Actually, I wasn't wearing any underwear at all when he asked me the last time."

Her sister's eyes widened, and she swished the end of the towel toward her. "Okay, forget my stupid dress. Tell me everything."

Jillian laughed. "Don't you have to go to work or something? I'll tell you all about it later."

"Okay. I can wait. But you're not wiggling out of this one. I expect details," Carley said, pulling her dress over her head as she followed her sister into her bedroom. She rifled through Jillian's closet, pulled out a red sundress, and wiggled into it. "For now, you can tell me who the hot guy was who sprayed me with the hose."

A knock sounded from the front room, and Knox's voice carried into the bedroom. "Jillian?" he called into the house.

"Be right there," she answered as she gave her sister a thumbs up at the dress, then left the bedroom.

Knox had his hat in his hands as Jillian let him in the front door. A lock of his black hair fell across his forehead, and Jillian was pretty sure he blushed as Carley sashayed into the living room a few seconds behind her. And yes, her sister was doing all kinds of sashaying. "I'm awful sorry I sprayed you with the hose, ma'am."

Carley's eyes widened, and she planted a hand on her hip. "I'll forgive the hose thing if you promise never to call me 'ma'am' again."

Knox's lips tugged up in a grin. "Yes, ma'am...I mean, yes, okay. What should I call you?"

"I don't really care, honey, as long as you call me." Carley may have actually batted her eyelashes.

"This is my sister, Carley Chapman," Jillian said, stepping in to save the deputy. "She runs Carley's Cut and Curl downtown. Carley, this is Deputy Knox Garrison."

Even though his hat was in his hands, Knox tipped his head as if he were wearing it. "Pleased to meet you, Miss Chapman. And I do hope you can accept my sincerest apologies. I swear I did not see you on the other side of that horse."

Carley waved his concern away. "I accept. And I'm fine. Like Brody said, it was just a little water."

"Maybe I could buy you a coffee sometime to make up for my mistake. Or dinner?"

"Maybe you could," Carley said with a nonchalant shrug of her shoulders. "But for now I've got to get to work. I've got a client meeting me at the salon in fifteen minutes." She turned and gave Jillian a quick hug. "I just wanted to make sure you were okay after last night."

"I'm fine," Jillian told her as they all trooped back outside and headed toward Carley's car. "I'll call you later."

"You don't have to," Carley said as she opened her car door. "I'll be back out for supper. Tell Milo I'm picking up cheeseburgers from the diner and to text me what kind of shake he wants." She gave a little wave to Knox, who was standing next to Jillian, then got in her car and took off.

"Wow," Knox said, as they walked back toward the corral. "I feel like I just got whipped around in a tornado. But like, in a good tornado kind of way."

Jillian raised her eyebrows as she peered at him. "A *good* tornado?"

He laughed as he shook his head. "Okay, yeah. That sounded weird. But you know what I mean."

She nodded. She knew *exactly* what he meant.

Brody was just finishing his exam by the time they reached the fence of the corral. "Other than being malnourished and her upkeep neglected, she's not in too bad a shape. I think cleaning her up and the work Knox did on her hooves will help her disposition, and she seems to be managing the food you've given her. You all are doing the right thing by going slow and letting her body adjust. I gave her a dewormer, talked through the feeding schedule with Ethan, and took some samples. I'll run her bloodwork and get back to you all and Bryn in the next day or two."

"Thanks, Brody," Jillian told him. "And thanks for keeping Milo last night. We'll plan to take Mandy to the pool with us later this week."

"Sounds good. And he was no trouble. We love having him. And Applejack was a perfect gentleman. The three of them, plus the two puppies, slept out back in a tent." After waving goodbye, the veterinarian and his daughter took off.

Ethan had taken Sienna back to her stall and come out of

the barn to where Jillian and Milo were standing with Knox. "I should probably take off," he said. "Let you two get on with your day. But I can come back over tonight to help if you need me."

"I'll text you and let you know," Jillian said. "Bryn and Zane are supposed to get back sometime tonight." She needed to call them and tell them about the new horse.

Ethan nudged Milo's arm. "I was going to ask you if you'd be willing to watch Frankie for me during the day tomorrow. I've got to be out of town all day. I talked to your mom, and she said she's okay with it if you are. And I would pay you, of course."

Milo frowned. "No way."

"Oh, okay. No problem. I can ask someone else."

"No, I mean no way, you don't have to pay me. I love your dog. She can hang out with me and Gus whenever she wants." He nodded to the puppy, who had his paws on the lowest rung of Tiny's sty as he and the pig sniffed at each other's noses. "And Monday is our Funday, so it's perfect."

"Why? What happens on Funday?"

"Mom has Monday afternoons off, so we get takeout or order pizza and get to spend the whole afternoon just lying around and reading. It's the best. And Frankie will fit right in."

Ethan nodded. "She is pretty good at lying around."

Knox frowned. "So you all have a *whole* day dedicated just to reading? And you think that sounds like fun?"

"I *wish* it were a whole day," Milo said. "But usually it's just for the afternoon."

"I think it sounds awesome," Ethan told them, and Jillian's

heart melted just a little more at the way he stood up for her son. "Can I come over and hang out on a Funday with you guys sometime?"

Milo shrugged. "Sure. Just bring a book."

CHAPTER 19

Taco Tuesday was in full swing when Aunt Sassy and Carley walked in the door a few nights later. Bryn crossed the room to take the cardboard box Sassy was holding and gave both women a hug.

"Sorry we're late," Carley told the group of women already sitting at the table. "It's my fault. I had an emergency color situation. One of the Baker girls tried to dye her ends pink and they ended up bright orange."

"Oh no," Elle said, jumping up to get them each a margarita. "What did you do?"

"I used a purple hair system on her, then gave her an adorable cut that got rid of the majority of the ends. Thankfully, she *and* her mom were happy with the results. But it made me late to pick up Aunt Sassy."

Sassy took the offered drink and sank into the chair next to Jillian. "It worked out fine. I needed the extra time to finish printing out the flyers for Ethan's campaign." She nodded to the box over the rim of her glass as she took a sip. "Hope you girls are up for some envelope stuffing tonight."

"Envelope stuffing?" Jillian said. "Why?"

"Because we need to get these flyers out as soon as possible."

"But why are *you* printing out flyers for Ethan's campaign?"

"Because I'm on his campaign committee. Geez, where have you been?"

Obviously not in on the conversation where everyone else, who took this knowledge in stride, must have been. "Okay, we can come back to that information later, but now I'm back to why do we need to send flyers out for him at all?"

"Because we need to bolster his reputation. We've already scheduled him for extra appearances at the Women's Club, the Rotary, the Elks Lodge, *and* he's cutting the ribbon for that new bakery downtown next week. He's a hometown hero, especially after saving that horse the other night, and we need to remind the town of that. They need to be thinking about all the good things he does for us instead of focusing on all the garbage that came out in that article today."

Jillian's heart skipped a beat. "What article? What kind of garbage?" She prayed it didn't have to do with her or Rad.

"It came out in the paper this morning," Elle said. "I figured you saw it and we just weren't talking about it."

Jillian shook her head. "No, my day was crazy at the library today. I stopped at the bunkhouse to check on Milo and change my clothes, then I came straight here."

Bryn got up and rummaged through the stack of mail on the counter. "Here it is," she said, holding up the weekly edition of the *Creedence Chronicle*.

Aunt Sassy snatched it from her hand. "Don't even waste your time reading the article. It's all drivel. I'll bet my best girdle that no-good snake Conway Peel had something to do with it. I remember him running for city council a few years back. He pulled out all the stops—digging into the past of the other candidates and sneakily leaking all sorts of stuff about them. He's a real weasel."

"But what does it say?" Jillian asked, her pulse pounding through her chest. "Does it have to do with me? Or Milo?"

Aunt Sassy's features softened, and she passed her the paper. "Oh no, honey. I'm sorry. It doesn't have anything to do with you. It's about Ethan's past. It's trying to claim that Ethan is soft on criminals because he was trying to help out an old friend."

"Soft on criminals?"

"It's laughable," Elle said. "We all know Ethan is a total stand-up guy. He apparently went down to testify in some guy's parole hearing yesterday. And the article claims that since the guy used to be a friend of Ethan's, he somehow goes easy on criminals he knows."

"Ethan went to a parole hearing yesterday?" Jillian asked.

Elle nodded. "I figured you knew that too. Didn't you say you and Milo watched his dog yesterday so he could go out of town?"

"Yes, and he told me he was going to Cañon City to see a friend. But he didn't say the friend was *in prison*." She swallowed. "Isn't Cañon City where the state penitentiary is? And the supermax prison where all the really violent criminals are?"

"Yes, but that's not where Ethan's friend is," Bryn told her. "Brian is at one of the medium or lower security ones, Fremont Correctional, I think. And he's not a bad guy. We went to school with him. He and Ethan were good friends growing up. Brian just got into some trouble a few years ago."

"What did he do?"

Bryn wrinkled her nose in concentration. "If I remember right, it seems like he got messed up with drugs and got caught trying to steal his neighbor's television. He had a bunch of drugs on him, so I think they got him for theft and possession. But I heard his mom talking about him at the diner the other day, and she said he's really gotten his life together. Which I'm sure is why Ethan went down to testify at his parole hearing. Because he would want to help him. Not because he's soft on crime."

"It's all nonsense," Aunt Sassy said. "Which is why someone needs to pass Carley and me some tacos so we can eat and then get to work stuffing these envelopes. We need to have this mailing ready to go out tomorrow."

"Okay, we're on it," Nora said, passing the women the plate of tacos. "Is there something else we can do to help with the campaign, Aunt Sassy?"

"Sure. There's always something to do. We set up Ethan's campaign headquarters in the back offices of the Elks Lodge. There's always room for folks who want to make calls, help with the polling, knock on doors, or put signs up. Lots of volunteers come in there to help. Even some of the other deputies."

Carley looked up from her taco. "Other deputies? Maybe I should stop in and help. I'm always looking for volunteer opportunities."

Jillian arched an eyebrow at her sister. "Especially opportunities that might involve a certain cute deputy who happened to see your underwear this weekend?"

Carley grinned. "That deputy also sent a gorgeous bouquet of flowers to the salon yesterday."

"Hold up," Bryn said, reaching for the margarita pitcher. "Underwear? Flowers? I leave for two days and I miss everything." She refilled Carley's glass. "Swill it and spill it, girl."

———

The next morning, Ethan had just come out of the barn after feeding and brushing his horses when he saw Jillian's car pull into his driveway. A flurry of butterflies took off in his gut and his palms started to sweat.

When would his body stop reacting so strongly to the presence of this woman? He hadn't gotten butterflies over a girl in years. Yet every time he was about to see the curvy librarian, the things took off in his stomach, swirling and dive-bombing his gut as if they were trying to get out.

His lips were already curving into a smile as she exited her car and strode to him. But that smile fell at the serious expression on her face.

"Hey, Jillian," he said, trying to keep his voice light. "I wasn't expecting to see you out here this morning."

"I wasn't expecting to watch your dog while you went down to testify for a parole hearing."

Ah. "You saw the article, I take it." Was that why she hadn't texted him back the night before?

She planted a hand on her hip. "Yeah, I saw it. Why didn't you tell me that's why you were going to Cañon City?"

"I did. Sort of."

"You said you were going down to see a friend."

"I did see him."

"At his *hearing*." Her voice raised an octave.

"Okay. You're right. I probably should have told you. I guess I didn't want you to worry. Or think less of me."

"Think less of you for trying to help your friend?"

"Sounds like you've been talking to Aunt Sassy." He scrubbed a hand across his jaw. "More like because I had a friend who was serving time."

"I don't care about any of that. I've had friends of questionable standing too."

"Brian Ross is of a little more than 'questionable standing' status. But we grew up together. He used to be my best friend."

"Then I think it's good you went to help him."

"But?" He could already feel the word coming on. She was shifting from one foot to the other, and she hadn't come any closer to him.

"But I still think this is too much."

"Too much?"

"Yeah, too much. This article stinks of that Conway Peel. The other night, he was threatening to dig into your past, and it looks like he's making good on that threat."

"Is that what this is about? Con playing dirty politics? He's an idiot. Who cares about him?"

"I care about him. And I care about what he can do to both of us. That's why I told you the other night that we need to cool things between us. But now I think we need to stop altogether."

"*Stop*? You mean stop seeing each other?"

"Yes. Ethan, you told me how much this election means

to you. I don't want to be the reason you don't fulfill your dream of becoming the sheriff like your dad."

"That's nuts. How could you and I seeing each other mess that up?" He took a step toward her, but she backed away.

"You know how. This guy seems slicker than a pocketful of pudding, and he is trying to dig up any dirt on you he can find. And we both know he doesn't have to dig very far to figure out the baby daddy of the woman you're seeing is in prison for an armed robbery that included hostages and a guard getting shot."

"So what?"

"*So what*? So, besides the fact that people may question your judgment, I'm also the new head librarian and my son is just starting school in the fall. I don't want a bunch of rumors going around that could affect my job or his life *or* cause you to lose the election. There are just way too many negative variables to make this all worth it."

"But I care about you, and I think we have something pretty great here, so that makes it worth it to me." The butterflies had changed into a ball of anxious nerves. Was she really shutting them down before they'd even had a chance to see where this could go? He took another step closer, close enough to reach her, and he pulled her into his arms. "Jillian. I don't care what anyone thinks or says about me. I'm falling in love with you, and that's all that matters."

"That's *not* all that matters." He heard the tremble in her voice, and she reached up to touch his cheek. "I'm sorry, Ethan. We can't do this. It's too risky. For all of us, but especially for you. I wish I could just tell you to fall in love with me *after* the election, but even then, you're still going to be under the microscope. Plus you're going to have the really important job of taking care of this town. I just can't get in the way of all that. I care about you too. I do. That's why this is so hard."

Was she really breaking things off with him? For good? This felt different from the other night—like a pizza and a cute line wasn't going to win her over this time.

"No, Jillian. This isn't hard. This is easy. We're good for each other. This is right. Don't do this."

"I don't want to. This is tough on me too. But I can't be responsible for you losing out on your dream." She pushed up on her toes and pressed a kiss to his cheek. "I'm sorry, Ethan."

He tried to hug her but she pulled away and got into her car. Slamming the door, she started the engine and then drove away, leaving him standing in the driveway wondering what the hell had just happened.

———

Jillian went through the next few days as if on autopilot, going to work and taking care of Milo, and doing her best not to think about a certain cowboy.

"I don't know what's wrong with me," she'd told her sister when she'd stopped by the night before. "I think I'm coming down with something. I swing from fine to totally crabby in seconds, I'm not sleeping, I'm not eating, and what I do eat makes me feel sick to my stomach. So I'm walking around either angry, tired, or nauseated, none of which is good for anyone in my life."

Carley had only laughed. "Poor girl. Sounds like you're coming down with something, all right. But it's not the kind of bug medicine can fix. I guarantee it's from the breakup with Ethan. It's called being *lovesick*."

Jillian had only groaned. She didn't have time to be lovesick or any other kind of sick. She had a job to do and her son to take care of.

She still wasn't feeling better that weekend when she walked down the hall of the assisted living center with a stack of books for Amos. He was the last one on her bookmobile route that day, and she hoped the visit with the old codger would cheer her up.

She was expecting to see Amos sitting in his chair with his pajamas and cowboy boots on, but she wasn't expecting to see the curly brown dog stretched across his lap with her head resting lovingly on his chest.

The dog looked up when she walked in, letting out a happy whine as her tail thumped Amos's bed.

"Hey, handsome. What's Frankie doing here?" she asked, reaching out to greet the dog, her pulse already racing at the idea that Ethan might be in the assisted living center and the dog must have got away from him.

Amos's brow furrowed as he scratched the dog's chin. "You mean Francesca? Nobody calls her Frankie except my grandson."

"Your *grandson*?" A dawning realization hit her like a brick to the chest as the door of Amos's room opened and Ethan walked in carrying a juice box and a bag of crackers.

"Sorry, Gramps, all they had were the cheese crackers, no

peanut butter." He stopped as he saw Jillian standing next to the dog.

"What are you doing here?" was all she could ask, but the answers were toppling over her like dominoes falling in a line.

"I'm visiting my grandpa. What are *you* doing here?"

"Apparently I'm visiting your grandpa too. Well, I'm bringing him some books. He's on my bookmobile route. And he's my friend."

Ethan's glance bounced from Amos to Jillian, then back to Amos again. "You told me a pretty gal had been bringing you books, Gramps, but you never said she was a librarian." Ethan laughed as he passed Amos the juice box and snacks. "You always were a sly one with the ladies, but I'm afraid this one's taken."

It was Jillian's turn to cock an eyebrow. "Oh really?"

Ethan nodded. "Yeah, really."

Amos held up his hand. "Hold up now. Are you telling me my grandson is *your* fella? The one you've been telling me about?"

She shrugged.

He turned his gaze on Ethan. "And this is the gal you've been clamoring on about for weeks now? The one who's got you all moony-eyed and falling in love?"

"Moony-eyed's a bit of a strong interpretation," Ethan protested.

But falling in love wasn't?

Amos slapped his leg, startling the dog as he let out a hoot of laughter. "Well, ain't that a helluva thing?"

"That wasn't exactly what I was gonna say," Jillian muttered.

"I've been trying to convince her to meet my grandson for weeks." He nudged Jillian's leg with the toe of his boot. "I told ya he was a handsome devil, didn't I?"

"Oh, you told me all right." And Ethan looked particularly handsome today. He wore jeans, boots, and a button-down blue collared shirt that made his eyes even more cerulean.

Amos frowned. "Now, hold on a minute. Ethan's just been telling me that the little gal he's falling for doesn't want to see him anymore. But that's you." He cocked his head at Jillian. "And you've spent the last few weeks telling me about how much you like this new guy. What gives?"

Ethan sat on the chair across from Amos's bed and peered up at Jillian. "Yeah, what gives? I for one think you should tell us a little more about how much you like this new guy."

"I *do* like this new guy," she told Amos, ignoring Ethan. "Which is why I'm backing off. I told you about my past, and with all the attention Ethan is getting with the election, I don't want something in my past to affect his chances of winning. Or mess up my new job. Being together could hurt both of us, but mainly it could be the cause of him not achieving his dream of becoming sheriff."

"She's upset about the article in the paper about Brian Ross."

"Only because it proves someone is digging up dirt on you and making you look bad for going to that parole hearing."

"But you *had* to go to the hearing," Amos said. "You owe that boy."

She frowned. "*Owe* him?"

"Didn't you tell her what he did for you?"

Ethan sighed. "No, Gramps. I haven't ever told anyone but you."

"Well, yeah, sure, I'm not talking about *that*," Amos said, obviously trying to backpedal. "I was just talking about what a good friend he was to you in school."

"It's okay, Gramps. I trust her," Ethan said, turning to face her. "You remember I told you how I got drunk and got into some trouble after I broke it off with Tina, the woman I was engaged to?"

She nodded.

"Well, Brian's the one I got into trouble with. It was the middle of the night, and we went looking for the guy she'd been…you know. I don't remember what we were going to do, but I was piss-drunk and looking for a fight. He lived in an apartment above the tire store. He wasn't there, and I'm ashamed to tell you we trashed his place. We didn't know we'd tripped the alarm at the tire store until we heard the cops pull up. Brian knew how much trouble I could get into—I hadn't been with the sheriff's office long. So he helped me escape out the back, then he surrendered himself to the police. He took the fall for me."

"What happened to him?"

"He spent a couple of days in jail, did some community service, and paid a fine."

"Which *you* took care of," Amos interjected. "*And* you

helped him do the community service. I remember you boys cleaning up all that trash along the highway."

"I don't want credit for that. He wouldn't have had to do any of that if it weren't for me." He hung his head. "After that, everything changed. Brian had met this guy in jail who he started hanging out with, and the guy was into drugs and that whole scene."

"Then Brian didn't want to be around Ethan because he started using and selling drugs himself."

"That was my fault too. I was involved in my own life, and didn't realize how bad it had gotten until they hauled him in for stealing that television. But going to prison was a real wake-up call for him, and he's changed and gotten his life together. Which is why I felt compelled to testify at his hearing."

"Of course," Jillian agreed. "I believe you did the right thing. And I admire you for sticking up for your friend. But this just shows how the press and some reporter can take a situation like that and turn it into something negative about you. I'm glad you told me, and I won't tell anyone else, but this just proves my point that they can easily twist *my* past and use it to hurt you. And I just can't be the one to mess up your chances to win this race."

―――――――――

Jillian wasn't feeling any better by the time Taco Tuesday rolled around, and she barely touched her food as Nora, Bryn, Carley, and Aunt Sassy gabbed about some funny thing that had happened at the salon that day and a big sale they were having downtown at the Ladybug Dress Shoppe.

Elle breezed in as they were cleaning up. "Sorry, gals. Meeting ran late." The light floral scent of her designer perfume wafted around them as she dropped her purse on the sofa, then grabbed a chip from the bowl still sitting on the kitchen island. "What'd I miss?" Bryn held up the pitcher of margaritas, but she shook her head. "Just water for me tonight."

"What's up with you? You didn't drink last week. And come to think of it, I don't think you drank the week before. And I know you weren't driving then." Bryn's eyes widened as if she'd just figured something out. And a broad knowing grin spread across your face. "Oh my gosh, Elle. Are you…?"

Elle tried unsuccessfully to hold back her smile as she nodded. "Yes. I am."

Bryn let out a squeal and threw her arms around Elle. "I'm so happy for you."

"What are we happy about?" Aunt Sassy asked, drying her hands on a towel as she turned from the sink. "Spill it. I want to be happy too."

Elle ducked her head as if suddenly shy. "I'm pregnant."

The kitchen erupted in cheers and hugs.

"I'm so happy for you too," Jillian said, hugging her friend. Elle had been through a lot in the last several years, including two miscarriages, before meeting and falling in love with Brody. "I'll bet Brody and Mandy are over the moon."

"They are. We all are. We weren't really going to tell anyone, until I was further along at least. Until we felt more confident that everything would…you know."

"It's all going to go great," Bryn said. "I have the best feeling about this. And we won't say a word until you give us the go-ahead."

Elle pointed at Aunt Sassy. "That goes for you too, Miss Sassy. You can't tell anyone, at least for the next few weeks. I can't handle going through the pain of telling everyone I'm pregnant, then weeks later having to explain that I'm not."

"That's not going to happen this time," Aunt Sassy said, reaching out to squeeze her hand. "And you can count on me. I won't tell a soul. But only if you tell us every detail now."

Elle laughed, the giddy kind of laughter of someone who is truly happy. "I don't know what to tell you. It just happened. We weren't planning it or anything. I didn't even know at first, but I was so cranky and moody, like fine one minute and growling the next. I wasn't sleeping, and I'd pretty much lost my appetite, mainly because nothing tasted good and everything I ate just made me feel nauseated. At first I thought I was coming down with a bug."

"Hey," Carley said, pointing toward her sister. "Jillian just said the same thing to me. That's exactly how she's been feeling this week."

Jillian felt the energy drain from her body as she listened to Elle describe her symptoms. The group turned to her as a whole as she mentally counted out the weeks since her last cycle. "Oh. No. I can't be."

"I just saw you counting in your head," her sister said. "Are you late?"

"I don't know. I mean, I'm not always right on schedule, and my cycle has been really wonky with the stress of the new job and moving here. But I think I should've had it by now." She dropped her chin to her chest and let out a groan. "How did this happen?"

"Well," Aunt Sassy said, "when a man and a woman care about each other, they—"

Jillian held up her hand. "I know *how* it happened, but I just don't know *how* it happened. I mean, we used protection. So I can't be pregnant. It doesn't make sense. I probably just have the flu."

"We have to find out," Carley said. "You have to take a test."

Jillian chewed on a loose cuticle on her thumb, then shook her head. "I can't. There's no way. How am I going to even *get* a test? There's only two stores in this town that carry them, the grocery store and the drugstore, and I can't walk into either one of them and make that purchase. I'm a single mom, the head librarian, and rumored to be dating a deputy who is running for sheriff."

"So what are you going to do?" Sassy asked. "Just wait nine months and see if a baby pops out?"

"No." She dropped her head into her hands. "I don't know *what* I'm going to do."

"Well, I love you, Sis, but I can't go into any of those stores and buy you one either," Carley said. "I'm single too. But I run my own business, and I don't even *have* a boyfriend. How fast do you think the rumor mill would start about me?"

Sassy shrugged. "That actually might be *good* for your business. Everyone will want to come get a haircut or color just to see if you've got a bun in the oven."

"That's why I made that spontaneous trip to Denver a few

weeks back, so I could get a test in a store where no one knew me," Elle said. "Normally, I'd be happy to go buy you one, but I'm not really ready for everyone to know about me either. I wasn't even going to tell you all for another few weeks."

Aunt Sassy slapped her hand on the counter. "Oh, for mercy sakes, I'll do it. I can go buy a dozen pregnancy tests and no one's gonna reckon Doc Hunter got me knocked up."

Jillian lifted her head. "You?"

"Sure. It'll be easy." She reached for her purse. "I can be to town and back in fifteen minutes. Then at least you'll know."

"Okay. But let me give you some money to pay for it."

Aunt Sassy waved her hand in the air. "Don't worry about that. We'll settle up later."

Twenty long minutes later, she walked back in the door and held up a red plastic bag from the Creedence Country Market. "Easy-peasy. I grabbed them off the shelf and went through the self-checkout. I even got the multipack in case you need an extra. Or…" She looked around the room. "In case anyone else needs one."

Bryn shook her head. "Don't look at me."

Nora held up her hands. "Me either."

Aunt Sassy dug into the box inside the bag, pulled out an individually wrapped test stick, and held it out to Jillian. "It's better to know than to sit here and wonder."

Jillian snatched the test from her hand and headed for the bathroom. "I grabbed a carton of cupcakes for us to eat while we wait," she heard Sassy say before she closed the door. *Ugh.* Just the thought of sweet sticky frosting made her stomach pitch.

Five agonizing minutes later, bile rose in her throat as they all gaped down at the plus sign in the middle of the stick.

"Maybe it's a false positive," Brynn offered.

Sassy reached into the box and passed her another test. "Try again."

Thirty minutes later, the group stared at all six tests lined up on the counter, the plus signs clearly evident on every single one.

Jillian was finding it hard to breathe, and her cheeks were tingling like she was going to hyperventilate. What the hell was she going to do? Right now, she felt like she was going to hurl. She'd brought the small pink wastebasket from the bathroom out with her just in case.

The screen door slammed, and she froze as she looked up to see Ethan walking into the room. What was he doing here?

He wore a sheepish grin as he held up a yellow and black cordless drill before setting it on the kitchen table. "Sorry to interrupt girls' night, ladies. I promise I'm not staying. I just needed to return this to Zane." His grin changed to a frown. "What's wrong? Haven't you ever had a man horn in on Taco Tuesday? I promise I'm not here to abscond with the guacamole." His gaze bounced from one woman to another, then dropped to the row of pregnancy tests lined up on the counter. His frown changed back to a goofy smile. "Aww. Wow. Who's pregnant?"

His smile faltered as the seconds ticked by, and his gaze again moved from one woman to the next, finally landing on Jillian.

She still hadn't moved. At this point, she wasn't sure she even remembered how to breathe.

The color drained from his face. "You? But how?"

Sassy sighed. "Well, when a man and a woman care about each other…" she began, but stopped at Jillian's hard glare.

Apparently her face *could* still move.

"I know *how*," he said, echoing her earlier response. "But *how*?"

She lifted her shoulders in a small shrug. "I don't know. I thought we were careful. We used something every time. The only thing I can imagine is that one was damaged somehow or the first one from my purse was too old."

"Do those things have expiration dates?" Sassy whispered to Elle, who shushed her.

Sweat broke out on Jillian's forehead, and her belly pitched and churned. She clutched the empty wastebasket to her chest, willing herself not to vomit.

Ethan stared at her, holding her gaze for a long moment, his expression changing from bewildered to thoughtful, then softening in tenderness. He took off his hat as he walked toward her, then went down on one knee. "Jillian Bennett, will you marry me?"

Her stomach heaved, and she lost the battle as she threw up into the pink wastebasket.

CHAPTER 20

JILLIAN'S PHONE BUZZED. IT WAS ANOTHER TEXT FROM Ethan.

She knew she was being unfair—she hadn't talked to him since the night before when she'd humiliated herself by vomiting as an answer to his proposal. She'd run out of Bryn's, locked herself in the bunkhouse, and made Carley tell him she'd call him when she was ready.

She still wasn't ready. She didn't know if she'd ever be ready. This was not in her five-year plan.

But she couldn't ignore Ethan forever. He was a good man and didn't deserve that. She peeked at her phone.

Please, Jillian. You've got to talk to me sometime. Call me, the text read.

She pressed the phone to her chest and fought another round of tears. She wasn't normally a crier. She was a fighter, a single mom who got shit done. But this morning, she was just a scared woman, holed up in her bedroom and hiding under her covers.

She'd called in sick to work, and Elle had offered to keep Milo for a couple of days.

But he'd looked a little worried when she'd picked him

up that morning. "You sure you're okay, Mom?" he'd asked before heading out the door.

"I'll be fine," she'd assured him. "Just got a stomach bug. You go have fun. Don't worry about me. I'm gonna go back to bed and sleep it off."

This wasn't something she was going to sleep off. In fact, this was something that was going to affect her sleep for years to come. She groaned at the thought of late-night feedings and early mornings. For just a moment, her traitorous mind let in an image of Ethan walking the floor, crooning to a swaddled infant, his hair doing that cute bedhead thing where it fell across his forehead. And another of the handsome deputy with one arm around her, laughing as he and Milo played peek-a-boo with a happy chortling baby.

She pushed the images from her mind. Not that she didn't *want* to imagine a future with Ethan, she just didn't believe it could happen. Her getting pregnant during the first few months of them dating was like another nail in his election coffin.

But a baby brought the relationship she'd just tried to end to a whole different level. They were going to *have* to talk about it. Eventually.

She blew out a breath as she tapped a message on her phone. I know we need to talk. We will. I just need a little time. To think. And to see a doctor. I'll call you tomorrow. I promise. She pressed SEND before she lost her nerve.

She'd scheduled a doctor's appointment for the following afternoon. Not that she doubted the confirmation of *six* freaking tests, but she still wanted to hear it from a professional.

After that, *then* she'd call Ethan.

———

The next afternoon, Ethan's mind was trying to process a million things as he walked into his campaign headquarters. He knew he needed to keep his focus on the election. It was less than a month away. But all he could think about was Jillian. And the baby. *Their* baby.

At first he'd been shocked, then scared, then tendrils of excitement had started to seep through him like bindweed vines taking over a flower garden. No, the situation wasn't ideal, and they definitely had some logistics to figure out, like the fact that Jillian wasn't talking to him yet, but he was still happy.

He and Jillian and Milo were going to have a baby. They were going to be a family.

Those words just kept playing through his head, and he couldn't stop smiling as he wound his way through the tables holding campaign buttons and posters. He spotted Aunt Sassy across the room and headed toward her.

She was sitting at a desk, stuffing flyers into envelopes, but stood when she saw him coming and reached for his hands. "Hello, Ethan honey. How you holding up? About the *election*, I mean." She leaned closer and gave him an exaggerated wink when she said "election."

He gently squeezed her fingers before letting them go.

"It's all I've been thinking about. And to tell you the truth, I'm actually pretty excited about *the election.*"

"It would be normal if you were a little nervous."

"I am a little nervous too. But overall, I just feel happy."

Aunt Sassy beamed up at him. "I feel happy too." She leaned closer again and whispered, "Have you seen her today?"

He shook his head. "No. I just stopped in at the library hoping to catch her, but they said she called in again. She's not answering my calls, and I'm a little worried about her."

"Aren't you going to see her at her doctor's appointment this afternoon?"

He narrowed his eyes and nodded slowly. "Yes. Yes, I am going to see her at the doctor's office. What time was it again?"

"Two o'clock."

"Two o'clock. Yep, that's what I had down. And it was with Dr. Hollis?"

"No, Dr. Thomas."

"That's right. Now I remember." He checked his watch. Her appointment was in thirty minutes. "I was just getting ready to head over there now."

"You do that. And don't tell her you heard about the appointment from me." She winked again.

———

Jillian sent up another prayer as she sat on the examination table waiting for Dr. Thomas to come in. The nurse had already checked her in, then taken her vitals and a small vial of blood.

She was nervous and scared and fighting another bout of nausea when a knock sounded at the door. "Come in," she said.

The door opened, and her heart leapt in her chest at the sight of Ethan poking his head around the door. "Okay if I come in?"

She nodded, unable to speak from the emotion in her throat. Tears filled her eyes, and she pushed off the table and threw herself into his arms.

"Hey now, it's okay," he said, smoothing her hair. "I've got you."

"I didn't know how much I wished you were here until you walked in the door," she said into his shoulder.

"That's nice to hear. I wasn't sure if you were going to throw me out or begrudgingly let me stay, but this is much better than what I thought was going to happen." He pulled back, then frowned. "Except for the tears." He tenderly touched her cheek. "Please don't cry. This is all gonna be okay."

"How is any of this going to be okay?"

"Because it's you and me and Milo, and the three of us can handle anything. Together."

Two more tears rolled down her cheeks.

"Oh no. That was supposed to make you feel better, not cry more."

She brushed the tears from her cheeks with the back of her hand. "It did make me feel better. You couldn't have said anything more perfect. Most men don't understand that Milo and I come as a set. He's part of me and has always come first."

"As he should. He's your son. I get that. Remember, I was raised by a single mom."

"And Amos." She shook her head. "I still can't believe he's your grandpa." It made a lot more sense now why Ethan would propose to her so soon after they met.

"He and my Grandma Gert taught me everything I know about what love and a marriage look like. And that's what I want for my life. Gramps didn't care what anyone else thought, when my grandma needed him, he showed up." His voice hitched a little as he looked into her eyes. "And that's what I'm doing. I'm showing up."

"*And* you're making me fall even harder for you."

"It's okay for you to fall," he said, his voice a husky whisper. "I promise I'll catch you."

She laid her palm on the side of his cheek. "Oh, Ethan, you really are just the best man."

"The best man, huh?" He grinned as he pulled her closer. "I'm kind of giving it my all here to actually end up as the groom."

She smiled back, that blossom of hope blooming again in her chest. "I'll think about it."

His grin broadened. "Yeah?"

She nodded. "Yeah."

"That's the best progress I've made so far with a proposal, so I'm gonna take it." He leaned in and kissed her.

The kiss was sweet and tender and so full of love that it almost made Jillian cry again. She kissed him back, her carefully guarded walls of defense crumbling as she let herself melt into his strong arms. Ethan was kind and thoughtful and cared not just about her but about her son as well. That meant everything to her.

She pulled away and peered up at him, trying to convey the depth of her emotion in her eyes. "I've always kept my heart locked away, but for the first time in a very long time, I'm letting myself really imagine a future with you. I mean with us. Not just as a couple, but as a family—you, me, Milo, and…"

"And our baby," he said, finishing her sentence.

Panic tightened her chest again, and her hands began to tremble. "Our baby," she repeated in a whisper.

Ethan took her hands and held them in his, quelling their trembling. His grip was firm and strong and stable. He was someone she could count on, someone who would be there. And who wouldn't expect her to drive the getaway car if he decided to rob a bank. There was always that.

A knock sounded on the door, then it opened and an older man in a white coat stepped in, followed by the same nurse who had drawn Jillian's blood. His eyes widened when he caught sight of Ethan. "Deputy Rayburn. I wasn't expecting to see you here. Is there some kind of problem?" he asked, then his glance dropped to their joined hands and his eyebrows raised. "Oh. I see."

"Hey, Doc. You know you can call me Ethan. You've been playing poker with my grandpa almost every weekend since I was a kid."

"Even before that."

Ethan gestured to Jillian as she let go of his hand and climbed back onto the examining table. "This is Jillian Bennett. She's the new head librarian over at the library."

The doctor shook her hand. "Good to meet you, Miss Bennett. I'm Dr. Thomas."

"Nice to meet you too." Now that they were done with the pleasantries, she just wanted to hear the results, get a prescription for prenatal vitamins, and get out of this room. There were too many people in it and the air was starting to feel too warm. She eyed the trashcan and the sink and calculated which she could get to first as the nausea swept through her again.

"So Miss Bennett, I first have to ask if you're comfortable with me discussing your health in front of Deputy... erm...Ethan?"

"Yes, I'm fine. He already knows I'm pregnant. He's the father."

Dr. Thomas's brow furrowed. "Oh?"

"Yeah, I was there after she took the tests," Ethan explained. "I think she took six of them. And they were all positive. So I don't think you're gonna tell us anything we don't already know."

The doctor leaned back against the door. His tone was serious as he stared directly at Jillian. "On the contrary, I believe I am."

Bile rose in her throat as she was struck with a terrible foreboding. What could be worse than confirming she was pregnant? Was she having twins? She reached for Ethan's hand and held it tightly. He squeezed back and offered her an encouraging nod.

"I'm sorry to be the one to tell you," the doctor said, then looked at Ethan. "Or maybe I'm not, but you're not actually pregnant."

She jerked back as if he'd slapped her. "What?"

"You're *not* pregnant," he repeated.

CHAPTER 21

"YES. I AM," JILLIAN SAID, BEWILDERMENT AND A DEEP
sadness coursing through her. "Ethan just told you—I took
six tests two nights ago. And they were *all* positive."

Dr. Thomas shrugged. "Well, I don't know what to tell
you about that. Those over-the-counter tests are usually
pretty accurate. But apparently not in this case. I just did a
quantitative blood test, which measures the exact amount of
hCG in your blood, and I can confidently confirm that you
are *not* pregnant."

"But I've been cranky and can't eat or sleep. And I've been
nauseated for days. And I've thrown up. More than once,"
she explained.

"All symptoms that can be brought on by stress. Or you
could simply have a stomach bug. There has been a nasty
one going around that seems to hang on for a week or so.
We've seen several patients with your same symptoms."

Her same symptoms? Her symptoms were that she was
pregnant. She'd taken *six* freaking tests.

He took a step forward and pulled his stethoscope from
around his neck. "It sounds like something viral, but why
don't I do a quick exam just to check."

Ethan had let go of her hand and was leaning back

against the counter, a pensive look on his face as he stared at the floor. He didn't look up the entire time the doctor was listening to her heart and looking into her ears and throat, but she noticed his shoulders seemed to get more and more tense.

She barely heard the doctor's words as he repeated his diagnosis of a stomach bug or something stress-related, then suggested she get some rest and stick to the BRAT diet. She was familiar with the bananas, rice, applesauce, toast plan and had already been implementing it. That and several sleeves of saltine crackers.

Did she really just have a stomach bug? But the positive tests…?

Ethan was quiet as she followed him out of the doctor's office and to where he'd parked his truck next to her car.

"You okay?" she asked, resting a hand on his arm.

"I don't think so," he said, shrugging off her hand.

She assumed he was feeling the same kind of sadness she was, but there was anger in his eyes as he lifted his head and glared at her. "Why didn't you tell me about your doctor appointment today?"

"Why would I?"

"So I could be there."

"It never even occurred to me that you'd *want* to be. I thought it was going to be simple and quick. Plus I assumed you had to work." She hadn't really stopped to think about how he'd known to show up there.

"Are you sure that's why? Or was it because you didn't *want* me there? Because you knew what the doctor was going to say."

She jerked back. "What? No. I'm just as surprised as you are."

He shook his head slowly back and forth. "No. I don't think you are." He tilted his head, studying her as if she were a suspect under investigation. "Why did you suddenly change your tune in there, and now all of a sudden you *can* admit that you have feelings for me and might want to marry me? The timing feels a little too convenient."

"Too convenient? What are you talking about?"

"This is just starting to feel really familiar. Like I've been here before."

"Been *where* before? In this parking lot?"

"No. In this situation where my girlfriend is suddenly pregnant and rushing me into getting married."

"Me? Rushing *you*? I didn't even know you considered me your girlfriend!"

"Oh come on, Jillian. We talk on the phone almost every day. We've spent the night together, we've slept together multiple times. But now that I think about it, you have been all over the place. You say you don't want to get involved one day, then we're in bed together the next. Is this all just some kind of game to you?"

"No, of course not," she sputtered. She reached for his hand again, but he pulled it back and crossed his arms over his chest.

"You push me away, then bring me back. Was that your way of drawing me in and keeping me off balance so I wouldn't suspect anything when all of a sudden you say you do want to get married?"

Nausea swept through her again, and she reached out for the side of the car to steady herself. She couldn't believe Ethan was saying these things. "No."

"I really cared about you. But now I'm wondering if this was all just a big lie. Was this just some elaborate scheme to make me think you were pregnant and trick me into marrying you?"

"Well, it would have to be pretty freaking elaborate to fake six effing pregnancy tests."

"Yeah, I'm still not sure how you managed that."

"I *managed* it by peeing on them. All six. Oh, yeah, then I purposely spread them out on the counter for you to see, even though I didn't even know you were stopping by. Come on, Ethan."

She reached for him again. But he held up his hands and took another step away, and the pain in his eyes almost destroyed her. "No. I can't do this. I thought you were something special. I thought we had something special."

"We did. We do."

She'd been telling him they needed to back off, but this felt different. This felt like he was really ending things. And she hadn't realized how much she wanted this relationship with him to work until it started crumbling around them.

"I gotta go," he said, jerking open the door of his truck. "I need some time to think." He stared hard at her, as if trying to see the inner workings of her mind, then he shook his head. "I thought you were different," he said softly, before climbing into his truck and slamming the door.

"I thought you were different too," she whispered, her heart shattering as she watched him drive away.

———

Jillian was surprised to see Elle and Carley's cars parked in front of Bryn's when she pulled into the driveway ten minutes later. Exhaustion and sorrow weighed down her bones as she got out of the car, and all she wanted to do was go to sleep.

But first, she needed to figure out what the hell had happened with those tests.

Someone must have picked up Nora and Aunt Sassy, because they were sitting in the living room with Bryn, Elle, and Carley, drinking iced tea and laughing when Jillian pushed through the screen door.

"Hey, there she is," Bryn called, but the cheer in her voice faded out as she must have taken in Jillian's crestfallen appearance.

"Oh my gosh," Carley said, bounding up from the sofa and hurrying toward her sister. "Honey, what's wrong?"

Jillian let her sister lead her to the living room where she sank down onto the sofa. "Ethan broke up with me."

"What? Why? I thought he was happy about everything," Aunt Sassy said.

"I thought so too," Bryn added. "He asked you to marry him last night. Why would he break up with you today? Because you're pregnant?"

"No," Jillian answered. "Just the opposite. He broke up with me because I'm *not* pregnant."

Carley pulled her head back. "Umm...*yes*, you are. We all saw the tests."

Aunt Sassy nodded. "All six of them."

"Well, the tests were wrong," Jillian said. "The doctor did a blood test today, and he confirmed that I'm *not* pregnant. I apparently just have the flu."

Carley shook her head. "But how could the flu make six pregnancy tests come out positive?"

"I don't know. Maybe we did them wrong."

"Did you pee on them?"

"Yes."

"Well, that's basically the only step."

"Then maybe we read them wrong."

"Because a plus sign equals negative?"

Jillian sank back into the sofa cushions, the exhaustion seeping further into her bones. "I don't get it either. That's why I'm here. To see what the heck went wrong."

"I've still got the whole box of them," Bryn said, pushing up from the sofa. "I think I put them in the recycle bin, and we haven't taken that out yet." She disappeared into the laundry room, then came back out holding up the red grocery sack. "Here they are." She set the bag in the sink and dug through its contents. Pulling the box out of the bag, she let out a cry of surprise. "Oh. My. Gosh."

"What?" Jillian said, hauling herself out of the sofa cushions.

Bryn's eyes narrowed as she stared pointedly at Aunt Sassy. "Cassandra James. Were you wearing your reading glasses the other night when you picked out this box?"

Aunt Sassy shrugged innocently. "I'm not sure. I *might*

not have been. I told you I hate wearing them in public. They make me look old."

"You *are* old. And if you *would* have been wearing them, you would have noticed that you did *not* buy a multipack of pregnancy tests."

"Yes, I did," Sassy insisted. "There was a baby on the box, and it was full of those little pee sticks."

"Those pee sticks weren't *pregnancy* tests," Bryn explained, holding up the box. "They were *ovulation* tests. They all tested positive for Jillian because she must be *ovulating*."

"Oh. My. Stars." Sassy covered her mouth with her hand as she turned to Jillian. "Oh, honey. I'm sooo sorry."

Jillian sank back into the sofa again, completely befuddled as she muttered, "Ovulation tests?" She turned to her sister who had her lips pressed tightly together. She blinked at the incredulous idea that her sister was finding this even slightly amusing. "Are you *laughing*?"

Carley shook her head and covered her mouth to smother a small snort.

Jillian swatted at her leg. "This isn't funny."

Her sister ducked her head, still fighting a smile. "Oh, come on, it's a little bit funny…"

Laughter tugged at the corners of Jillian's lips, the absurdity of the situation bubbling up in her like a fizzy soda.

Carley couldn't hold it any longer and another snort of laughter broke free. The sound of it released something in Jillian, and the stress of it all gushed out in a burst of chuckles.

Then the room erupted into laughter as one by one the women collapsed into giggles or cackled with glee until they were all howling with laughter, doubled over, clutching their stomachs as they fought to breathe.

As soon as they started to get themselves under control, someone would spout off another comment or Carley would let loose another giggling snort, and they'd dissolve into fits of hysteria again.

"Oh heavens, I think I wet my pants," Aunt Sassy said, pressing her thighs together and sending the room into another wave of hysterical mirth.

One minute Jillian was laughing and giggling with the rest of them, then suddenly her laughter dissolved into crying and she was sobbing into her hands.

"Oh no," Carley said, scooting closer and putting her arms around her. "Oh, honey, it's going to be okay."

The laughter died as the women realized Jillian was crying.

"It's *not* going to be okay. Before I met Ethan, I was doing fine. I had my job and my son and friends. Then he strolled into my life and everything changed, and I found myself wanting things I hadn't dared to let myself even dream about before. I didn't even think I wanted to get married, and I know I didn't want to get pregnant, but the last few days I've let myself imagine a life, a family, with Ethan, and I realized that *is* what I want."

Bryn sat on her other side and passed her a tissue. "That's good then, isn't it?"

"No," she sobbed, pressing the tissue to her nose. "Because now it's all ruined. Ethan doesn't want anything to do with me. And I have this horrible ache in my stomach for a baby that I wasn't even pregnant with."

"Oh, honey, I'm sure you can work things out with Ethan," Aunt Sassy said. "That man loves you."

She shook her head. "Not anymore. Now he thinks I betrayed him. And that I was faking a pregnancy to try to trap him into marrying me."

"That's ridiculous," Carley said. "He's the one who's been proposing to you."

"That doesn't matter. The last woman he proposed to was trying to trick him into a quickie marriage because she was pregnant with some other man's baby."

"But you're not even pregnant," Elle said.

"And you would never do that," Nora added.

"It doesn't matter what I *would* do," Jillian told them. "It matters what he *thinks* I could do. And I get it. I have trust issues too. The last time Ethan let himself fall in love, his girlfriend totally betrayed him. And now it seems—to him, at least—that I'm doing the same thing. You should have seen how hurt he looked. He's such a great guy, and he's been nothing but amazing to me. It makes my heart ache just thinking about how much I hurt him."

"But you didn't do this on purpose." Bryn darted a glare at Sassy.

"That's right, honey," Aunt Sassy said. "We can fix this. You can just go tell him what happened. Or I can tell him. I'll take all the blame. Then he'll be mad at me."

Jillian shook her head. "No. You're sweet to offer. But it's better this way. Now he can focus on the election, and all my dirty laundry won't mess up his chances of winning."

"But he has to know that you didn't try to trick him," Carley said.

"No, he doesn't. He has to focus on his career and winning the sheriff seat. That's the most important thing right now. The election will be over in a few weeks, and I can talk to him then, *after* he's won."

===

The following Tuesday night, Jillian was in the kitchen stirring a pan of spaghetti sauce when Carley came through the door.

"Hey, girl. It smells amazing in here. You must be feeling better."

"I am. From the flu, at least." She wasn't nauseated anymore, but her stomach still hurt and so did her chest. She didn't need to tell her sister she was still reeling from the heartache of losing Ethan. Carley could read her mood and expressions from a mile away. Plus she'd spent close to an hour on the phone with her the night before lamenting about it.

Ethan hadn't called or texted since he'd left her standing in the parking lot of the doctor's office. And she hadn't messaged him either. He'd asked for time and space, and she would give them to him. With only a few weeks left in the race, he needed to focus on his campaign, not on her. She knew their split was for the best, but it still hurt like hell.

She was doing her best to stay busy—to do anything to keep her mind off the handsome cowboy. Which was why she was making spaghetti and homemade sauce for dinner tonight.

With Elle having a doctor appointment in Denver and

Bryn and Zane spending the afternoon at a cattle auction, they'd decided to cancel that week's Taco Tuesday night. Which was fine with Jillian. The women were her best friends, and it would probably be good for her, but she wasn't in the mood to try to pretend everything was okay.

She didn't have to pretend with Carley. They'd seen each other through plenty of break-ups and tough times, and her sister was good about knowing how to make her feel better without being pushy.

"I thought I heard you drive up ten minutes ago," she told Carley as she passed her a relish tray to put on the table.

"I did. But I saw Knox's truck out front and figured I'd mosey through the barn just to say hello."

"I didn't know he was here."

"He said he just stopped by to check on the horse again."

Jillian smiled. "I think he may be checking on you again." It was obvious the two had chemistry, and flirting with the deputy looked good on Carley. Jillian hadn't seen her this happy in a long time.

She turned as the screen door slammed and Milo walked in, the puppy in his arms and Applejack at his heels. "Hey, honey. How was the pool? Did you have fun with Mandy?"

Milo shrugged as he set the puppy on the floor. Gus ran through the kitchen, stopping first to sniff Jillian's shoes before going on the hunt for any fallen morsels.

Carley giggled over Applejack nudging her in the side. "This horse is so cute. I can't believe you just take him with you to your friend's house like he's a dog." She nuzzled the mini-horse's snout, then Applejack sauntered over to the table and snuck a carrot off the relish tray.

"Hey," Jillian said to her son, pointing at the carrot poking out of the corner of the horse's mouth. "What have I told you about not letting Applejack eat off the table?"

The horse turned to her and stopped chewing as he offered her a look of innocence.

"I saw you," she told him.

Milo leaned on the counter, his brow set in concentration as he studied her. "So, are you pregnant?"

Jillian dropped the slice of French bread she'd been about to butter. It hit the floor with a spray of crumbs, and both the puppy and the mini-horse went racing toward it. "No. I'm not," she answered, scooping up the fallen bread and tossing it in the sink, much to the disappointment of the puppy and the horse who were frantically licking the crumbs off the floor. "Who told you I was?"

"No one told me. I read it in the paper."

Her stomach dropped. "Excuse me?"

"Yeah, there was a big article about Ethan and you in today's paper."

Carley gasped. "Oh no." She hurried toward the door. "I think I've got a copy of it in my car. I'm pretty sure there was one in the stack of mail I grabbed on the way out here. I'll be right back."

Jillian sank onto the bar stool. "Are you sure the article was about me too?"

Milo nodded. "Oh yeah, took up most of the second page. A bunch of people were talking about it in the diner this afternoon when Mandy and I stopped in to get shakes. We found a paper someone had left on their table and read the whole article."

She buried her face in her hands. "How bad was it?"

"Not gonna lie. It was pretty bad. The first part was a bunch of stuff about my dad being a hardened criminal and doing time in prison for armed robbery."

Hardened criminal? She groaned. This was exactly the thing she was worried would happen.

"It got worse," Milo said. "The second part read like one of those magazines at the grocery store. It basically said you faked being pregnant to get Ethan to marry you. Are you and Ethan getting married?"

"No."

"I didn't think so. Not that I mind. I love Ethan—he's cool. I just didn't think you'd get married without telling me."

"You're right. I wouldn't. And I'm not pregnant either. I thought I was for like a minute, but I did *not* try to trick Ethan into anything. I took a test, well, six actually, and they all said I was. But I made a mistake, and I was taking the wrong kind of test."

"Mom, I learned about this stuff in health class. How could you take the wrong kind of pregnancy test? It seems like there *is* only one kind."

When did her kid get so smart?

She sighed. "It's a long story. But suffice it to say, it was all Aunt Sassy's fault."

"Ah." He nodded. "That makes sense."

"I'm sorry, honey. I should have told you about the

pregnancy thing. It was all a big mistake and totally embarrassing, but I still should have told you. I hate that you found out by reading it in the paper."

"I got it," Carley cried, holding up the paper as she ran back into the bunkhouse. She turned and used it to swat at Otis, who was trying to sneak in after her. "What is it with this goat? He was milling around by your porch when I got here, but now there's also a pig waiting at the bottom of the steps."

"That's Tiny. She and Otis must've smelled Mom's spaghetti sauce. We sometimes let them in to watch television with us while we eat supper," Milo explained. "They love *Family Feud*."

"Forget the pig and the goat," Jillian said, holding out her hand. "Give me the dang paper." Her sister passed it to her, and she spread it open on the counter and flipped to the second page.

"Thank God for small favors that at least it wasn't on the front page," Carley said, peering over her shoulder.

Jillian wasn't surprised that the byline was Cynthia Dresden, but she gasped at the absurdity of the headline. *"Small Town Deputy, Big City Scandal: They say you can't judge a book by its cover, but have we been reading our new librarian all wrong?"*

CHAPTER 22

AS MUCH AS SHE WANTED TO CALL IN SICK TO WORK the next day, Jillian had never been one to shirk her responsibilities. And no matter what the *Creedence Chronicle* said about her, she still had a duty and responsibility to the library.

That didn't mean she couldn't hide in her office most of the day, she thought as she strode through the library lobby with her head held high. It wasn't that difficult; there were only three patrons in the library: a harried-looking young mom with two toddlers in the children's section, and the mom appeared to have enough on her plate without worrying about Jillian's problems.

She had a little harder time meeting Hazel's eye as she approached the volunteer sitting at the reference desk. "Good morning, Hazel," she said, ducking past her as quickly as she could without seeming like she was outright running. "I'll be spending most of the day in my office today working on orders."

"Hold it," Hazel said, pushing up from the chair.

Jillian's shoulders sank as she stopped and turned back to the volunteer.

"Now don't you let some durn fool who thinks it's fun to rip into other people's lives scare you into thinking you have to hide in your office all day. You hold your head up today and show this town that a stupid article doesn't faze you."

Tears sprang to her eyes at the volunteer's support, and she blinked them back. "Thank you, Hazel."

The older woman hustled toward her and pulled her into a hug. She was so tiny, Jillian could put her chin on her head, but the support of the hug felt like it was being delivered by a giant. "Don't worry, honey," Hazel told her. "Nobody reads that drivel. And the ones who do will forget about it before you know it."

"I'm not pregnant, and I swear I wasn't trying to trick Ethan into marrying me."

Hazel held up her hand. "I know, honey. And you don't have to explain anything to me."

"Thank you."

"Besides, I'm friends with Sassy James and she already told me the whole story anyway." She winked as she smiled. "And not in a bad way. Sassy is singing your praises and telling anyone who'll listen that the story in the paper is a load of malarkey."

Oh, Aunt Sassy.

Jillian took a deep shuddering breath. "The problem is that some of it *is* true. I do have this scandalous background, and my son's father is in prison. I tried to leave all that behind me in California. I thought I could come here and no one would even care about what happened in my past, but maybe I *don't* deserve this job. That article claimed that I'm just as guilty of theft as my ex because I stole this job from a local. Maybe I should just quit and make everyone happy."

"Don't you dare," Hazel said. "That article is just a bunch

of poppycock. Don't you believe a word of it. You got this job because you earned it. I was on the hiring committee, and you were the best candidate by far."

"Maybe I was, but not now. Not with all this hanging around my head. And not if I've lost the trust of the parents and the kids and the patrons who use the library."

"You need to give Creedence a chance. I think this town will surprise you. There will be some that'll gossip, but a lot of people will ignore the story for the hearsay that it is. Believe me, there are plenty of folks around here with more than a few indiscretions in their pasts they'd like to forget. And I'll bet there'll be plenty who show up to support you. Some might even think the story is exciting. An ex in prison and a romance with a deputy—I think it makes you seem a little dangerous and gives you more street cred." She nodded wisely. "I heard that on television. Look it up. It's a thing."

Before Jillian could argue that she was far from being dangerous or having any kind of street cred, the front door opened and two women entered. They glanced around, then headed toward the reference desk when they spotted Jillian. She recognized them as a couple of moms who frequently brought their grade-schoolers in to attend her library programs.

"Miss Bennett," one of them said, holding out her hand to grab Jillian's. "We're glad you're here. We just wanted to tell you that we saw the article and thought it was terrible that someone would bad-mouth you like that."

"Our children love you, and you've brought life and fun to the children's library program that's been missing for years. We love it that our kids are excited about books and reading, and that's because of you."

They continued to talk over each other, not letting Jillian get in a word.

"We decided we needed to come down and sit in the library today to ward off anyone who might come in and try to say something mean to you," the first one said.

"Yeah, like we'll be your badass book-mom bouncers."

"But with better hair and wearing great shoes." The first one held up a small padded cooler. "We even brought our lunches so we can stay all day. Don't worry, we're not letting anyone cause trouble for you."

Jillian was so stunned by their offer of support, she didn't even say anything about the *no eating allowed in the library* rule. She might just make an exception today. At least for her book-mom bouncers.

The second one reached into her bag and pulled out a business card. "And I also brought my husband's card. He's a lawyer. He said you can call him if you want to sue the paper and that wicked Cynthia Dresden for slander."

"Thank you both so much," Jillian said, taking the card and tucking it into her pocket. "I wasn't planning on suing anyone. I just want everyone to forget about the article. And forget about me."

"Forget about you?" the first mom said. "No way. We adored you before. But now you've suddenly become a lot more interesting."

Interesting?

The second mom waved toward a table in the center of

the library. "We'll set up over here. Come over and chat if you get a few minutes free."

Hazel nudged Jillian in the side and winked at her again. "Told you so."

———————

That Saturday morning, Ethan's heart rate sped up as he walked down the hall of the assisted care center and saw the bookmobile cart sitting outside his grandfather's room. He wasn't trying to run into Jillian, but the thought that the librarian might still be here had his pulse racing.

He took off his cowboy hat and smoothed his hair before pushing through the door. "Hey, Gramps," he said a little too brightly. Then his shoulders dropped as he realized the librarian standing next to Amos's bed was definitely not Jillian. "Oh, hi, Hazel."

The older woman raised an eyebrow at him. "Well, gee whiz, don't act so excited to see me."

"Sorry, it's not that."

Her expression softened. "You were just hoping I might be the other librarian—the one with long curly hair that you happen to still be sweet on even though you told her you weren't anymore?"

Ethan scrubbed a hand across his forehead. "Dang. Is there anyone in this town who *doesn't* know everything about my love life?"

"I know you're not gonna have much of one if you don't apologize and go after that girl," Amos said.

"How can I? I don't know how to trust her after what she did."

"*She* didn't do anything," Hazel said. "It was Sassy James. She's the one who screwed up those tests. If you want to be mad at someone, be mad at her."

"How did Aunt Sassy screw up a bunch of pregnancy tests?"

"Because they *weren't* pregnancy tests." Hazel filled him and Amos in on the debacle with the reading glasses and the mistaken purchase.

Ethan sank into the chair opposite his grandfather's bed. "So Jillian really didn't know?"

"No. She was just as disappointed as you were that she wasn't pregnant."

I doubt that.

"How do you know all this?" he asked.

"Because Sassy told me. We play pickleball together Monday mornings, then we go out to brunch. She told me the whole story. And Jillian was just sick about the mix-up."

"Then why didn't she tell me about it herself?"

"Haven't you been paying attention at all, son?" Amos said, rolling his eyes in disgust. "She's told you a dozen times already. She's trying to protect you and give you a better chance at winning the election."

"Maybe. But thanks to that dang article, everybody and their dog knows our whole story. Why wouldn't she come to me after that?"

"Same reason," Hazel said. "She's trying not to make it worse. Plus she's embarrassed. I think she's just trying to lay low and hope this whole thing blows over. But she's really worried that the stuff about her hurt your chances."

"It didn't. In fact, you should tell her that it did just the opposite. People have been coming up to me all week telling me how much they respect Jillian and thought we were good together. More people are angry at Conway and Cynthia Dresden for orchestrating the trashy article than there are people upset about Jillian's past. My press guy said I'm up even further in the polls this week, so he thinks the article actually *helped* my campaign."

"And Sassy's been setting folks straight about that pregnancy thing all week," Hazel said. "I'm surprised you haven't heard about it by now."

He leaned back in the chair. "What am I going to do now?"

"Seems like you've got yourself in a fine kettle of fish," his grandfather said. "I think first you need to decide what you want."

"That's easy. I want Jillian. Always have. Even when I was royally pissed and accusing her of faking the pregnancy, there was still a part of me who knew she could never do that. I was just so danged shocked. And all that stuff with Tina came rushing back. Then I said a bunch of stupid stuff I don't know how to take back."

"I think an apology will go a long way."

"It's gonna take more than an apology to make up for what I did. And it's not like you and Grandma Gert. I can't just ride up in a beat-up old pickup and drive her off into the sunset to live happily ever after."

"Are you sure?" Amos asked. "Because there's all kinds of

'old pickups' out there. It doesn't have to be a truck that gets you to happily ever after."

———————

It took several days to put everything in place, but Ethan had come up with a plan. He walked into the courthouse that Tuesday morning, the envelope in his hand the last piece to his version of an "old pickup."

He still had a few things to do to really be ready, but this was an important one. This step was the one that would truly prove to Jillian that she and Milo were the most important things in his life.

He turned down the hall and was surprised to see Aunt Sassy sitting outside the door to the mayor's office, thumbing through a magazine. "Hey Aunt Sassy. What are you doing here?"

"Oh, hi, Ethan." She jerked a thumb at the closed door. "Just waitin' to talk to Eugene…er…I mean, Mayor Lloyd." She pointed to the light-blue envelope, the Sheriff Department seal prominently displayed in the corner, that he held in his hand. "Whatcha got there?"

He peered down at the envelope that held so much of his plans for the future. It wouldn't hurt to tell her. She was on his campaign committee, she'd find out soon enough anyway. "It's my official withdrawal from the race."

Her eyes widened. "The race for sheriff?"

He nodded.

"Oh no. Why?" She pressed her hand to her chest. "Not because of that stupid article."

"In a way, yeah, I guess. That article may have spurred my decision on. But I'm really withdrawing to prove to Jillian she's more important to me than the race or the election or being sheriff."

"Can't you just *tell* her that?"

"I could. But I think it'll go a long way further if I show her."

"But this is your dream, to build on your dad's legacy. Are you sure you want to give that up?"

"A hundred percent sure. What I really want is a life with Jillian and Milo. I'll still be a deputy sheriff and get to help people, and that's enough for me. At the end of the day, the job doesn't matter, the people do. I'm in love with Jillian, and sacrificing this job is my way of proving to her that she matters to me more than anything else."

"If you're sure..."

"I am." He gave her a rundown on the rest of his plans for the day.

"All right. Give it here then," she said, holding out her hand when he'd finished. "Sounds like you've got your hands full getting ready and you need to skedaddle, so I can give it to the mayor. I'm up next, but he's been in there a while and I don't know how much longer he'll be."

Ethan shook his head. "No, that's okay. I can wait."

She huffed. "What? You don't trust me now? I make one little mistake reading a label on a box and now I'm not capable of handing someone a gall-danged letter?"

He held his hand up. He did have a million more things to do. And Sassy loved Jillian, she would do what was best for her. He passed her the blue envelope. "Okay, fine. Take it. But make sure he gets it *today*." He narrowed his gaze. "I mean it."

"I'll give it to him as soon as I see him. I will. You can trust me."

―――――――

Jillian sat on her sofa that afternoon trying to read a book. And failing. She'd read the same page three times now. She just couldn't seem to concentrate. All she could think about was Ethan. And how she'd lost the best man she'd ever known.

But thinking about him being the "best man" only brought up more memories of his earlier proposals and of the time she'd called him the best man and he'd told her he was aiming to be the groom.

She let out a sigh, the sandwich she'd eaten an hour ago sitting like a rock in her stomach as she started over at the top of the page again. Milo was helping Zane work on the tractor in the barn, and she'd silenced her phone and drawn the curtains, trying to block out the rest of the world as she sulked and licked her wounds.

The sound of a car honking in the driveway got her up off the sofa and walking out onto the porch to see what was going on. She was surprised to see Elle's SUV pulling up in front of the bunkhouse. Nora was in the front seat and Aunt Sassy was in the back, crammed in next to about a million shopping bags.

She'd been sequestered inside for the last few hours, but now noticed that there seemed to be an awful lot of activity happening around the ranch. Cade's pickup was pulled up in front of the barn and the sound of hammering and the whir of a circular saw cut through the air.

Tiny was sitting on the edge of the porch, as if she were the official greeter to the newcomers. She had a new flower fastened to her ear, an elaborate glittery white and pink peony tied with satiny white bow.

"Well, aren't you looking fancy today?" Jillian asked.

The pig gave a snort and offered Jillian one of her trademark smiles.

The three women jumped out of the SUV and hurried toward her as Carley's car turned in and sped down the driveway. The screen door slammed at Bryn's farmhouse as she came flying out and practically sprinted toward the bunkhouse.

"What is going on?" she said, as the group of women came bustling up the steps. She might have been alarmed or wondered who died if they didn't all have weird goofy grins on their faces.

Her sister braked to a stop, then jumped out. "Has she read it yet?" she called, her voice a fever pitch of excitement, as she reached into the backseat and hauled out a giant bag of hair and makeup stuff from the salon.

Read what?

"Where's Milo?" Bryn asked, looking over her shoulder into the bunkhouse.

"He's with Zane. What is happening?" Were they planning some kind of surprise spa day to cheer her up? Is that why Carley had all that stuff? But why would they need Milo?

"There he is," Elle said, pointing toward the barn door where he, Zane, Gus, and Applejack had just emerged. "Hey Milo, come over here real quick."

Her son ran toward the porch, the puppy yipping and tumbling next to him and the mini-horse trotting along at his heels. "What's up?" he said as he scrambled up the porch steps.

"Don't look at me," Jillian told him. "I have no idea." But anxiety was starting to build in her chest.

"Why don't you sit down, honey?" Aunt Sassy told her, gesturing to the glider swing on the porch.

Oh no. It was never good when someone said to sit down before they shared what was going on.

She perched on the side of the glider. Milo must have felt the frenzy in the air because he lifted the puppy onto the cushion, then sat down next to her. Gus wiggled in between them to rest his head on Jillian's leg.

"Okay, I'm sitting," she said, her anxiety starting to rise. "Now somebody better tell me what the heck is going on before I scream."

"Okay, geez, calm down," her sister said, dumping the salon bag into the chair. "Somebody give her a paper."

A paper? Oh no. Her shoulders tightened as her nerves ramped up.

Nora passed her that day's edition of the *Creedence Chronicle*. "Page four."

Jillian held the paper in her lap, afraid to open it. "Don't tell me there's another article about Ethan and me."

"No. Something better," her sister said, practically shaking with excitement. "Just read it. Page four. You too, Milo."

Jillian took a deep breath, let it out slowly and opened the paper.

But nothing could have prepared her for what she saw inside.

CHAPTER 23

At first she couldn't figure out what she was supposed to be looking at as her eyes skimmed over the headlines. Then she saw it—a quarter page ad on the bottom right. Surrounded by a thick black box, her gaze caught on their names at the top of what looked like a form letter.

Milo leaned in closer, and Jillian blinked back tears as she read the words aloud.

Dear Jillian and Milo Bennett:

I know how important letters are to both of you so I thought this was the best way to publicly tell you how much I love you and to ask you both to marry me...one more time... but this time with the whole town as our witness.

Jillian, I am madly, desperately in love with you and don't want to go another day without you being my wife.

And Milo, I love you too, kid. I think you're awesome, and I want to spend every day trying to be the kind of dad you deserve.

Jillian, I told you once that it was okay for you to fall because I promised I would catch you, but today instead of falling, I want you to take a leap with me.

In the tradition of the men in our family, who know when we know, I'm asking you to jump all in and marry me TODAY.

I know how skittish you get, so don't overthink it, just show up.

If the answer is YES, meet me at the Heaven Can Wait Horse Rescue ranch at six o'clock and let's get hitched.

My Gramps said all we need for a wedding is some food, some flowers, and a whole lot of love, so I'll bring all the love in my heart and I'm inviting the whole town, anyone who wants to show up with a hot dish or a bouquet of flowers and a kind word to witness our union.

Hoping to see you there.

All my love,
Ethan

Tears were falling freely down her cheeks as Jillian read the letter a second time. She realized she was holding Milo's hand, and she squeezed it now as she looked down at him. "Well kid, what do you think? Should we marry this guy?"

"What do you think?" he asked. "You're the one who has to listen to him snore."

"Why do you think he snores?"

He shrugged. "On television, it seems like the dads always snore." He looked down at the letter, then back up at her. "Do *you* want to marry him?"

She nodded. "Yeah, I do. I'm madly, desperately in love with him too. And I believe he'd be a good dad, even if he snores. But you're my first priority, and if we do this, we do it together."

"I love him too. I say we go for it."

"Okay," she said, her face breaking into a happy grin. "I guess we're getting married today."

A round of cheers went up around them, and Jillian looked up to see her friends gathered around them and grinning like loons. She'd been so focused on the letter and on her conversation with Milo, she'd almost forgotten they were there.

"How long have you all known about this?"

"Ethan called us a few hours ago," Elle said. "We've all been racing around trying to get things ready. Nora and I have been pulling together decorations."

"And I've been prepping food," Bryn said. "And the guys are focusing on the music and all the setup."

"I think Ethan's got half the town working to pull this thing off," Aunt Sassy said.

Carley picked up her bag and opened the screen door. "I brought everything to do your hair and makeup, so my entire job is getting you and Milo ready. And we've only got two hours to do it so we'd better get a move on."

"Oh gosh. Okay. I guess we're really doing this." She pushed up from the chair, then stopped in her tracks. "Wait. What about a dress? Don't I need something to wear to this shindig?"

"Don't worry," Carley said. "I've got that covered too. Remember a few weeks ago when we were having lunch downtown and you saw that gorgeous white dress in the shop window and said wouldn't that be perfect for a summer wedding?"

Tears filled her eyes. Again. "You didn't?"

Carley grinned. "Oh, I did. It's in the car. We got clothes for Milo too. Now go get in the shower."

The next few hours flew by in a whirlwind of laughter, makeup, and hair products. The women had set up the front room of the bunkhouse as spa central, and Nora had painted her nails as Carley worked on her hair and makeup. Elle had helped Milo to get ready, and he was in his room, reading a book after promising not to get his clothes messed up.

It seemed that between her sister and their friends, they'd thought of everything.

"I brought you Grammy's pearls to wear," Carley told her, lifting a small satin jewelry box out of her bag.

"So that's something old," Jillian said, clutching the box to her chest.

"And the dress is something new," Elle added.

"So now I just need something borrowed and something blue."

"Oh, I've got both of those covered," Sassy said, reaching for her purse and pulling out a light-blue envelope with the sheriff department emblem in the corner.

"What's this?" Jillian asked, turning the sealed envelope over in her hands.

"It's a letter Ethan wrote to the mayor withdrawing his name from the race for sheriff."

"What? Why would he withdraw his name?"

"For you. I was sitting outside the mayor's office this morning when he brought this in. He told me he was giving up the position to prove that you and Milo were more important to him than any job."

"Oh gosh. I would *never* want him to do that."

"I know," Aunt Sassy said. "That's why I never gave it to the mayor, and I took it with me instead." She winked. "See, something 'borrowed' *and* something blue."

With only thirty minutes to go, Elle, Nora, and Sassy headed over to Bryn's to get dressed, leaving Jillian alone with her sister to finish getting ready.

They stood in her bedroom, both staring at the gorgeous white dress that hung on the closet door. It was simple, yet elegant with touches of lace embellishment.

"You're going to look beautiful," Carley said, wrapping an arm around her sister's waist.

"I can't believe I'm getting married," Jillian said. "And I couldn't have done any of this without you. Heck, I wouldn't even be in Colorado if it weren't for you." She turned and pulled her sister into a hug. "Thank you for everything you've done today. So far, you've done everything exactly as I imagined my wedding would be, even down to the colors."

"That's because we've been talking about our weddings since we were little girls and playing dress-up. It wasn't that hard. I knew you would want pink and white, and you practically picked that dress out yourself."

"Well, I hope you have a gorgeous dress here for you too, since I'm going to need you to be my maid of honor."

Carley grinned and pulled a beautiful flowing pink sundress from the closet. "As luck would have it, I did happen to buy a new dress for me too. I was just waiting for you to ask."

They laughed as they hugged again. Then Jillian turned toward her dresser. "Okay, now which mock superhero undies should I wear for today?"

"Forget those. I bought them for you to wear when you need to feel brave, but you don't need them today. I feel like you're going into this with your eyes wide open, and you're brave enough on your own."

"I really do love him."

"I know you do. And he loves you. Which is why it doesn't matter which pair of undies you pick. Because I doubt you'll be wearing them for very long." She grinned as she peered into Jillian's drawer. "But you should still pick those white lace ones."

"Good call."

"And I know that Sassy already gave you something borrowed, but I also brought you my white cowboy boots, just in case you wanted to borrow those as well."

"The ones with the silver embroidery?"

Carley nodded. "I thought they'd be fitting since you are marrying a cowboy."

"They're perfect."

It was five till six when Carley straightened the rhinestone tiara nestled in her hair, then Jillian opened the front door and stepped out on the porch. Her hand flew to her mouth as she gasped at the transformation of the ranch.

The grassy meadow next to the farmhouse had been mowed and chairs were set up on either side of a burlap and lace lined aisle leading to a giant cottonwood tree. One huge branch jutted out to the side and pink and white flowers were affixed to the trunk and up along the edge of the branch, then a long flowing length of fabric was wrapped around it, then draped down one side to form a gorgeous arch. Mason jars containing glimmering tea lights hung from the other branches of the tree.

It was all so beautiful, it took her breath away.

Twinkling fairy lights crisscrossed above a dance floor and stage that had been set up in front of the barn. And she could hear the low melodic strains of a cello playing somewhere—the music floating to her on the gentle summer evening breeze.

Milo was waiting for her on the porch holding a gorgeous bridal bouquet filled with pink and white roses and wrapped in a satiny pink ribbon. Gus and Applejack were with him, both wearing matching white bow ties around their necks.

"Wow Mom, you look like a beautiful princess," Milo said as he handed her the bouquet.

She leaned down to hug her son. "Thanks honey. You sure you're ready to do this?"

He grinned up at her. "Heck yeah."

She squeezed his hand as she looked out over all the people still busily putting the finishing touches on the preparations. Everything was perfect and beautiful, and she couldn't imagine how they all pulled it together. It looked like half the town was there helping, from Bryn's coworkers from the diner, to Sassy's actual nephews, the James brothers and their significant others.

Her closest friends stood in a group gathered at the base of the porch steps. Bryn and Zane, Brody, Elle, and Mandy, Cade and Nora and his daughter Allie. Even Hazel was there.

Jillian let out a happy gasp at the sight of the elderly man standing next to Hazel, wearing a light gray cowboy hat, a pink rose boutonniere in his jacket, and a proud grin the size of Montana on his face. "Amos, you handsome devil, who broke you out?"

"I needed a best man, didn't I?" a man's voice said, stepping out of the crowd.

"Ethan," she breathed his name, her heart taking flight at the sight of him in jeans, boots, a white button-down shirt with a white vest, and a white cowboy hat on his head.

His gaze held all the love she felt as he peered up at her. "Wow. You look amazing."

"So do you."

His gaze dropped to her son. "Hey kid."

Milo, who was dressed in an outfit similar to Ethan's, ran down the stairs and threw his arms around the deputy. "Thanks for the letter. We really liked it."

"I'm glad. I meant every word of it. I know I'm marrying your mom, but I aim to be the best dad to you that I know how."

With Milo at his side, Ethan approached Jillian, and drew a small ring box from his pocket. He bent to one knee as he pulled the lid open and held it up to her. Inside was an antique engagement ring with a solitaire diamond at its center and two smaller diamonds set into either side of the band. "It belonged to my grandmother," he said, turning his head to smile at Amos. "Gramps gave it to me to give to you."

"Oh, Ethan, it's perfect," she said, the sentiment of his grandmother's ring touching her heart.

"So is that a yes?"

"Not yet. First, I need you to do something for me." She took the folded blue envelope her sister was holding and held it out to him. "I'll only say yes if you rip this up and agree to stay in the race."

His eyes widened as he saw the envelope. "How did you…?" Then they narrowed as he turned to level a stare at Aunt Sassy. "You were supposed to turn that in to the mayor."

"I must've forgot," Sassy said with an innocent shrug. "Apparently I'm getting old."

Ethan turned back to Jillian. "I handed in my withdrawal to prove to you that you and Milo are more important to me than any job."

"I think you've proved plenty to me." She peered around at the festive wedding preparation. "And that *job* is import-ant to you. I don't want to stand in the way of you fulfilling your dream."

"Building a life with you and Milo *is* my dream."

"Then tear up that envelope and put that gorgeous ring on my finger."

He laughed as he handed the ring to Milo. "Hold this a second." He took the envelope from her, ripped in half, and then dropped it on the porch by her feet. Taking the ring back, he held it out to her once again. "Jillian Bennett, I love you with everything I have, and I want to spend the rest of my life with you. I know I'm asking you to take a big leap here, but I promise I'll spend every day of my life showing you that it was worth it. I know I've asked you before, but I'm asking one more time. Will you marry me?"

She beamed down at him, her heart overflowing with so much love for him. "I love you with everything I have, too."

"So is that a yes?"

She took a deep breath and this time she answered, "Yes, yes, a thousand times yes."

Then she took his hand, and she leapt.

━━━━━━━

Two weeks later, the society pages of the *Creedence Chronicle* featured this story.

The Town of Creedence Gives 'Credence' to Our Newest Blessed Union

Gabby Grapevine here, the *new* reporter for community happenings, happily reporting that our newly elected sheriff, Ethan Rayburn, has left for a long honeymoon with his blushing bride, our favorite head librarian, Jillian Bennett Rayburn.

After the whole town gave 'credence' to their blessed union, the happy couple and their son, Milo, took off to spend time camping in the mountains.

It was leaked to this reporter, but hasn't been confirmed, that along with two dogs, a cat, and Ethan's grandpa, Amos, that a mini-horse may have accompanied them on their honeymoon trip as well.

Signing off for now, but this new society writer is wondering who will get married next...

THE END...
...AND JUST THE BEGINNING

ACKNOWLEDGMENTS

As always, my love and thanks goes out to my family! Todd, thanks for always believing in me and for being the real-life role model of a romantic hero. You make me laugh every day and the words it would take to truly thank you would fill a book on their own. I love you. *Always.*

I can't thank my editor, Deb Werksman, enough for believing in me and this book, for loving Ethan, Jillian, Milo, and Applejack, and for making this story so much better with your amazing editing skills. I appreciate everything you do to help make the town of Creedence and my motley crew of farmyard animals come to life. Huge thanks to Dawn Adams for this gorgeous cover and every other awesome cover you've given me! I love being part of the Sourcebooks Sisterhood, and I offer buckets of thanks to the whole Sourcebooks Casablanca team for all of your efforts and hard work in making this book happen.

A big thank you to my parents—all of them. I appreciate everything you do and am so thankful for your support of this crazy writing career. Special thanks goes out to Dr. Rebecca Hodges, my sister, and Dr. Bill Bryant, my dad, for always being willing to listen and offer sound veterinarian council when I call with frenzied questions about my farmyard crew of animals and rescues.

Enormous shout-out to my plotting partners and dear friends Ginger and Annie. The time and energy you take to talk through scenes and run through plot ideas with me is invaluable. Your friendship and writing support mean the world to me—I couldn't do this writing thing without you. Annie—thank you for the amazing writing retreat marathon we had while I worked on this book—for the cookies and the pizza and the margarita-fueled sing-along! For the late nights and the Pico-cuddles and the constant encouragement—you are the best! Don't stop believin'!

Huge thank you to my agent, Nicole Resciniti at The Seymour Agency, for your advice and your guidance. You are the best, and I'm so thankful you are part of my life.

Special acknowledgment goes out to my writer besties—the women who walk this writing journey with me every single day—the ones who make me laugh, who encourage and support, who offer great advice and sometimes just listen. Thank you, Michelle Major, Lana Williams, Anne Eliot, and Ginger Scott. XO

Big thanks goes out to my street team, Jennie's Page Turners, and to all of my readers: the people who have been with me from the start, my loyal readers, my dedicated fans, the ones who have read my stories, who have laughed and cried with me, who have fallen in love with my heroes and have clamored for more! Whether you have been with me since the first book or just discovered me with this book, know that I write these stories for you, and I can't thank you enough for reading them. Sending love, laughter, and big Colorado hugs to you all!

ABOUT THE AUTHOR

Jennie Marts is the *USA Today* bestselling author of award-winning books filled with love, laughter, and always a happily ever after. Readers call her books "laugh out loud" funny and the "perfect mix of romance, humor, and steam." Fic Central claimed one of her books was "the most fun I've had reading in years."

She is living her own happily ever after in the mountains of Colorado with her husband, two dogs, and a parakeet who loves to tweet to the oldies. She's addicted to Diet Coke, adores Cheetos, and believes you can't have too many books, shoes, or friends.

Her books range from Western romance to cozy mysteries but they all have the charm and appeal of quirky small-town life. She loves genre-mashups, like adding romance to her Page Turners cozy mysteries and creating the hockey-playing cowboys in the Cowboys of Creedence. The same small-town community comes to life with more animal antics in her new Creedence Horse Rescue series. And her sassy heroines and hunky heroes carry over in her heartwarming, feel-good romances from Hallmark Publishing.

Jennie loves to hear from readers. Follow her on Facebook at facebook.com/jenniemartsbooks, or Twitter at @JennieMarts. Visit her at jenniemarts.com and sign up for her newsletter to keep up with the latest news and releases.

RELENTLESS IN TEXAS

Bestselling author Kari Lynn Dell puts you right in the
middle of the action with her thrilling Texas Rodeo series!

Gil Sanchez was once rodeo's biggest and baddest hotshot. Now he's
thirteen years sober and finally free of the pain that ended his sky-
rocketing career. Given one last shot to claw his way back to rodeo
glory, he can't let fantasies of happily-ever-after dull his razor edge...
but Carmelita White Fox is every dream he's never let himself have.

Carma may come from a Blackfeet family noted for its healing
abilities, but even she knows better than to try to fix this scarred,
cynical cowboy. Yet she's the only one who can reach past Gil's
jaded armor. Gil needs Carma just as much as she needs him, but as
the pressure builds and the spotlight intensifies, they'll have to fight
like hell to save the one thing neither can live without.

"Look out, world! There's a new cowboy in town."
—Carolyn Brown, *New York Times* bestselling author,
for *Tangled in Texas*

For more info about Sourcebooks's books and authors, visit:
sourcebooks.com

COWBOY TOUGH

Sparks fly in this opposites attract cowboy romance
from bestselling author Joanne Kennedy.

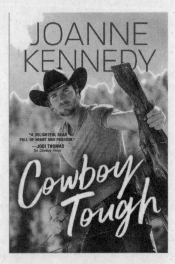

Mack Boyd might be able to ride a wild stallion to a standstill, but
he won't ever say no to his family. When his mother asks him to
help manage the family ranch, Mack arrives just in time to prepare
for an upcoming artists' retreat and to meet Cat Crandall, a pas-
sionate art teacher who can't be more different from him. But when
the ranch is threatened financially, can Mack and Cat set aside their
differences and work together?

"Full of heart and passion."
—Jodi Thomas, *New York Times* bestselling author,
for *Cowboy Fever*

For more info about Sourcebooks's books and authors, visit:
sourcebooks.com

CHARMING TEXAS COWBOY

At Big Chance Dog Rescue, you can always count on a cowboy to teach you a thing or two about life and love...

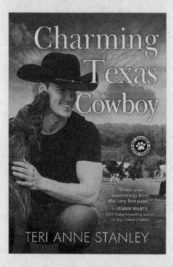

After an embarrassing blunder on her web show, lifestyle influencer Jen Greene attempts to outwait her notoriety by homesteading in Chance County, Texas. Jen has never lived this remotely before, but she doesn't want—though she might just need—help from Tanner Beauchamp, the handsome cowboy army veteran who lives down the road.

"A real page-turner with a sexy cowboy you can root for."
—Carolyn Brown, *New York Times* bestselling author,
for *Big Chance Cowboy*

For more info about Sourcebooks's books and authors, visit:
sourcebooks.com

COWBOY HEAT WAVE

Love is catching fire in Kim Redford's
Smokin' Hot Cowboys series.

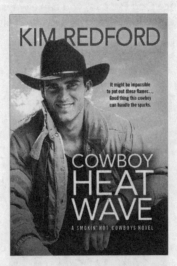

When Audrey Oakes witnesses a mustang herd theft, she looks to hunky cowboy firefighter Cole Murphy for help. Cole is out to protect the last of his mustang herd, and he isn't sure that Audrey is an innocent bystander. But he does know two things—that Audrey is hiding why she's really in Wildcat Bluff County. And, that there's a red-hot connection between them…

**"Scorching attraction flavored with just
a hint of sweet innocence."**
—*Publishers Weekly*, Starred Review,
for *A Cowboy Firefighter for Christmas*

For more info about Sourcebooks's books and authors, visit:
sourcebooks.com

JACKSON

From award-winning author LaQuette: Can he learn
to trust love, even when the law tells him not to?

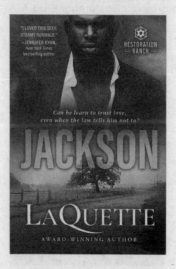

Texas Ranger Jackson Dean doesn't trust love. He made that
mistake once, and eight years later he was still paying the
price. So when he's tasked with finding out who is vandalizing
Restoration Ranch, a place where ex-cons can go to reinvent
themselves, he has a hard time believing in second chances...
until he meets Aja Everett, a former criminal attorney whose
passion for rehabilitation just might be Jackson's key to finding
love again.

"I loved this sexy, steamy romance."
—Jennifer Ryan, *New York Times* bestselling author

For more info about Sourcebooks's books and authors, visit:
sourcebooks.com

HOPE ON THE RANGE

Welcome to the Turn Around Ranch: charming contemporary cowboy romance from *USA Today* bestselling author Cindi Madsen.

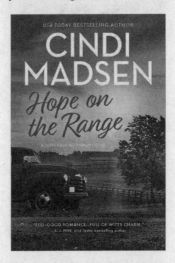

Brady Dawson has been in love with Tanya Greer for as long as he can remember. But running the Turn Around Ranch with his family doesn't leave much downtime for relationships. Now that Tanya is contemplating a move to the city, it looks like he might never get his chance... Faced with the realization that he might lose Tanya forever, he'll have to cowboy up and prove to Tanya that the Turn Around Ranch is the perfect place to call home.

"Feel-good romance...full of witty charm."
—A.J. Pine, *USA Today* bestselling author

HOLDING OUT FOR A COWBOY

First in a brand-new, compelling cowboy romance
series from *USA Today* bestselling author A.J. Pine.

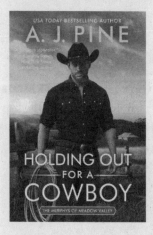

In high school, Boone Murphy and Casey Walsh were the couple
most likely to tie the knot, until tragedy tore them apart and
upended Casey's future. Now, more than a decade later, the beauty
school dropout runs Meadow Valley's family tavern and steers clear
of the cowboy who once stole her heart. What Casey doesn't know
is that she is the only reason Boone hasn't left behind his life in
Meadow Valley. He's never stopped loving her, and if she would give
him a second chance—this time, he'll never let her go.

"A fabulous storyteller."
—Carolyn Brown, *New York Times* bestselling author

For more info about Sourcebooks's books and authors, visit:
sourcebooks.com

Also by Jennie Marts

COWBOYS OF CREEDENCE
Caught Up in a Cowboy
You Had Me at Cowboy
It Started with a Cowboy
Wish Upon a Cowboy

CREEDENCE HORSE RESCUE
A Cowboy State of Mind
When a Cowboy Loves a Woman
How to Cowboy